MURDER
in the
Village

MURDER
in the
Village

LISA CUTTS

bookouture

Published by Bookouture in 2021

An imprint of Storyfire Ltd.
Carmelite House
50 Victoria Embankment
London EC4Y 0DZ

www.bookouture.com

ISBN: 978-1-80019-733-6
eBook ISBN: 978-1-80019-732-9

This book is a work of fiction. Names, characters, businesses,
organizations, places and events other than those clearly in the
public domain, are either the product of the author's imagination
or are used fictitiously. Any resemblance to actual persons, living or
dead, events or locales is entirely coincidental.

In loving memory of my mum
and Major

There is sorrow enough in the natural way
From men and women to fill our day;
And when we are certain of sorrow in store,
Why do we always arrange for more?
Brothers and Sisters, I bid you beware
Of giving your heart to a dog to tear.

The Power of the Dog, Rudyard Kipling

NO DOGS were harmed in the making of this story.

PROLOGUE

The naivety of the middle classes always meant a healthy profit.

Safe in that knowledge, the driver of the black SUV circled the estate twice before coming to a stop outside the target premises. It was perfect – almost too perfect. The yellow roses had the audacity to climb happily, almost arrogantly, up the front of the cottage, allowing their scent to fill the air.

What was the point? It was gone four in the morning, not long until the sun came up, so who was actually here to smell them?

With well-practised care, the passenger silently opened the car door and stood on the pavement. The whole of Little Challham was shrouded in sleep. Treading as lightly as he could manage, with almost feline dexterity, he made it to the edge of the driveway.

A quick glance left and right, and with one gloved hand, he pulled the aerosol can from his pocket.

In less than ten seconds, he had sprayed a yellow symbol on the road, and he was back in the car. The marker he had left was far enough to the side of the driveway to prevent the occupants noticing and yet close enough that his conspirators would know their objective on another street of unnumbered houses.

The only living soul he had alerted was the no longer slumbering pooch inside the house. The sound of voracious barking was canine music to his ears, if indeed there was such a thing. Bach, perhaps? He laughed to himself when he thought about the house-protecting hound whose fortune was about to change.

With no further concern other than their own finances, they drove home to get some sleep before another big day began.

CHAPTER ONE

Belinda Penshurst always looked forward to nights out in the village, and nothing pleased her more than a few hours on a Thursday night listening to live music in the New Inn.

She strolled along the pathway from her front door towards the centre of Little Challham, the beautiful and comforting English village she was lucky enough to call home.

For most of her forty-one years, she had lived in the village, although there were periods of time she had spent abroad, frequently travelling by herself, sometimes enjoying the company of someone she'd met. Usually it was short-lived company, except for her last relationship. It had ended more suddenly than she would have liked, but at least it had propelled her home, this time for good.

Probably.

Belinda was always happy being on her own, yet she always felt as if something was missing, as if there should have been more going on. She had seen enough of the world to know it was not wanderlust, more curiosity and intrigue.

The route she was now walking was one she knew well, and her path was lit by the late evening sun. It was warm on her face and made her spirits soar as high as the cloudless sky.

Things were really looking up for her, and everything seemed to be falling into place with her family, their home. She wanted to stay in Little Challham and make her mark, a positive mark, with all that she had planned for the local community.

Belinda, dressed in jeans, a white shirt and red wedge sandals, felt more at ease than she had for a long time. A lot of planning had gone into the evening and she wanted to make sure that everything was absolutely perfect.

When she reached the edge of the green, she stopped and ran an eye across the village. *Her* village.

The delicatessen, the tea room, the Women's Institute, the village hall, the post office, the Gatehouse and both pubs. All were nestled around the green, a large communal area usually scattered with families, dog walkers and couples strolling from one part of Little Challham to another. Hanging baskets bursting with colour and fragrance adorned the edges of the green, as well as every lamp post and street light along the pavements.

An unusual sight greeted her, in a spot where the street lighting didn't quite illuminate every single inch of the grass. Two figures stood close to one another chatting. On the face of it, it seemed innocuous, but the two people chewing the fat were Lennie Aisling, landlord of the Dog and Duck, and Anthony Cotter, owner of the village's microbrewery.

For the briefest of moments, Belinda considered the sight and then wrote it off as nothing more than two local rivals checking out their competition. A smile broke out across her face as she took it all in, before turning her attention to the competition Lennie and Anthony were looking at: the New Inn.

A huge banner across the front of the black-and-white seventeenth-century former coaching inn informed everyone of what was on offer inside. In two-foot-high purple lettering, the pub proudly announced that, for one night only, the tribute act was none other than Ed Sheernanigans.

With a feeling of contentment, Belinda put one heel in front of the other and strode across the grass towards the busy pub.

The doors were propped open, and a number of drinkers spilled onto the pavement, sitting on the pub's wooden benches or perching on the windowsills. A few regulars said hello as she cut a swathe through the throng, and a couple stopped to chat and ask after her and her family. She politely turned down the drinks she was offered as she made her way towards the entrance.

Once inside, Belinda edged her way to the already busy bar. At over five foot ten, and with years of practice under her belt, she managed to get to the counter with minimum effort.

'Belinda, my love,' said Tipper Johnson, the New Inn's middle-aged, slightly out of shape landlord. 'Wonderful to see you. What can I get for you?'

His unruly grey hair sprouted over his collar and framed his drinker's cheeks. At least he had put on a clean T-shirt for the occasion, even if it hadn't seen an iron since its creation.

He grabbed the tea towel from his shoulder as he spoke and wiped down the bar top in front of her, presumably hoping she would be pleased with his dedication to cleanliness and all things customer-focused.

She started to give him a withering stare, thought better of it under the circumstances, and turned it into a smile, teeth and all. 'Good evening. A large Sauvignon Blanc for me. And make it the good one.'

'They're all good, my lady.'

'Less sarcasm, if you would,' she called after his retreating back as he went in search of his stash of wine for the discerning customer, one who could tell Lambrusco from Listerine.

Belinda sensed someone was looking at her and turned her head sharply to the left, her straight, black, shoulder-length hair falling across her face as she did so.

Sandra Burgess, Tipper's longest-serving barmaid, was holding a pint glass under the Sun Over the Yardarm beer tap, her eyes fixed on Belinda.

The cold stare Sandra was giving her felt like a challenge. Belinda stared back at the younger woman's prominent cheekbones, dark complexion and mess of blond hair, streaked pink on one side.

Not wanting to appear rude, Belinda nodded at her and watched as the beer began to pour over the sides of the already full glass. As the cold liquid ran over Sandra's fingers, it shook her into action: she turned the tap off and, with reddening cheeks, carried on serving the customer patiently waiting for her drinks before they ended up in the slops bucket.

Belinda felt someone brush against her right hip as they moved closer to the bar. She glanced across to see a man in his early fifties, a little over six feet tall, with a solid build, red hair and stubble the same colour.

'Would you recommend the local beer?' he said, leaning across so he could speak in her ear.

As she opened her mouth to answer, Tipper stepped into view with a large glass of white wine. He put it down on the counter, looked at Belinda's new acquaintance and said, 'Well, hello to you, Harry. What can I get you?'

'I haven't paid for this yet,' said Belinda, pulling a wad of notes from her jeans pocket.

'Let me get that,' said Harry.

'No need,' said Tipper. 'It's on the house for you, Belinda.' He put his hands out towards her and waved away any chance of payment.

'In that case,' said Harry, 'she'd like a pint of Sun Over the Yardarm to go with it.'

Belinda turned in his direction and leaned back against the bar on her elbow, one hip pushed forwards.

'You've more front than most,' she said. 'I'll give you that.'

'I'm Harry, Harry Powell,' he said, extending a hand towards her, which she took.

'I'm Belinda. What brings you to Little Challham?'

She studied his lined face as he looked over her shoulder towards the bar, presumably to where Tipper was pouring his pint. In the harsh light, the grey in his red hair was easily visible, as was a speck of blood on his collar, presumably from shaving although the stubble on his chin belied that.

Harry turned back towards her, catching her reading him.

They both awkwardly glanced down at the sticky pub carpet.

'I don't live very far away,' he said, 'and I'm meeting someone here.'

'Don't let me keep you,' she said.

'It's only my friend Eric,' said Harry. 'And when I say friend, he's my boss really, so it's more of a business thing.'

'You've picked a great night to meet up here,' said Belinda, scanning the pub to find a better spot to move to.

'So, er, is it always this busy when there's live music?' said Harry as he took the pint from Tipper and exchanged it for a ten-pound note.

'Yes, always. It's good to see the local pubs doing so well.' Taking this as her chance to get an ideal position to watch Ed Sheernanigans before he started his set, Belinda said, 'Enjoy your evening, Harry,' and pushed herself away from the bar.

He appeared torn between leaving his change with Tipper and continuing talking to her, but his social life was not her concern. Not at that moment anyway.

She was very much a woman comfortable in her own skin, and needed no one beside her, especially here, in her home village.

Barely aware of whether Harry was following her or not, Belinda moved behind one of the stone pillars, knowing that the angle would give her a good vantage point when the music started.

As she took a tentative sip of her wine, trusting her palate's reaction that it wasn't being flooded with Sarson's, she crowd-watched.

Nothing unusual was going on in her peaceful world.

Not if Belinda didn't count that there was something very familiar about the tall, red-haired stranger and it was tying her stomach in knots. She needed to give herself time to process the idea that he had walked back into her life after all these years. Plus, the fact that through the open front door, while admiring the softly lit sixteenth-century facades of the buildings across from the pub, she had just seen her brother Marcus drive past in his black Mercedes.

On almost any other day, that wouldn't have been a surprise. Except only two hours ago, he had called her to say that he was stuck in Madrid, that his plane was delayed, so she shouldn't expect him home for hours.

The last time he had lied to her like that was when he had crept home unexpectedly and put the roof over their heads up for sale. The first thing she'd known about it was estate agents visiting and potential buyers knocking at the door. It had taken all of her skills and savvy to rectify the dire financial situation he had brought upon them.

With a sigh, she realised Marcus was up to his old tricks again. Someone was bound to get hurt.

This would only end badly.

CHAPTER TWO

While the day after the village's tribute act wasn't the first morning that Harry Powell had woken up free from his police force shackles, it was certainly the most positive he had felt since handing over his warrant card.

For a moment he nestled back into the duck down pillows, sun streaming in through the gap in the curtains, and thought about what an adventure his new life was going to be. It was definitely time to start again. He liked change, he told himself, and here it was in abundance.

He had moved on since retiring from the police, and most people would pinch themselves for finding such a wonderful place to live in as the Gatehouse of Challham Castle. It had character, it had a garden, it was in one of the county's most beautiful villages and, above all, it had central heating.

Positive thoughts, yes, positive thoughts.

He let out a sigh when the thought struck him, for about the thousandth time, that he had been a police officer for longer than he had been a civilian.

And that's what he was again, a *civilian*.

Quite frankly, what was the point of that? He had no powers, no responsibilities, no team, no—

Purpose, he had to think about purpose.

What he wouldn't give to solve a crime just one more time. Nothing too demanding. It didn't have to be a murder, nothing taxing. He was retired, after all.

He closed his eyes, concentrating on the sounds of the countryside and the village of Little Challham as it came to life. The chattering birds flying in and out from under his bedroom windowsill had annoyed him at first, until he had decided to find it charming. After all, they had picked *his* crumbling wall to nest in.

He heard the delivery van pull up beside the rear entrance to the nearby tea room and the slam of its door as the driver started to unload. For the last two weeks Harry had been up with the sun and had found himself at his desk in the corner box room, staring out of the window, watching the middle-aged driver – Max Fish, apparently, according to the side of his van – flirt with Angie, the young woman who ran the bustling quaint premises. He listened to the unmistakable sounds of a market being set up, only a few feet from his front gate.

He had a front gate – a wrought-iron front gate at that. It separated his new residence from the peaceful community he was learning to call home. So far, he had made a point of using the post office with its small stock of pricy goods, had sat in the tea room and paid for a drink he could make fifty yards away in his own kitchen for a fraction of the cost, and had made himself known in both pubs and the microbrewery. Somehow, he didn't mind spending money there. It was the social aspect, he supposed. Having people to talk to was important.

There was a part of him that had been concerned about spending all his spare time in the pub chatting to locals, but he had been a part of some truly fascinating discussions. At least, he had thought he was fascinating. He hadn't been barred so he must have behaved and mostly kept his opinions to himself.

'Breathe,' he said to himself. 'Deep breaths like the nice lady counsellor told you. Breathe in through your nose, out through your mouth.'

Harry could do this.

Next step: up and dressed. He had to get ready for work.

He threw back the duvet, swung his legs over the edge of the mattress and said, 'That's right. I am not a fifty-year-old retired detective inspector, I'm a Doggie Delight food delivery associate. Nothing to see here, move on.'

Harry would be damned if he had spent three days on the training course designed and taught by his regional manager, Eric Whitley, learning how to pick up bags of dry food, make a fuss of the customers' pets and look good in his corporate uniform, and not get to his full potential.

He pushed his feet inside his memory foam slippers, ran a hand through his hair – once a shock of red, now more shockingly grey – and walked towards the bathroom.

Today was going to be a good day.

Within ten minutes of leaving home, Harry pulled onto the driveway of his first customer of the day.

He liked Ivy White, a sweet and cheerful woman in her seventies, and not too mean with the tea and biscuits.

Harry got out of the car, closed the door and walked up the gravel pathway.

After a loud, insistent rapping on the door knocker, Harry stood back and waited for Mrs White to open the door. He was sure he could hear some sort of movement from the other side.

'Mrs White!' he shouted. 'It's Harry, Harry Powell. I've got your Doggie Delight.'

Harry stood and waited while he heard the noise of bolts being pulled back and the turning of a huge metal key that he knew Mrs White kept in the lock.

'Harry, love, I won't be a minute,' she called before the door creaked open and she shuffled backwards to let him in. Her Cavalier King Charles spaniel Bonnie sat obediently beside her slippered feet.

Mrs White looked up at Harry, whose huge frame filled the doorway, his bulk blocking out the light and casting a shadow over her.

'You all right?' he said, bending forwards to peer at her lined, fragile face. 'You look very pale. Did I wake you up?'

He looked over her shoulder into the living room.

'Why are the curtains closed, Mrs White? Are you feeling poorly?' He stood up back to his full height. 'Want me to call someone for you?'

She shook her head, soft grey hair immaculate in spite of her obvious troubles, and said, 'No, really, Harry. It's kind but I don't want to put you out. My dog food is plenty, thanks.'

'If you're sure,' Harry said, 'but I'll take it round the back for you. Give you time to get to the kitchen and put the kettle on.'

'You're a cheeky soul,' she laughed. 'I've got custard creams too.'

'Music to my ears,' he called as he went to unload the nine-kilo bag of dry dog food from the boot of his car.

He opened the boot remotely as he got closer, whistling tunelessly to himself as a black SUV drove towards the front of Mrs White's house, slowing as it got level with the top of the driveway.

For a second, his eye was drawn to a yellow mark on the road close to the top of the driveway. From where he stood, it appeared to be paint from an aerosol, something he probably wouldn't have noticed had it not looked like the letter 'D'. He stood pondering it briefly, barely giving it much thought, before the approaching car grabbed his attention again.

The house was set thirty yards from the bend in the country lane that led out of Little Challham and towards the more rural part of the area. It was one of a cluster of older houses on the edge of the village, each sitting on an acre or two of land. It was a fairly secluded spot, with the nearest neighbour a couple of hundred yards further along the route.

The fact that the SUV slowed did not give Harry too much cause for concern; after all, the contour of the lane didn't encourage speed.

What did make him look twice was the screech of tyres as the driver steered the car into the top of the driveway and then reversed and gunned off at speed.

It did not take thirty years of police work to guess someone had been about to pay the lonely, isolated old lady a visit.

And that someone hadn't wanted a witness.

A few minutes later, Harry sat on one side of the wooden kitchen table, dainty cup and saucer at his fingertips, fluted plate of custard creams midway between himself and Mrs White.

He nodded towards the bag of dog food he had placed against the cupboard door. 'Once I've had my tea and eaten these biscuits, I'll empty what's in your dog food bin into a carrier bag, give the container a quick clean and fill it with the new food.'

'That's very decent of you.' Mrs White smiled at him. 'The last delivery man used to leave it on the front doorstep.'

'Well,' he said, as he leaned across to pick up a custard cream, 'I expect your weight training days are a few weeks behind you, so it's no bother.'

He heard her laugh as he examined the pale snack, complete with sickly yellow filling. He dunked it in his tea, shoved the whole thing in his mouth and winked at her.

'And while I restock Bonnie's food bin,' he said, 'you can tell me what's really bothering you.'

Mrs White's gaze shifted to the diminishing plate of biscuits. She opened her mouth to speak, then closed it again without a word.

'I'm guessing it's something to do with the black car I watched try to pull into your driveway and make off like the devil was chasing them when they saw me.'

Harry wasn't surprised to see Mrs White's face drain of what little colour it had, and tears cascade down her sallow cheeks.

'You must think me so stupid,' Mrs White said after a minute spent delicately crying into a white lace handkerchief. If Harry wasn't very much mistaken, a Cavalier King Charles spaniel was embroidered in the corner. He was trying not to stare in case Mrs White wondered what on earth he was peering at.

Truth be told, he had never been very good with people crying. One of the bonuses of being a detective inspector had been that he could make his excuses and leave a member of his team to deal with the waterworks. Now, he was a team of one.

Not to mention his job was to deliver dog food. Run-of-the-mill, ordinary employment that shouldn't cause him any stress or anxiety. Yet, at this moment, he felt more anxious than he had for some time.

Harry suddenly knew what the problem was with raw displays of emotion – he felt powerless. Suddenly, he was struggling with what to do or say. His working life had been filled with taking action: investigating crimes, most notably murders, protecting the vulnerable, arresting the perpetrators. Now it was dropping bags of pre-ordered kibble at doors and in kitchens.

There was no way he would walk away and not do everything in his power to help someone, especially when that someone had no one else.

He put his hand out to touch the sleeve of Mrs White's mauve cardigan and said, 'Tell me what's happened, and I'll do what I can to help you.'

'There's not much you can do, Harry.' She smiled through her tears, rapidly blinking again. 'It probably feels worse because it's a year ago this week that the police found Peter Clayton's body in the lane.'

Mrs White wiped her nose on her handkerchief.

'You probably don't remember it as you weren't living in Little Challham at the time,' she said. 'It was reported as a hit-and-run, but he'd been out walking his dog Scooter, a beautiful West Highland terrier.'

'I do remember a dog walker being run over,' said Harry. 'It's something I'd have been aware of because of my job, but I saw it on the news too.' He chose his next words carefully. 'I really don't recall it being anything other than an awful tragedy that no one ever took responsibility for.'

'A couple of people around here thought there was more to it,' said Mrs White with a sniff. 'One or two of the other dog owners had seen a car slow down or pull alongside them in the lanes when they walked their dogs. Just last week, a couple in their sixties had their springer spaniel snatched by someone on a walk near here. And now I keep noticing cars and think they're coming to take Bonnie from me. Peter had seen a car outside his house a couple of times, and like me, he lived in a fairly quiet spot. When Peter was found, Scooter was nowhere to be seen.'

'The dog was found later though, I think,' said Harry, not entirely sure that Mrs White was being at all rational. At the same time, he allowed the comforting feeling of a crime that needed solving to creep through him.

'Yes,' she said, leaning forward in her chair, her bloodshot eyes staring at him. 'Poor little Scooter was found tied to a post in the field, some distance from where Peter lay.'

Harry shifted in his chair. One thing he hated – other than people murdering one another, obviously – was animal cruelty. There had been times in his thirty-year police career when he had all but given up on the human race... Hurting animals deserved a special place in hell.

'Any idea who found Scooter?' said Harry.

'No one really talked about that,' said Mrs White. A frown creased her forehead and she fiddled with her handkerchief. 'Most things get around the locals here, but that always struck me as strange because it was never mentioned again. There was a wall of silence around it. That's why a few of us thought there was more to it than an awful accident.'

'Any idea where Scooter is now?' said Harry, hating seeing Mrs White so clearly upset but needing some answers.

She shrugged and said, 'I heard from another neighbour whose bulldog went missing that Scooter was rehomed, although the neighbour's moved away now. She was too distraught by Beau's disappearance to carry on living here.'

'Mrs White,' he said, leaning across the table to place his hand on hers, 'I promise you that I'll look into this and get you some answers.'

The briefest of smiles greeted his answer until it was replaced by another frown.

'I'm just not sure anyone can stop them.'

He leaned closer, his interest piqued. 'Who? Stop who?'

'You really don't know?' Mrs White said with a shake of her head. She spoke slowly, enunciating every syllable.

'The dognappers are back in Little Challham.'

CHAPTER THREE

Even though Belinda had stayed at the New Inn until closing time and drunk another large glass of white wine – not entirely convinced that Tipper had given her the 'good stuff' on her second and final libation – she had been awake since four that morning.

After a couple of hours of tossing and turning, she gave in and decided to get up and mull over how to put an end to what could only be another of her brother's ridiculous schemes.

At least she could take comfort in the beautiful view from her bedroom window. As she got out of bed and made her way towards the bathroom, she stopped as she did every morning to savour the lush green landscape before her. The downs were a gorgeous sight, especially on another relentlessly sunny day: the myriad trees, fields dotted with sheep and the river were all bathed in sunlight.

For a moment, Belinda drank in the scenery and steadied her thoughts.

Then she took a deep breath, walked towards the shower and steeled herself for dealing with her brother Marcus's fallout again.

Twenty minutes later, Belinda was dressed and downstairs, ready to face the day. Her impressive three-inch heels were a real and present danger to the wooden floors as she stomped up and down the kitchen.

Aware she was wearing herself out, she stopped and sat down at the table. This wasn't the first time she had managed to rescue the family from an impending disaster, and it sure as hell would not be the last either. The problem was, she was unsure what this one even consisted of.

Anything, she hoped, except more trouble with the bank.

She folded her arms and leaned back in the chair, clearing her mind of all thoughts of how she was, once again, putting her own life on hold, and focusing on what she already knew about her brother's latest folly.

There were a couple of occasions when she had heard a van or truck trundling up the driveway late at night, yet she had chosen to ignore it. Something she'd known would come back to bite her.

Belinda chewed on the side of her fingernail, a sure sign that things were not going according to plan.

What exactly was her brother up to? His last hare-brained scheme had almost got them all evicted from their family home, something their father had chosen to ignore and never speak of again. It was only Belinda's quick wit and business sense that had kept the roof over their heads after Marcus had destroyed their financial security.

To be fair, it was a resplendent roof, one that could be seen from the whole of Little Challham, from some parts of Great Challham, and on a good day even from as far afield as Upper Wallop.

Still, it didn't stop her anxiety levels from heading towards that very roof.

Determined that she was going to get Marcus to explain what he was up to and why he had lied to her, she stood up to go and look for him.

Pre-empting her move, the kitchen door opened, and Marcus walked in, sunglasses pushed to the top of his head and glee all over his face.

'Good morning, Bel,' he said, swiftly changing direction to kiss the side of her face before he swerved towards the kettle. 'Want one?' he said, waving it in her direction.

'I presume you mean a tea, and not an actual kettle?'

'Always smart-mouthed, aren't you?' he said with a wink.

Belinda felt her resolve diminish. Marcus's messy blond hair, dimples, piercing blue eyes and all-round good looks had always got him out of mischief. If that was not enough, he was charming to boot.

Yes, he lacked intelligence, but she had that in spades, so it really hadn't mattered when they were growing up. She was the younger sister; he was the big brother. The five years between them hadn't meant they had drifted apart, far from it.

Belinda had followed him everywhere at one point. Not now though: she didn't fancy getting arrested again. She certainly would not follow him to prison.

'You know who I miss?' said Marcus, his back to her now.

Belinda knew with a sinking feeling where this was going.

'Ivan,' said Marcus. 'He brought out the best in you. I've never seen you so happy as when you were with him.'

She took a deep breath and said, 'Except he's still in Africa and I'm here in Little Challham.'

Her brother turned and gave her a wink before returning to make his drink.

'Marcus,' she said after a short silence.

'Oh, dear,' he said, hand poised on the cupboard door as he went in search of a cup. 'I know that tone.' He turned round to face her. 'Got to hand it to you, sis. You manage to say so much with only one word.'

She gave him a rueful smile.

'Please don't tell me that you've borrowed money again,' she said. 'You do recall what the bank was about to do last time, don't you?'

'Borrow money?' said Marcus. 'Of course I haven't. Anyway, we're doing very well with the income from the tours and hiring out the grounds.'

Belinda felt a headache coming on. The only reason they still had a home at all was because she had ensured it was booked solid for events for the next two years, to say nothing of the regular tours of the gardens and the castle which paid for the staff and general upkeep of the place. None of which Marcus helped with.

'Why did you lie to me about being stuck in Madrid when you were here in Little Challham?' she said, preferring not to explain for the hundredth time that their financial salvation was all down to her.

'Ah.' Marcus opened the cupboard, took down a mug and went about making his drink. 'I didn't want to spoil the surprise.'

'What surprise?'

'I've bought you a present.'

'You have?' she said. 'What is it?'

'Well, if I told you, it wouldn't be a surprise, would it?'

'You know I hate surprises.'

'Not this one,' he said, beaming at her. 'If you really want to know, I'll tell you.'

Belinda outstared him.

'All right, all right,' he said. 'I've bought you a puppy.'

'A puppy? What on earth for?'

'You've been on about it for ages. Don't mention it.'

With his drink completely forgotten, Marcus gave her another of his winning smiles and walked out of the kitchen.

As much as she loved her brother, Belinda had to admit he was harder to hold down than a greased weasel.

What in heaven's name was she supposed to do with a puppy? Knowing her brother, he had paid over the odds for it, and she was going to have to look after it – the last thing she wanted was responsibility for another life. What if she actually did want to go travelling again? She shook her head at that idea. What if she wanted to get married or settle down? While that wasn't impossible, there was definitely no chance of her being remotely attracted to a man who didn't love dogs, or in fact all animals. That was what had made her fall in love with Ivan in the first place. The fact that he was probably the most handsome man she had ever had the good fortune to set eyes on obviously helped.

Belinda opened the kitchen door which led to the gardens, taking comfort in the verdant views and subtle fragrance of the roses in full bloom. A cascade of colour from the rose garden led towards the middle terrace with its box hedges, framing the view across the valley. The only things between the edge of her family's land and the beautiful blue sky were the forest and river in the distance.

If she couldn't enjoy the grounds of Challham Castle, her family home, what was the point of constantly bailing out the family?

CHAPTER FOUR

The conversation with her brother had unnerved Belinda. Exactly what was he up to, buying her a puppy? For starters, where was he going to get a puppy from?

She made herself a hot drink, more for something to do than because she wanted one. It at least occupied a few minutes as she took the packet from the fridge, spooned some of the rich, dark, ground beans into the percolator and waited for the aroma of freshly brewing coffee to fill the room.

Black coffee. That was what she needed, not because of her two large wines the night before but because she needed to wake up and put everything into place.

It was going to be an uphill struggle, no matter what path she now chose. Still, it would not sort itself out and Marcus had added to her problems with a puppy, in addition to whatever lies he was no doubt telling her.

It still did not explain why he had pretended to be in Madrid when he was clearly close by. None of it made sense.

Coffee in hand, she made her way up the main staircase. Three flights of stairs took her to the uppermost part of the castle, to the attic room she had loved to visit as a child to escape the constant noise and bustle floors below. When they were children, Marcus had sometimes joined her, but mostly she had sat alone and envisaged a life free of all the responsibilities the Penshurst family brought her way.

Decades on, and she was still here.

If it hadn't been for the enterprising schemes Belinda had launched to make money, they would have been forced to move out long ago. She had arranged for parts of the grounds to be hired out for private events, such as weddings and parties, a modest fee for tours of parts of the castle, plus entry to the gardens on certain days of the weeks and some sporting events held on their land.

It was another reason she was so keen to keep investing in local businesses and make the place thrive. The community had supported her home and family so the least she could do was make sure they reciprocated.

It was unlikely she would ever leave, not permanently anyway. If she did, she'd be leaving Marcus in charge, and that thought made her shudder. As much as she loved her brother, he was totally hopeless and had failed in his last three attempts to fly the coop and make a go of it. The family probably couldn't afford to let him try again.

Belinda reached the attic room door and pushed it open.

Over the years, Belinda had cleared the junk from the room, pushed it away into corners or cupboards, reluctant to throw too much away yet keen to create her own space. It was clean, functional and, most importantly, it was hers. Now, no one else ever came up here.

She kicked her shoes off and walked across the rug that covered most of the twenty-by-twenty-foot space.

Settling her coffee mug on the small occasional table salvaged from one of the garages before it was cleared, she sat in her favourite pale blue Chatsworth chair, a little frayed around the edges, patchy where the sun had charmed its way through the tiny leaded window panes, but nevertheless the most comfortable seat in the castle. At least, it was for her.

Belinda sank down into the cushions, released that morning's tension and reached down beside the chair to the wicker box where she kept so many of her mementos: snapshots from a time in her life when she had tackled everything with the cheery optimism of youth.

There were so many to choose from. Without even peeking over the edge of the chair's velvet arm, she allowed her fingers to find their way through decades of her life. They settled on a scrapbook filled with newspaper cuttings.

Book open on her lap, Belinda leafed through the pages. She had browsed through her keepsakes so often over the years. It was her escape from reality. Now she allowed her mind to take her back to one of the most defining moments in her life. But surely, it couldn't be that – after all this time – he had stumbled his way back to her. Not after all these years.

Her breath caught as she turned the page.

Page eight, top right.

A newspaper article with the headline: FROM THE DOCKS TO THE DOCK – LANDED GENTRY GETS LANDED IN THE NICK.

Beneath the title in all its tabloid subtlety was a partially accurate account of how Belinda had been arrested on her twentieth birthday.

And underneath that was a photograph of her being led away in handcuffs.

The person holding her arm was a younger, slimmer Police Constable Harry Powell.

CHAPTER FIVE

Belinda had managed to turn the morning to her advantage. If nothing else, she was very organised. The coffee had revived her more than she could have thought possible. Sun blazing down upon her, she walked down to the village and queued up at the post office to get that morning's correspondence despatched, before heading to the tea room to get herself some breakfast.

Even the short stroll across the green from the post office warmed her as she paused to take in the line of shops, welcoming pub fronts and the pristine displays of flower boxes along the pavements.

What today needed more than anything was a free-range egg on toast with avocado.

It cheered her to see that the single-storey stone tea room was bustling and still half-full despite the usual lull after the breakfast rush. Market day always brought in more customers.

It lifted Belinda's spirits even further when she saw that her favourite table by the window was free. It gave her a bird's eye view of the village green and the comings and goings of others.

Belinda pushed open the door to the tinkle of chimes and the scent of cinnamon. She smiled at Angie, who waved back from behind the counter and jabbed with her pen in the direction of the window table, all the while managing to repeat back a large order into the phone she had clamped to her ear.

Angie Manning was a young woman with a kind face and a heart to match. Her calm and engaging manner had no doubt worked wonders in bringing in new customers, retaining loyal patrons and cajoling a few into spending more money than they had anticipated before walking through the door.

Not for the first time, Belinda gazed at the counter where the display of cakes and cookies promised a sugar rush like no other. Behind the glass was row after row of rich and decadent chocolate cakes oozing with cream filling, enrobed with chocolate ganache and topped with chocolate sprinkles, irresistibly light and moist sponge with lemon zest and lime juice, not to mention fluffy cupcakes with sun-ripened fruit and thick icing, topped with fresh berries.

Willpower made Belinda walk away and vow to stick to her original breakfast choice, as tempting as the array of treats looked.

Within a few seconds, Angie was on her way to Belinda's table, order pad at the ready.

'Morning, Bel,' said Angie, already a little flushed for someone who was only twenty-three and less than halfway through their working day. 'What can I get you?'

With a laugh, Belinda said, 'You won't need to write this one down.'

Angie tucked a strand of mousy blond hair behind her ear and said, 'Should have guessed, but one day you'll surprise me. The cinnamon buns are fresh if I can tempt you? Max delivered them this morning.'

She shifted her weight from one foot to the other, Birkenstock sandals in contrast to the rest of her outfit. The tea room manager was dressed in a black short-sleeved T-shirt, tight across her chest, and a silk skirt of approximately twelve inches in length. Belinda owned bigger handkerchiefs although in her youth had been seen in public wearing much less.

With a deep breath that Angie appeared surprised she had been holding, she tucked the errant strand of hair behind her ear again and said, 'One egg on toast with avocado coming up, boss.'

With an absent-minded smile, Belinda turned her attention back to the green, where she continued to watch the morning shoppers milling around the village.

While the breakfast had very much hit the spot, it was time to get up and leave before she caved and ordered a slab of Victoria sponge cake. At risk of salivating, she watched the woman on the next table pop a morsel of light butter sponge, strawberry preserve and vanilla buttercream in her mouth. Belinda decided to make her way back outside before it was too late.

Besides, it was getting busier inside the modest tea room. She didn't want to take up a table that could host paying customers. So, with a wave towards Angie, Belinda stood in the doorway of her inaugural Little Challham business venture, congratulating herself on how well it was doing.

Belinda strolled towards the village green, the hustle and bustle of the swelling crowd of shoppers on all sides of her. She ran an appreciative eye over the thriving businesses nestled around the green, all benefiting from the footfall the market brought in.

Who didn't love a jar of local honey or artisan bread?

With a glance at her watch, Belinda stopped to consider how much longer she had before she had to be back at home. There were so many tasks she had to take care of, there surely weren't going to be enough hours in the day. It simply would not do to have her plans disrupted.

The most important thing she had to take care of was at the New Inn. Last night had brought in so many drinkers, it would have been impossible to get Tipper on his own. He had made her angry, although a packed pub was not the ideal spot for confrontation. There was also the matter of Sandra.

That was another awkward conversation that she needed to get out of the way.

CHAPTER SIX

Buoyed up at the thought of dealing with Tipper the landlord once and for all, Belinda walked over to the New Inn. Like last night, the front doors were propped open, and drinkers and a stream of early lunchtime diners were making the most of the outdoor seating.

Belinda noticed that the Ed Sheernanigans banner had been taken down; Tipper had at least been on top of that. He sometimes needed a prod in the right direction, more due to drunkenness than laziness. When he was sober, there was no stopping him, although his drinking had seemed to get worse of late. Perhaps Belinda shouldn't have invested in a business with someone whose entire life consisted of alcohol, something that was clearly Tipper's downfall. If he had been this bad twelve months ago, she might have had more reservations.

She had trusted her instinct, and usually it didn't let her down. A confrontation with Tipper was the last thing she was after, but the man could be so uncompromising at times.

Determined, she headed across to the pub and through the doors.

Tipper and Sandra stood side by side behind the bar, both serving customers while two of the pub's waiting staff took care of the diners already sitting at tables and perusing the menus.

'Belinda,' said Tipper, concentration torn between her and the pint he was pouring. 'Twice in two days. Can I let Sandra serve you? I'm in the middle of a large round here.'

Belinda looked in Sandra's direction and couldn't have failed to miss the intense stare the young woman was giving her. Her face was almost as fuchsia as her highlights and the brilliantly pink top she was wearing.

The dispute with Sandra would have to wait for another time: she had bigger fish to fry.

'As great as it would be to have a chat with Sandra,' said Belinda, returning the look across the beer-stained countertop, 'I need to speak to you.'

'All right,' huffed Tipper, demonstrating little in the way of landlord dexterity as he thumped the pint down onto a beer towel and slapped the list of drinks next to it. 'Sandra, take over when you've finished serving your customer, if you would. I've got as far as the fourth item on that tab.'

As Sandra stepped towards the order pad, a pile of cling-filmed sandwiches stacked up under the optics came into Belinda's view. Belinda felt herself bristle.

Tipper indicated the side door leading to the staircase that connected the cellar, the pub and the private flat he occupied on the top floor. Belinda followed him up the stairs; his footsteps were slow and weary on the worn brown carpet.

Once inside his living room – with dusty curtains keeping the daylight at bay, a stack of old newspapers and magazines in one corner, dirty plates and used mugs and glasses on the table in the opposite corner – Belinda felt her patience run out.

'What an absolute heap!' she said in bewilderment. 'What happened to the money I gave you to do this place up?'

'Whoa, hang on. Gave me? You didn't give it to me!'

'OK, it was not a gift. But you understood what you were supposed to do with it, right?'

She stood with one foot in front of the other, toe tapping the floor, and hand on her hip. The rest of her resolve went into holding back the full force of her fury.

'This is not on, Tipper. It's not the first time we've had this conversation about the state of the place, and it's a far cry from what we agreed.'

He snorted with laughter. 'This place is a gold mine and I'm the miner, only you can't see it.'

'What I can see,' she said, taking a step closer to him, 'is that you are taking liberties with my generosity, something I won't keep extending. Make no bones about it, I am not a soft touch. This ends now.'

'Or what?'

'Or what?' Belinda repeated. 'I'll tell you what. No more money and you'll be out on your ear. I invested in this pub to make Little Challham a better place to live for all of us.'

'I'm trying, aren't I? I got the tribute act you wanted.'

'The man wasn't even a natural redhead,' said Belinda. 'And I hope you at least paid him. His roadie was bigger than a barn door and didn't appear the sort to take kindly to being had. And something else I've told you about repeatedly,' she went on, unable to control her fury, 'is wrapping rolls and sandwiches in cling film and leaving them behind the bar. It's unhygienic if they're not refrigerated and you'll get us shut down. And I hate cling film, something you're also fully aware of.'

'I should stick to doing business with your brother,' said Tipper, taking a step towards her. 'I know where I stand with him. At least he knows—'

Something over Belinda's shoulder caught Tipper's attention.

'Erm, I need a hand downstairs,' said Sandra from the doorway. 'It's got busier, the beer needs changing, and I've not had a chance to go into the cellar at all today. Oh, and Anthony from the microbrewery is here needing a word with you.'

'Belinda was just leaving,' said Tipper, red face now scarlet.

Knowing that this wouldn't be the end of it, Belinda turned towards Sandra as Tipper pushed past her to get downstairs.

Both women stood within touching distance of each other, neither sure what to say.

'Look, Sandra,' said Belinda, not one comfortable with silences at the best of times, and certainly not now. 'We need to talk, only I don't think that today is the right day for it, especially if you've got your hands full in the bar.'

Belinda studied Sandra's face as her lower lip trembled and her eyes filled with tears. She stepped towards the barmaid, put a hand on her arm, felt her try to move away. 'We'll talk tomorrow,' said Belinda, voice so soft it was barely audible. 'Please.'

Sandra fished a tissue from her pocket and wiped at her mascara.

'I may look as though I'm upset,' said Sandra, 'but it's only fair to tell you that I'm actually furious with you right now.'

'I'm really not sure what to say that would make this any better,' said Belinda. 'If you give me a chance to explain, I will.'

'Don't patronise me!' shouted Sandra, shrugging her arm away from Belinda's grasp. 'You've always looked down your nose at me.'

'Now you're being ridiculous,' said Belinda. 'I've done nothing of the sort. Like everyone else in this village, I gave you a fair chance. It didn't work out and that was all there was to it. There's only so many times I can tell you I'm sorry.'

'Sorry!' said Sandra. 'I'll give you sorry. I'll get a proper apology from you over my dead body.'

Belinda opened her mouth to say something but before she could utter another word, Sandra slapped her hand away and ran from the room.

CHAPTER SEVEN

After spending as much time with Mrs White as he could spare and leaving her his phone number in case she needed him, Harry dragged himself away to finish his day's work. He hated leaving her when she was so upset, but he also felt the old familiar lure of investigating a case. Of course, it was only a possible dognapping and not an actual murder, but still, perhaps it was the stopgap he was looking for.

Harry made his mind up that when work allowed, he would find out all that he could about Peter Clayton's unfortunate hit-and-run and then visit Mrs White again. That was what years of detective work had taught him: build your case and take nothing at face value.

Weirdly, he felt more optimistic than he had in a long time. In fact, since the day he had handed back his warrant card. His police exit interview had involved an awkward tug of war with Loretta Bannister, the assistant chief constable. Harry had underestimated the powerful grip of the five-foot-two senior officer. It seemed that she had wanted the black leather wallet containing his warrant card more than Harry had. His police career hadn't ended on the high he had always hoped for, and he really didn't want to contemplate his non-existent love life for too long.

Keen to get the rest of his Doggie Delight delivery round wrapped up as soon as possible, Harry wasn't wasting any time. He even managed to pick up two new customers from one of his drop-offs. It paid to be up and out early, catching people before they got distracted by their busy lives, and a free sample usually helped to clinch the deal.

He had handed out most of his free samples so now had to head home to restock before his next port of call. He could hardly expect to land a huge order without giving away some of the products. The sight of hungry hounds gobbling up the goods would melt any loving owner's heart.

Harry turned his Audi in the direction of his house, smiling to himself at the thought of calling picture-perfect Little Challham home. He had lived in the county all his life, most of it in the coastal urban sprawl of East Rise, where his incident room had been. Even though the move to Little Challham had been a knee-jerk reaction, he was determined to make it work.

It had never been part of his plans to use his own car for sacks of dry dog grub, but picking up a van from the depot was a twenty-minute round trip and seemed totally pointless when part of his route was in the village. And he kept a supply of everything a dog's stomach could desire in his garage.

Harry indicated right, stopped at the junction and looked across to the corner of the street. Two young men standing on the pavement caught his eye, the taller of the two glancing quickly left and right, dark blue hoodie pulled up over his head, face partially obscured. The other one stepped closer, shoved a hand inside the front pocket of his jeans and leaned across to the hooded one.

Harry paused, cancelled the indicator and considered his options. He knew his policing days were behind him. He really shouldn't stop and deal with what was clearly someone else's problem.

'Report it and carry on, you old fool,' he muttered to himself as Hoodie turned his attention towards Harry, a scowl trained on the retired DI. Not one to back down, Harry stared as he weighed up his options.

This wouldn't end well.

Deliver the dog food, take the money and go home.

Harry turned the Audi away from confrontation. It would have to wait for another day. He had somewhere important to be.

*

Harry drove through the centre of Little Challham, circumnavigating the market crowd. Hordes of lunchtime shoppers all eager to pay three pounds for a loaf of bread and part with a king's ransom for some chutney with a made-up name that would probably sit at the back of the cupboard until it was well past its best-before date.

He drove slowly around the edge of the village green, eyeing the stripy blue-and-white tops of the market stalls in the distance. As the day was getting on, the crowd was beginning to build up, young and old shoulder to elbow in their search for a beeswax candle or pair of alpaca wool mittens.

The best thing of all was that Harry loved every bit of it. It was people buying goods that they didn't really need, certainly had lived for many a long year without, and often didn't actually want.

It warmed his heart. It was so simple, so reassuring. These folks were truly happy. They had homes full of superfluous knick-knacks and it made them get out of bed in the morning and enjoy life. That was Harry's purpose from now on, whatever fate chucked his way.

Whistling tunelessly as he so often did, Harry remembered his positive-thought mantra and imagined himself pushing all negative ideas clear from his mind. Deep breathing was trickier while whistling so he stopped to open the window for a lungful of countryside air.

Harry slowed the car at the edge of the green a few metres from the post office, the sight of Belinda subconsciously forcing his foot from the accelerator.

Her black shoulder-length hair caught the sunlight as she strode across the road towards the village green.

'Won't get far across the grass in those heels,' he muttered to himself, calming breathing technique out of the window as he found himself fixated on her calf muscles, visible between the hem of a dark green pencil skirt and three-inch black heels.

Angry with himself that he had to stop his eyes from travelling any further skyward, he took some more deep breaths.

A face appeared in the open window.

'Hell's teeth, Harry. Are you having some sort of fit?'

Harry's view was completely obscured by the saggy cheeks and bulbous nose of Tipper Johnson. The pub had barely been open an hour, yet Harry caught a waft of stale alcohol float towards him.

'Afternoon,' said Harry, catching himself trying to crane his head. 'Practising my calming breathing techniques.'

'Well, don't do it here, man,' said Tipper, waving an arm in the direction of the queue that had started to form behind Harry. 'Come and join me in the pub for a pint. I should get back inside. It's busy as you like but I, er, came out to get some fresh air.'

'That's kind of you,' said Harry, as a driver a couple of cars behind him finally lost their patience and sounded their horn, 'but I'm supposed to be working. Quick stop at home and then off to the castle.'

'Ah, well, good luck,' said Tipper as he moved back onto the pavement. 'I take it that's your first visit?'

'Yes,' said Harry, watching Tipper's expression harden with a glance towards the castle gates.

He made a mental note that his next visit to the New Inn would involve a surreptitious scout for information. He felt the need to explore Tipper's reaction to his mention of the castle.

Harry waved at the increasingly impatient motorists stacking up behind him and drove around the green to the Gatehouse.

Not wanting to waste time, and now bordering on an impression of Pavlov's dogs at Tipper's mention of a pint, Harry grabbed what he needed from his kitchen, locked the door and drove to the castle.

Even though he lived next door, he had had no interaction with its residents. It was another reason he had decided to use his Audi that morning rather than his work van with its Doggie Delight logo emblazoned on the side. It was cute and said, *Stop me and buy one*, while making him feel like an imbecile driving it.

Harry wanted this job to work out. The firm had taken him on for a trial period and the last thing he wanted was to let them down. It was the change he was searching for, and he got to meet a lot of dogs. He liked dogs. It was easy to tell what a dog wanted from life: they let you know when they were hungry, wanted walking, needed to empty their tanks, and the rest of the time they slept. But the thought of driving his van through the restored oak gates, along the sweeping gravel pathway and the double avenue of limes flanking it on either side, made him shudder. He might as well make his entrance in a clown car complete with amusing horn and exploding wheels. In fact, why not go the whole hog and get himself one of those plastic flowers that squirted water and a fire bucket filled with glitter?

Captivated by the majesty of the castle, Harry made his way through the open gates and along the pathway towards the broad gravelled forecourt, with its impressive views across the gardens and formal terraces.

Next to the castle's entrance, he got out of his car and stood for a while gazing at the beauty of the lush green valley, catching a church spire in the distance and a glimpse of the river as the sunlight caught its lazy meanderings.

He marvelled at the tranquillity.

'Gorgeous, isn't it?' breathed a voice in his ear.

'What the—' Harry turned to look at whoever had sneaked up on him and stared a little dumbly at Belinda, the last person he had expected to see.

CHAPTER EIGHT

'Sorry,' said Belinda, feeling a slow smile spreading across her face, long mascaraed eyelashes fluttering at him. 'Did I startle you?'

'You could say that.'

She watched Harry pull back his jacket to reveal Doggie Delight's cartoon logo.

'I say,' she said, 'the Masons have really let themselves go.'

He stared at her.

'You know,' she said. 'Baring your chest.'

'I'm not a Mason,' he said. 'And my chest isn't bare.'

'Oh.' She took a tentative step backwards and tilted her head to one side. 'Well, the fact that you're wearing clothes is a good start. What sort of a world would it be if we all walked around naked?'

'Who mentioned being naked?' said Harry, his eyes down at her feet.

'I know what you're thinking,' she said, enjoying watching him squirm, all the while waiting for a reaction to her comment. It was a little unnecessary, but she had been desperate to read his expression.

'I was wondering how you got up here so fast in those shoes,' said Harry, his confidence seemingly reinstated. 'Along with your stealth approach on this gravel pathway in vertigo-inducing footwear. I thought you might be some sort of high-heeled ninja.'

'I'm light on my feet,' she said. 'Cat-like tread.'

'No,' said Harry. 'Dogs.'

'Pardon?' Belinda was now beginning to wonder if Harry Powell was, in fact, a little bit of a simpleton.

'I've come to speak to someone about a dog food order. Apparently, it's something that needs discussing. In person.'

They stared at one another.

'In person,' repeated Harry. 'As in with a person. That person being Marcus Penshurst.'

She smiled again, burgundy-painted lips stretching across her face, as she wondered what Marcus was up to this time. 'That will be my brother Marcus. Come with me and I'll get him for you.'

Belinda led Harry around the side of the building, listening to him as he trotted along behind her, sounding like a lame donkey, scrunching and kicking gravel as he went.

More than once, a couple of stones ricocheted off the back of her calves. It crossed her mind that perhaps he was aiming for her. Something she dismissed as unlikely. Harry just seemed clumsy.

Belinda slowed a little and they fell into comfortable step. She pointed to the huge gate on their left-hand side and told him it led to the formal gardens. With a wave towards the parts of the grounds that were obscured by the castle, she explained it contained the barns, garages and fields.

'And here,' she said, sixty feet or so further along the castle exterior, indicating a large wooden door set back in the stone wall, 'is the entrance we tend to use if we're on this side of the grounds.'

'So, you live here?' said Harry.

'Yes. With my brother and father, although you probably won't see *him* very much at all. He's hardly ever here.'

Belinda stopped, turned the black metal handle and ushered Harry inside. 'This is really the gardeners' kitchen, but it has all of the essentials and it's a lovely cosy spot. Coffee?' she asked, walking towards a percolator on a granite worktop on the far side of the room.

'Please,' he said. 'Milk, no sugar.'

'Take a seat,' she said, nodding at the square kitchen table, a high-backed chair tucked in on each side. 'I'll get Marcus.'

She put the drink down in front of him and he took a moment to savour the strong aroma before lifting the cup and taking a sip.

Belinda walked out of the kitchen, deliberately leaving the door open behind her.

If Harry was anything like the curious detective she thought he was, she would bet he was about to go wandering in the corridor. For an inexplicable reason, she wanted him to show an interest in her home.

Amused at how easily she might be able to coax Harry along, Belinda thought she should probably reconsider her brother's ridiculous notion of a puppy. If men were this simple, how tough could dog-training be?

A couple of feet from the living room, Belinda heard voices, raised voices at that, and stopped in her tracks.

The thick carpet masked any sounds of her approach. One of the voices belonged to her brother, that was easy to identify. The other was a little harder to place, due to it being so out of context.

It was the slurred shouting that gave it away.

Tipper Johnson was in her home raising his voice to her brother.

He must have all but followed her home after she confronted him in the New Inn. Tipper's earlier comment about Marcus had totally slipped her mind, what with the surprise at seeing Harry. She really had to focus.

The voices were getting louder as the two of them moved towards her.

'I'm telling you,' said Tipper, 'it's not right, not right, I tell you.'

'I'm sorry to inform you that your opinions don't count for much,' said Marcus in a cold, clipped tone. 'This is what I do and what I have been doing for some years, so it's unlikely that you will have any sway over me or my business.'

'Listen, I won't sit back and let you do this. I know things.'

A sharp laugh cracked the air.

'Really? You're resorting to blackmail?'

From the far end of the corridor behind her, Belinda heard Harry call out, 'Blimey, Belinda, these photos on the wall are extraordinary.'

Belinda felt satisfaction that Harry had taken the bait. She did, however, have a more pressing concern that his curiosity would extend to wanting to know why Tipper was in their home, when she didn't know herself.

She acknowledged Harry by flapping her hand in the air, hoping that if she disappeared around the corner, he would carry on looking at the collection of photos stretching many feet in either direction.

As Belinda rushed around the corner, out of Harry's sight, Tipper flung open the morning room door and barrelled towards her. The red flush on his face and neck was not the only indication of his rage: his expression was pure anger, accompanied by mutterings of strong language.

Her brother stood a couple of feet behind him, appearance one of equal fury, something she had only seen once before.

Tipper muttered something, his anger so great that he didn't seem to be forming coherent words.

With a snarl, he turned in the direction of the front entrance and was gone. The sound of the door slamming shot through the great hallway.

'Marcus,' she said, keeping her tone as light as she possibly could, 'Harry is here from the Doggie Delight food place and says he has an appointment with you.'

She studied her brother's face. If she hadn't witnessed the end of the heated exchange for herself, she would now be totally oblivious that anything untoward had taken place.

'Of course,' said Marcus, rubbing his hands together. 'How remiss of me to have forgotten.'

'He's in the kitchen,' she said, a little in awe of how quickly Marcus had recovered his composure.

'Let's not keep him waiting any longer,' said Marcus, walking up to her and putting an arm around her shoulder. 'Is he a decent sort?'

Belinda nodded and said, 'The only encounters I've had with him have been memorable for all the right reasons.'

She was glad her brother's arm was still around her: there was no chance of him seeing the concern etched on her face over Tipper's rant and hurried departure.

CHAPTER NINE

Belinda and Marcus walked side by side to where Harry was still peering at the photographs on the wall.

Belinda could see from his gaping mouth and face inches from the glass that he was smitten with them.

'Sorry, sorry, sorry,' said Marcus as he hurried towards Harry, holding out his hand. 'I managed to get myself caught up in a bit of business. I'm Marcus.'

'Harry Powell,' said Harry. 'These are incredible. I expected the place to be adorned with suits of armour and oil paintings of dour-faced, uptight aristocracy in enormous wigs. Instead, here's photo after photo of dogs.'

'Do you sell much food, Harry?' said Marcus, a seemingly innocent question that made Belinda smirk.

'Yes, my round's increasing all the time.'

'Incredible,' muttered Marcus.

Harry leaned towards the display and pointed to a photo of a cocker spaniel beside a silver trophy almost as big as the dog, which was being kissed by its ruddy-faced owner.

'This one, for example,' said Harry. 'It's obvious from the enormous Crufts sign in the background where it was taken. But who's this man fondling the dog?'

'That's our Aunty Clarissa,' said Marcus.

Belinda's shoulders shook with silent laughter.

'Anyway, let's talk dog food,' said Marcus. He placed a hand on Harry's shoulder and steered him back through the kitchen door.

Without drawing any more attention to herself, Belinda stepped into the kitchen behind them. The meeting had nothing to do with her, but she wanted to know more about her brother's plans.

Marcus looked surprisingly gleeful at the idea of chatting about all things beef and carrot, turkey and rice, salmon and potato. 'Take a seat and we'll talk figures.'

Once they were sitting opposite each other, Belinda hanging back in the doorway, Harry said, 'I understand that you're looking to place a substantial order for the next few months.'

'Absolutely.' Marcus nodded. 'We love dogs here and hope to have plenty more in the coming weeks.'

'Coming weeks?' said Harry. 'How many do you have now?'

'Oh, well, none right now.'

'I'm easily confused,' said Harry, 'but—'

'Yes, I gathered.' Marcus smiled, head to one side.

'You want the first delivery to be made in two days' time, but you don't have any dogs at present?'

'Spot on,' said Marcus.

'And you're after a delivery of,' Harry glanced down at his tablet, where he had been busy tapping in his customer's requirements, 'three eighteen-kilo bags of sensitive adult food, turkey and veg flavour; six twelve-kilo bags of grain-free working-dog food, beef flavour; and five twelve-kilo bags of high-performance dog food, chicken flavour.'

From her vantage point in the doorway, Belinda could see that Marcus's face was a mask of sheer delight.

'Winner, winner, chicken dinner,' said Marcus.

'But there are no dogs here?' said Harry again.

'No, not yet, but mark my words, there soon will be.'

Marcus stood up, pushing his chair back across the ceramic tiled floor, a movement Harry mirrored.

Belinda stepped forward, unsure whether this would be the right time to ask her brother why he was buying so much dog food. It was probably a question for when they were alone, but she knew she wouldn't like the answer and could only put it off for so long.

'Oh, sis,' said Marcus, 'I'd completely forgotten you were there. Is it OK if you see Harry out? I have some other business I need to run out and take care of.'

Silently, she watched them shake hands and inched out of her brother's way as he headed out of the kitchen. She wasn't sure whether her feelings towards her brother's business matters were that of curiosity or of fear. Nothing he did ended well and the row with Tipper had unnerved her.

'Well,' she said.

'Well,' Harry said. 'I'd better get out of your way.'

'Or you could stay and have another coffee?'

Harry gave her a smile that she could only interpret as pity as he fiddled with the off button on his tablet.

'It's a fairly large order,' he said. 'I should really get home and put it through. Besides, I need to refill the car for tomorrow, plus look into something a customer told me about this morning.'

Belinda tilted her head to the side, gave what Harry had said some thought and asked, 'Anything I can help with?'

Harry gave the smallest of shrugs and said, 'Thanks, but no. I've got this one in hand.'

He inched towards the door.

'You really didn't know who I was?' she asked.

He glanced across at her, one hand on the door that would take him back out into the gardens.

'Last night in the pub, you didn't give me your surname,' he said. 'In all honesty, I'm not sure I would have immediately twigged that you were related to one of my customers either.'

So, he still didn't know *who* she was.

Belinda took a deep breath and said, 'Please sit down, I have something I need to tell you.'

She watched Harry as he let go of the door handle and walked back over to the table.

What exactly was she going to say to him? *Funny you don't remember that time on the freezing cold docks when you handcuffed me?*

'You're smiling,' said Harry once he had sat down in the same chair. 'I'm guessing it's not that bad.'

Could he be that adept at forgetting something that had been such a huge deal to her? Perhaps he was extremely gifted at pretending? Some sort of amateur dramatics buff?

Belinda sat opposite Harry, folded her hands in her lap and said, 'I haven't been completely honest with you.'

He raised an eyebrow.

'When we met in the pub last night, I wasn't sure who you were, but it didn't take me long to work it out.'

She risked a glimpse at him from under her fringe.

So far, no reaction.

'The Gatehouse is owned by my family,' she said. 'I decided to have it renovated and rent it out. I knew who was renting it, but it didn't register with me at first.'

'Right.'

Belinda ran a finger around the corner of the table. Although she was focusing on tracing an imaginary pattern back and forth, she saw Harry move back an inch or two in his chair.

'And when I said met you in the pub last night,' she said, looking up at him, 'I should have said met you again.'

'Again? As in, we've met before?'

She nodded. 'We have.'

Silence.

'Go on,' said Harry eventually.

She knew she would feel better for getting this out in the open. 'Twenty-one years ago. You arrested me.'

Harry folded his arms and said, 'You're going to have to give me a bit more than that to go on. I've arrested hundreds of people over the years and I can't remember them all, although I'd be sure to remember someone who lived in a castle. That doesn't happen every day.'

'It was at Dover docks.'

She left the words hanging there, waiting for the penny to drop.

The realisation was all over Harry's face in an instant.

'You were… I remember… You must have been a kid.'

Belinda roared with laughter, relieved to have told him, and in all honesty, relishing Harry's discomfort.

'I was twenty, Harry. And you were the perfect gentleman, even then.'

He fidgeted in his chair and slowly blew the air out from his reddening cheeks.

'What a day that was,' said Harry. 'I was a DC by then, but we were all called back into uniform to cover the demonstrations at the docks.'

He gave a slow shake of his head.

'Is it really obvious that I now can't look you in the eye?' he asked.

'You struggled to look me in the eye on that day too.'

Now she was enjoying herself.

'There was a damned good reason,' he said. 'In my thirty years as a police officer, that was the one and only time I arrested anyone who was naked.'

Belinda was struggling to stop herself from guffawing: the sight of Harry averting his eyes twenty-one years later was too funny.

'You can look now,' she said. 'I'm dressed. And I wasn't completely naked that day either.'

'That's true,' he said. 'I seem to remember you were wearing boots and a hat.'

'We thought naked women on a January day would be more impactful, draw more attention to what we were doing. You've forgotten that we were draped in a banner. It covered a lot of, well, you know.'

'There's no way I could have remembered you,' said Harry, a little composure regained. 'There was something like thirty of you and I was back and forth between the docks and the police van. I seem to remember I arrested about four of you.'

'I know you did. I was the only one you gave your coat to though.'

'I only had one coat. And by the way, you still owe me for the dry cleaning.'

CHAPTER TEN

Belinda watched Harry drive away, expecting to see gravel flying in all directions as he spun along the path in an attempt to put as much distance between them as he could manage.

She'd thought she would have to remind him of how he had led her away, as she shouted and protested her innocence. Being hauled into the back of the police van was as fresh in her mind as if it had happened that very day. Yet Harry seemed to recall the arrest perfectly, just not *her*.

She stood watching his car as it disappeared from view behind the lime trees and around the curve of the driveway.

For several more minutes Belinda remained rooted to the spot, trusting her revelation had not made her appear a little on the odd side.

She made for one of the benches nestled to the side of the driveway and lost track of time dissecting their conversation in her mind: what she had told him, how she had said it and whether it was usual for police officers to bump into people they had arrested decades earlier. Perhaps on their next encounter she would need to show that he hadn't got to her with his casual remark about his dry-cleaning bill. Arresting people may not be a big deal to him, but it was the one and only time she had been in trouble with the police. Maybe she should have laughed at what she hoped was his idea of a joke to lighten the mood.

Her mind raced when a flash of a car in the distance drove back into view and she jumped up. Except the car wasn't Harry's but her brother's Mercedes.

Belinda was not prepared to leave things as they were with Harry. He had said very little after hearing about one of the most defining moments of her life, and after a time, he'd simply got up and left.

She wanted the last word; she couldn't leave it there.

Marcus drove towards Belinda, slowed, pulled round her and said through the open window, 'You quite all right, sis?'

'Give me a lift down to the village, would you?' she said, rushing around to the passenger door and jumping in before he had a chance to answer.

She looked across at his puzzled face before turning her attention to clicking the seat belt into place.

'What?' she said. 'It saves me getting the Land Rover out. Besides—'

Her head snapped towards him.

'Have you been drinking, Marcus?'

With a sigh, Marcus released the brake and said, 'I popped into the pub for a quick pint.'

'After the unfortunate incident earlier with Tipper?'

Marcus glanced across as she nibbled on the side of her nail, something they both knew she did when stressed. She dropped her hands into her lap.

'That man's always three sheets to the wind,' said Marcus, face clouding over. 'Drink will be the death of him.'

They both fell silent until the car reached the gate. 'Drop me here, would you?' Belinda said.

'Are you sure you're all right?' her brother asked. He had a genuine look of concern on his face, which was rarer than hens' teeth.

'Don't worry about me, I'm fine.'

To prove her point, she leaned across and ruffled his hair, gave him a grin and got out of the car.

Belinda stood for several seconds while Marcus turned the car around once more and headed home. Then she walked towards the green, deftly avoiding the remaining market shoppers, who were trotting along on the grass with bags of local goodies, so enthralled with their purchases they paid little attention to anyone around them.

Belinda, however, could not fail to miss the small crowd forming outside the New Inn. A single glance told her that this was not hordes of happy customers gathering outside with their drinks, but disgruntled customers who could not get in through the locked doors. Even George Reid from the butcher's shop next door, which appeared to be closed for the day, had come out to see what was happening. His tattoos were hidden by his blood-stained white overalls, which was more than could be said for his bulk and demeanour.

One thing Belinda thought she and Tipper had agreed on was that on market days, the pub stayed open all day. Her visit to Harry in the Gatehouse momentarily forgotten, she marched towards the pub.

Once she was an arm's distance from the closed doors, she heard a woman say to her friend, 'The landlord's not very well, so the barmaid said.'

'Not very well?' her friend replied. 'We've got a table booked. I've got a voucher, so I hope he starts feeling better. It runs out this week.'

Puzzled at the woman's comments, having seen a perfectly healthy Tipper a little over an hour ago, Belinda made her way past the dozen or so people who were taking it in turns to try the door handle, press their faces up against the window or phone the landline only to hear the answerphone.

Making sure no one was following her, she made her way inside the pub via the tradesmen's entrance. The last thing Tipper needed if he had developed a mystery illness in the brief time since he'd slammed out of her home was to be greeted by a dozen bad-tempered customers.

The cellar steps ran alongside the wall of the side alley, leading below. Clutching the handrail, trying to ignore the whiff of stale ale, Belinda made her way down towards the solid wooden door, her feet finding it difficult to gain purchase on the narrow stone steps. Three steps from the bottom, her foot slipped and – in an effort to prevent herself from falling backwards – she pitched forwards, colliding headfirst with the door.

The force threw the door wide open and for an instant, Belinda couldn't quite believe the scene in front of her.

The cellar, which should have been packed with beer, wine and spirits – all paid for by her – was instead littered with a few crates holding empty mixer bottles and a couple of boxes of bar snacks scattered around a large beer barrel.

It was what was in the barrel that made Belinda stop in her tracks and shake her head in disbelief.

Tipper Johnson's legs were sticking straight out of the top of the barrel of beer, liquid sloshing on the cellar floor as his body bobbed up and down.

CHAPTER ELEVEN

Momentarily, Belinda froze. Then she covered the distance between her and the protruding limbs, unsure whether to grab Tipper's feet and pull him clear of the barrel or leave him. Her mind made up, a wave of stale beer drenched Belinda as she tried to pull him from the rancid ale.

There was little hope he was still alive, but she was not about to leave it to chance.

As Belinda slid around on the cold, wet floor, achieving little but feeling a strong sense of duty to at least try, she heard footsteps rushing down from inside the pub.

She looked up at two pairs of feet on the steps: one a pair of black men's shoes, the other a pair of pink mules.

The mules made it down first and brought Belinda face to face with the barmaid, Sandra.

Her face wasn't difficult to read, but the sterner expression on Harry Powell's was.

'How did you get inside the pub?' said Belinda.

'Never mind that,' said Harry. 'Let's get him out.'

Belinda and Sandra stood back as Harry grabbed one of Tipper's ankles, put an arm around his waist and yanked him from the barrel.

'What are you doing?' said Sandra, looking down at the soaked and very lifeless body of the pub's landlord.

'Making sure he's dead,' said Harry.

'Pardon?' said Sandra, pushing herself back against the cellar wall.

'No, no, not *making sure* he's dead,' said Harry. 'You know what I mean.'

He turned his attention to Belinda. 'How did *you* get in here? Sandra saw me on the pavement outside and let me in, but she definitely didn't let you in.'

'Oh, stop eyeing me up like a suspect, Mr Used to Be a Detective but Not Any More,' said Belinda with a grimace. 'The door leading to the alley was open.'

'She didn't kill him,' said Sandra. 'Tipper was already in the barrel when I came downstairs to check the delivery had arrived. They were supposed to be here first thing, although for some reason they didn't turn up. We're running out of almost everything, what with it being market day too. I saw… you know… and went straight back upstairs to get help.'

All three of them peered at his clearly lifeless face, almost as red and bloated now as it had been when he was alive.

'We'd better not disturb the crime scene any further. It's time to call the police,' said Harry, wiping his wet hands on his trousers.

'Here,' said Sandra, who handed him a bar towel that had been hanging over the end of the bannister.

'Put that back,' said Harry, scowl on his face. 'We can't move or contaminate anything. We need to leave it all exactly as it is.'

Belinda made a point of allowing Sandra and Harry to ascend the steps ahead of her.

If she wasn't very much mistaken, there was something even Harry Powell had failed to spot in the cellar.

A few minutes later, cellar doors secure, massing herd outside dispersed and the police on their way, the three of them sat in a line at the bar, elbows resting on the counter.

'So, what exactly *are* you doing here?' Belinda asked Harry.

'I was about to ask you the same thing,' he said.

'You didn't say earlier that you were heading to the pub,' she said, interest piqued, and a little worried that Harry had heard Tipper rowing with Marcus only that afternoon.

'Well, I asked you first,' said Harry.

'Don't be so childish,' said Belinda. 'You're not a policeman now. You sell dog food for a living.'

'Something wrong with selling dog food?'

'There's no need to be touchy, I was only asking,' said Belinda.

'Will you two stop rowing?' said Sandra. 'You are doing my head in.'

'Sorry,' they mumbled in unison.

After a brief silence, Belinda said, 'So what made you come to the pub?'

Harry rubbed his temples and sighed. 'I wanted a drink. Is that unusual? This is a pub, isn't it?'

'I only saw him at lunchtime,' said Sandra, picking at a loose piece of cotton on the hem of her pink blouse. 'He told me to take a break when the place emptied out after the Friday lunchtime rush. It was very unusual for him to lock the doors on market day. I should have known something was up.'

Belinda turned on her stool to face Sandra on her left-hand side. 'What makes you say that?'

It was Sandra's turn to let out a sigh. 'He's been a bit down lately. Not able to pay his bills, in debt to the brewery, and I heard him on the phone discussing other money he owes. I mean owed. It's no wonder he took his own life.'

Harry's head snapped towards Sandra. 'You think he committed suicide? That's not really likely.'

'Why do you say that?' said Belinda.

'Who'd drown themselves in the slops bucket?' said Harry. 'You'd at least use something with a touch of class.'

'That is hardly the point,' said Belinda, scanning the bar for some sort of tissue to hand to the now weeping barmaid.

'And what on earth was he doing with a huge open barrel of beer? Don't tell me he was pouring that back into the Sun's Over the Yardarm barrel. I've been drinking that…'

The rest of Harry's sentence was lost in the banging coming from outside.

Belinda heard a couple of voices shouting, 'Police,' and got off her stool to open the main bar doors. Two police cars were parked directly outside, and a small group of locals had started to gather again at the sight.

Within a short space of time, the three of them were each sitting in front of a police officer.

Belinda eyed the young officer designated to take her statement. PC Green, according to his name badge, although he had introduced himself as Vince. She supposed in another space and time, he might have had the potential to fill Harry Powell's shoes.

'So,' said Vince, 'can you tell me what happened?'

With a glance over at Harry – who seemed to be attempting to bond with his assigned officer through humour, which wasn't going all that well – and then at the ashen face of Sandra, Belinda explained how she had come to be in the cellar.

'How well did you know the landlord?' said Vince.

'I'd known him for some time,' she said, 'but it was more of a business association. I invested some money in the pub, and he was running it for me.'

She glanced down at her hands on the table, then up at the brown eyes of the youthful police officer. 'I don't suppose I'm going to be making much of my money back with the landlord dead and the pub closed.'

Belinda watched him nod thoughtfully and then write down her answer. Satisfied she had his full attention, she leaned across the table and in a conspiratorial whisper said, 'There is one thing I need to tell you though.'

The wait for the police had given Belinda time to think about her brother's possible involvement. He had rowed with Tipper shortly before his death and had smelled of beer minutes before she'd found his body. The least she could do was speak to Marcus – maybe even find the real killer – before she burdened the police with this information. She owed him that much.

She risked another peek across at Sandra to make sure she was still out of earshot. Sandra's face was a mask of horror as she insisted she had no idea how Tipper had met his untimely end.

Vince leaned closer to Belinda.

'One thing I noticed as I came through the cellar door,' she said, 'was an open wooden crate.'

Another check to make sure Sandra couldn't hear her.

'Caught on the edge of the box is a bright pink piece of cotton, the same colour as the barmaid's top.' Belinda nodded knowingly. 'She told me that she ran down the stairs, saw Tipper and ran straight back up to the bar. If that's true, how did she rip her blouse on a crate on the other side of the room?'

CHAPTER TWELVE

It was some time before Harry was allowed to leave the pub, and even then, he left Belinda and Sandra being interviewed. His experience told him that they would be more useful to the police than him, what with Sandra having found Tipper's body initially, and then Belinda happening upon him and trying to get him out of the barrel.

If Harry was completely honest with himself, he also felt a little swell of pride that as a retired detective inspector, the officers had taken his evidence at face value.

His intentions of an afternoon pint had completely left him. Now, wired and unable to sit still, work seemed the only solution. He had a couple more local customers he could fit in, so he collected his car and drove back through the village, cautious eye on the New Inn. He told himself it was to see how many police officers and crime scene investigators Tipper Johnson was worthy of, but in truth he was hoping that Belinda would walk out of the pub.

He sat in his car at the edge of the village green, trying to convince himself that he really wasn't stalling to see Belinda. If there was anything she could tell him, he could pass it back to his former colleagues. He was a retired police officer, someone had been murdered in his village, and Belinda knew everyone. He could use her local knowledge to his advantage. That was what he told himself.

Harry let the engine idle, staring at the New Inn, and as if summoned, Belinda stepped through the doorway.

Without giving it any further thought, Harry drove towards the pub, window open, hand out waving. When that didn't attract her attention, he leaned on the horn.

Startled, Belinda's head snapped in his direction with such speed her hand automatically went up to support her neck.

Harry pulled to a stop beside her and peered through the open window. Belinda bent down and locked eyes with him.

'That was discreet,' she said. 'Did you do much undercover work when you were a policeman?'

'I thought we could chat things over,' said Harry.

'Chat what things over?' said Belinda, a smirk of amusement creeping across her face.

'Do you want to get in?' he said, moving across to open the door.

'Get into the car with a stranger?' she said. 'This could look as though you're picking me up.'

'I am picking you up.'

Belinda laughed. 'Not something you really want to brag about, but I'll humour you and get in.'

Within a couple of minutes, Harry had pulled into the car park of the local nature reserve. There were only a few other vehicles and no other people in the tarmacked area set aside for ramblers, walkers and those wanting to get in amongst the Kent countryside rather than see it from their cars.

It would have felt like a perfect summer's afternoon with the dappled sunlight falling all around them, birds chattering in the branches overhead, a gentle breeze through the open window.

Except they had just found a dead body.

'Are you doing OK?' Harry said. 'Shock's a funny thing.'

'You're sweet,' she said, 'but honestly, I'm doing all right. I simply can't think who would have wanted him dead.'

'I'd bow to your better judgement, but he didn't strike me as the most likeable of people.'

Belinda seemed to consider this for a time.

'I'm not sure I can think of anyone who despised Tipper enough to do that to him,' she said, tucking her hair behind her ears. 'Although now I come to think of it, on my way to the pub last night, I saw Anthony Cotter and Lennie Aisling chatting on the green.'

Harry gave a shrug and said, 'The owner of the microbrewery and the landlord of the Dog and Duck speaking to one another isn't that intriguing, especially on an evening when most of their trade was taken by their biggest rival. It's really not enough to want the man dead.'

'You've got a point,' said Belinda. 'They certainly weren't the only ones who seemed interested in what was happening in the New Inn this afternoon.'

'Most of the village was out at some point,' said Harry. 'It's murder – it attracts the crowds.'

'Yes, I keep forgetting your background is murder.'

'Investigating them,' said Harry. 'You make it sound as though I killed people for a living.'

She laughed. 'The last thing anyone would ever mistake you for is a hitman,' she said, twinkle in her eye. 'Do you miss the police much?'

Harry thought about lying, but there was little point.

'Yes,' he said, voice a touch more miserable than he would have liked. 'There are times I regret leaving. But it was for the best.'

Belinda placed her hand over his. 'It sounds as though it didn't end on a high for you,' she said.

He didn't really want to talk about it, and yet he liked talking to Belinda. It felt natural. Perhaps it was sitting in one of the county's areas of outstanding beauty, or the shared trauma at the afternoon's events, but whatever it was, he told Belinda more than he intended.

'A member of my team was killed,' he said, pausing only when he heard the sharp intake of breath from his passenger. 'And then another member of the team was involved in something a little murky, and she also got hurt.'

They sat in silence until Belinda said, 'You know what'll help us both?'

'Go on.'

'A good murder to solve. How about it?'

Harry had already thought about it, but he made her wait for his answer. He had already showed his hand about his departure from the police; the last thing he wanted was to come across as desperate to fill his days.

'Murder investigations are a tricky business,' he said. 'I was thinking of looking into something a little more straightforward, such as dognapping. Care to join me in that?'

'Dognapping?' said Belinda. 'I'm more interested in who thinks they can start bumping people off in *my* village.'

When Harry made no comment, she raised her eyebrows at him and said, 'Go on, I'm intrigued.'

'This morning,' he said, 'a while before I came to talk to your brother, I was at Ivy White's house delivering her dog food. She told me about some concerns she had around Peter Clayton and what led up to his death.'

'Poor Peter,' said Belinda. 'I knew him, and we were all sad about what happened to him, but wouldn't you rather spend your time trying to solve Tipper's murder?'

'Belinda, I'll admit that I miss my old job,' said Harry, shifting in his seat to face her as square on as he could manage. 'That's why I want to look into the dognapping. Murder is different. We should leave that to the police.'

She put a hand up to her chin and nodded thoughtfully.

'Look,' she said after a few seconds, 'I know everyone, and I was living here when Peter was killed. I can help you with the dognapping, but you have to agree to help me work out who killed Tipper.'

Harry let out a long, slow breath.

'Not sure I like that idea,' he said. 'It's going against protocol and we could unintentionally jeopardise the investigation and contaminate any potential evidence.'

'Harry, that all sounded extremely boring, and again, if you want my help with the dognapping, you have to investigate Tipper's murder with me.'

'I don't think the two are connected, but I'll help you as far as I can.'

Belinda grinned at him, prompting him to hold up a hand.

'But we'll have proper briefings to discuss what we find out,' said Harry, knowing he could not allow her to go off track. 'You don't do anything dangerous or go anywhere without discussing it with me first. Agreed?'

She took a little longer to answer than he would have liked, but she eventually said, 'Agreed.'

'Mrs White was adamant someone was trying to steal Peter's West Highland terrier and that's why Peter was run over,' said Harry. 'It sounds as though the dog was unscathed.'

Belinda pondered this for a moment and then said, 'Scooter ran away by all accounts, which is hardly surprising. The little mite was found by a local lad in a field with his collar caught on a branch.'

'Caught on a branch?' said Harry. 'I do remember that the dog was nearby, but the details escape me. Mrs White said earlier that Scooter was found tied to a post. However, it sounds more likely he was terrified, raced off and got his collar snagged. That makes a big difference. The devil is very much in the detail.'

'I completely agree. I'm sorry to be the one knocking down Ivy's theory, but if the objective was to take the dog, why not simply take him then and there rather than walk him to a field, tie him up and then go back for him?'

Harry considered this and said, 'Who found the dog?'

'I'm not entirely sure,' she said. 'Whoever it was was fairly young and so his details weren't made public. We can ask around; it shouldn't be too hard to find out.'

Harry pondered her latest suggestion, in two minds whether he should be teaming up with Belinda. His intention had been to get as much information from her as he could, then pass back anything he found out to the police.

It was abundantly clear that he needed to get his teeth into something other than delivering dog food. Belinda just might help stave off the boredom. Life seemed like it could be more fun with her in it, and she had offered to help him. He would no longer be a team of one; she seemed desperate to find out who had killed Tipper – they both stood to gain from partnering up.

'What's the deal with Sandra?' said Harry, aware he was jumping topic and hoping it would get him a genuine reaction.

'How do you mean?' said Belinda, narrowing her eyes.

'Tell me about her.'

They stared at one another, with the birds tweeting loudly in the silence. All rather pleasant, apart from the tension in the car.

Belinda moved back in her seat, shuffling against the car door. 'Sandra and I don't really see eye to eye, although she's pleasant enough. I've tried to be friends with her, even though she seems to have taken a dislike to me. I don't think she enjoyed working for Tipper and that seemed to bring out the worst in her. Tipper could be difficult, and his drinking had apparently spiralled out of control of late.'

'So she had a reason to kill him?' said Harry. 'That seems too easy.'

'By itself, not liking your boss is hardly a reason to kill them, let alone drown them in a barrel of beer,' said Belinda. 'Although there was a piece of pink cotton on the crate in the cellar, the same colour as Sandra's top.'

Harry had missed that. He was really slipping.

'Don't look so disapproving,' laughed Belinda. 'I told the nice police officer. I think they'll be having words with Sandra before long – she's definitely got some explaining to do.'

'It could be her then,' said Harry, wondering if this was the fastest murder investigation he had ever worked.

'I tend to agree with you. Only how are we going to prove it?'

'We don't need to,' said Harry. 'That's the police's job.'

'Oh, they're completely use—' Belinda executed a truly wonderful goldfish impression at the expression on Harry's face.

'OK then, DCI Penshurst,' said Harry. 'What are you going to do first?'

'Interview the suspect?'

'And what are you going to ask her?' said Harry.

'I'd start with… "Did you do it?"'

Harry hadn't laughed so hard in ages.

'And if she says no?' he asked, loving how the day was panning out.

'I suppose I'd have to prove her motive for wanting Tipper dead,' said Belinda, a smug smile on her face.

'Good start,' said Harry. 'You said that she didn't like working for him, especially with his drinking getting worse. If she killed him, what would she do for money?'

'Tipper certainly didn't have any,' said Belinda with a scowl. 'He used the money I lent him for the pub on doing up the garden and buying some new furniture for the bar. It wasn't what we'd agreed and I know there was virtually nothing left in the business account.'

'So, perhaps Sandra lost it and pushed him into the barrel,' said Harry, considering his own suggestion. 'But she'd have to have been really angry for some reason; she wouldn't have gained from his death, as far as I can see. She's out of a job at the moment.'

'Mm,' said Belinda. 'Until there's a new landlord, anyway.'

'Unless she had something lined up…'

'You've given me an idea,' said Belinda, 'and it involves you dropping me at the Dog and Duck. I can see if Sandra had a new job arranged there, and throw in some subtle enquires about how profitable killing off his competition at the New Inn would be.'

Not entirely certain how he'd ended up her chauffeur, Harry started the engine and drove Belinda back to Little Challham, all the while wondering what he had got himself involved in.

CHAPTER THIRTEEN

There was no doubt in Belinda's mind that Harry was coming around to her way of thinking. He hardly said a word on the way back to the village, so she surmised he was 'working the case'. She tried to tell him that she had derived no pleasure from telling PC Vince Green about Sandra's torn blouse, but even that didn't elicit a response.

'Drop me here, would you?' said Belinda, indicating the car park of the Women's Institute. 'I don't want Lennie to see us together.'

She unclipped her seat belt and stole a glance at Harry.

'What?' she said, when she saw he was staring at her.

'Has anyone ever told you you're extremely bossy?' said Harry.

'Why is it that women are bossy when they're clear about what they want, and men are assertive?' Belinda pushed the car door open and added, 'You don't have to wait for me, not if you've got things to do.'

With that, she was out of the car and about to head to the Dog and Duck when Delia Hawking, one of the WI trustees, caught her attention. Delia was kneeling on the ground, weeding one of the flowerbeds. There must surely have been someone who could have helped her, if not done it for her, but even at eighty years of age, Delia wasn't one to sit idle.

Delia's neat, short haircut was coiffed to its usual perfection and her light blue cotton trousers and floral-print velour sweatshirt were very much in line with her habitual crease-free look.

As Belinda approached her across the gravel car park, Delia called out, 'Lovely day for it.'

Belinda crouched beside her. 'Fine job you're doing there, Delia.'

'We simply can't let these things get the better of us,' said Delia, manoeuvring herself slightly on the cushioned kneeling pad. 'I was only out here a couple of days ago, but apart from the number of weeds, someone has graffitied over there by the door.'

Belinda looked at where she was pointing.

'I'm sorry,' she said, craning her neck. 'I can't see anything.'

'It's very small, but I notice these things, and it's the start of the village going downhill,' said Delia as she took her gardening gloves off. 'But I don't think you're bending down in that awkward position to ask me about weeds and graffiti. You should really join us one evening for Pilates.'

'Yes, I'll definitely do that,' said Belinda, with no intention of ever doing so. 'You remember the tragedy of Peter Clayton's death?'

A sad nod from Delia was followed by a sigh.

'Do you recall who found his dog?' said Belinda.

Delia pulled herself up from the ground with the agility of someone several years younger. Perhaps Belinda should reconsider the Pilates after all.

'I don't think anyone mentioned who found the dog – a West Highland terrier, I think,' said Delia, now face to face with Belinda. 'Why? Is it important?'

'I'm not sure,' said Belinda. 'Anyway, I'm sorry for disturbing you.'

'That's quite all right, Belinda. It was time I had a break. If I find out who found Scooter, I'll let you know.'

Belinda thanked her, smiled at the sight of Harry still sitting in his car waiting for her, and then carried on with her original mission to speak to Lennie Aisling, landlord of the Dog and Duck.

What had seemed like a straightforward morning had soon seen events spiral out of control. Belinda would rather have shared the next part of her plan with Harry, but she sensed he was still trying to keep her at arm's length. Until he was completely on board, she would do a bit of digging by herself. Besides, she had the feeling that he would respond better if he thought she would leave him behind otherwise.

Once at the end of the road, she glanced over at the New Inn before steeling herself for a visit to the Dog and Duck, nestled happily on the far end of the green.

As Belinda rounded the corner, she made out the figure of someone outside the Dog and Duck.

She felt herself bristle as she realised that Lennie was watching her make her way towards him. She had always tried not to think of the village's other pub as a competitor yet couldn't quite reach the level of benevolence required.

Lennie stood motionless, leaning against the door frame, his arms crossed over his pigeon chest, the start of a smile on his thin lips.

At forty-five years of age, he had done well to buy the pub outright and he turned a good profit, although the money never seemed to cheer his joyless face up.

There had always been something about him that put her on edge, although she failed to put her finger on what it was. The man was awfully fond of dogs, so he really couldn't be that bad. Even so, despite the sun shining upon her as she approached him, she felt as if a cloud were passing over. He had never liked her, and she hadn't taken much of a shine to him.

With only two metres between them, Belinda paused, opened her mouth to say something and watched as Lennie pushed himself from the door frame, turned and walked inside the pub.

'Rude,' she muttered.

Once inside, she was surprised to see that the place was reasonably quiet. Of the thirty tables, only three were occupied and the bar area itself was deserted.

Lennie had done a fine job of the interior, she had to admit. The wood panelling was a warm shade of light green, the wooden floor newly installed, and he had spared no expense with the soft furnishings. A mixture of low sofas and mismatched tub chairs at intervals across the enormous fireplace area and the far side of the restaurant gave a casual impression. Something that was far from simple to pull together.

The place even had the smell of hops from the thick garlands hanging from the ceiling. It had the markings of a quintessentially Kentish pub with the modernisation of an upmarket bar and restaurant. Perhaps Belinda should have asked Lennie to lend a hand with the New Inn.

'Hello, Lennie,' she said, taking one of the bar stools.

''Lo,' he said from behind the bar. 'That right Tipper's dead?'

'Yes,' she said. 'I found him.'

'Oh.'

He placed both of his hands flat on the counter and bowed his head towards her. This was the first flicker of interest he had shown her since she had suggested investing in his business some time ago.

'You all right?' said Lennie.

'It wasn't the most pleasant of experiences,' she said with a sigh, 'but I'm OK, thank you.'

'Nasty shock. Brandy?' He indicated the optics behind him. 'On the house, of course,' he added.

'Thank you, that's kind.'

Belinda studied his thinning hair as he took a bottle from the shelf and poured her a generous measure.

Her eyes were drawn to the framed photo of Lennie's German shepherd, which took pride of place in the centre of the wall.

Lennie turned to put the amber tot of spirit down in front of her.

'Have you ever thought about getting another dog, Lennie?' she asked, peeking at him from under her fringe as she took hold of the brandy glass.

The corners of his mouth turned down, and he shook his head. 'No, no, I couldn't. Howler was the best dog ever. I could never replace him.' There were tears in his eyes. 'Very big paws to fill.'

'Sorry,' she said, 'I didn't mean to upset you.'

Belinda took a sip of brandy, enjoying the feeling of warmth spreading along her throat, the liquid flame enlivening her.

'Are you working by yourself today?' she said, trying to start a conversation while steering it away from Tipper.

'Yes,' he said, with a worried glimpse at the empty tables. 'Just as well my last bar supervisor left – I'd hardly enough business to keep him employed this week.'

Lennie gave her an angry look. It put her on edge but gave her the impression he was cross with himself for giving too much away. That was hardly her fault, although it was what she had come here for in the first place. Clearly, she was better at this than she thought.

'Well, I expect business will pick up now that the New Inn's shut, at least until the police have finished there.'

'That's true,' he said, smile brightening his greying face and momentarily lifting the bags under his eyes. 'Nothing like a murder to bring the locals in too.'

'Who said it was murder?' said Belinda, taking another sip of her brandy.

'All those police officers?' he scoffed. 'Give me a break. If he'd fallen down the stairs of the cellar and broken his neck, they would have taken him away and that would be that. No, there's more to this than an accident.'

Belinda considered her next words carefully.

'The last time I saw Tipper alive, we had a row,' she said, thinking Lennie seemed clueless about Tipper's death, yet wondering if he was bluffing. She lifted the brandy to her lips and used the opportunity to peer at him over the rim of the glass, before saying, 'I hope the police don't suspect me.'

He opened his mouth to answer but a noise behind her distracted them both.

Lennie's face hardened and he indicated one of the far tables in the restaurant area.

Unable to see clearly in the mirror behind the bar, Belinda turned on her stool in time to see Sandra scurry towards the back of the pub.

'Interesting,' Belinda whispered to herself as Lennie went to join Sandra.

So, the police had not yet arrested her, but surely that was a matter of time. And now here she was in the village's only other pub. There was the microbrewery, of course, but that had never been serious competition. Still, Belinda should at least check that out. Once she had finished her brandy, obviously. This murder wasn't going to solve itself, so she might as well enjoy her libation, as well as the show.

Timing her intervention to perfection, Belinda gave them enough time to start a conversation, downed the rest of the brandy and eased from her bar stool towards the table Lennie had indicated.

Sandra was sitting with her back to Belinda while Lennie was partially hidden by the pub's fireplace.

Try as she might, Belinda was only able to get so far before Lennie saw her and widened his eyes, shaking his head at Sandra to stop her from speaking.

'I think we should keep up the walking,' said Sandra as Belinda approached them.

'Sandra,' said Belinda, and the young barmaid turned towards her. 'Are you OK? It was all such a horrible shock, wasn't it?'

Belinda placed a hand on the younger woman's shoulder and felt her recoil at her touch.

'Yes, yes, it was,' said Sandra. 'I wanted to speak to Lennie about a couple of things.' She stared up at Belinda. 'In private,' she added.

'Of course,' said Belinda after a brief pause. 'I'll leave you to it to chat about your walking.'

She turned to move away, wondering when Lennie and Sandra had started rambling together, and whether it was code for something else.

'Oh, just one other thing,' said Belinda. 'It's probably best you don't go too far – I imagine the police will be wanting another word with you soon.'

CHAPTER FOURTEEN

Once Harry had watched Belinda stop chatting in the Women's Institute car park and walk out of sight towards the Dog and Duck, he thought about what to do next.

Even though he wanted to follow her to the pub, he resisted the urge. Belinda struck him as the sort to get herself into trouble without really trying, and he probably shouldn't have let her go and speak to Lennie on her own. They hadn't had a chance to talk through everyone who might have had a reason to kill Tipper. Pub wars shouldn't be the reason, but he'd known people murder over less.

Still, Harry had other tasks to take care of. For a start, he was determined that he would look into the source of Mrs White's earlier distress, Belinda's contribution only adding to the uncertainty of Peter Clayton's death and his wandering pooch.

If Belinda could go off and make her own enquiries, he would be damned if he'd sit in the car and wait to see if she came back. She had told him he didn't have to wait for her if he had things to do. But did she really mean that, or was she hoping he would still be there? From what he had already learned about her, she was belligerent enough to leave him hanging. Or worse, she'd simply forget about him and go home.

That thought spurred him into action: whether Belinda came back or not, he mustn't forget he still had jobs he should be doing. Before Tipper's murder, he had planned for an early finish, but now he wanted to keep busy and get on with his round. Unfortunately, there were only so many more 'leave in a safe place' drops he could do before the work ran out for the day.

Harry drove towards the cluster of thirty or so more modern houses, the castle looming in the distance. Even though the more recently built bit of the village had been constructed over forty years ago, it was still referred to as the new part. This grouping of houses was home to a number of couples, young families and a few older inhabitants. It was mostly the older residents who added to Harry's round.

He had three more deliveries to make at the new houses and that would leave the boot of his shiny new car empty.

Within a few minutes, Harry had pulled up outside The Windchimes in Carringbrook Road. Professional face on, he popped open the boot, pulled out the eighteen-kilogram bag of sensitive adult dog food, turkey and vegetable flavour, and lugged it along the driveway.

He had only walked six feet or so towards the front door when it was pulled open, and a young girl ran towards him screaming.

In one swift movement, Harry shifted the bag of food from his shoulder to the side of the path, put his hands out and stepped in front of her.

'Hey, hey,' he said to her. 'What's wrong? Is your mum home?'

Her panicked brown eyes focused on him and then her pony-tailed head jerked in the direction of the house.

'No, she's gone out, and she's going to kill me when she gets back.'

The young girl's sobbing made her words incoherent. Harry bent down to her level and said, 'No one is going to kill you. You need to tell me what's wrong.'

Her face paled and she shook, bottom lip trembling.

'He's gone,' she whispered. 'Our dog Colonel. He's been stolen and Mum's going to kill me. I've let someone take him and she loves him more than me. My life's over.'

Two people crying in one day was a record for Harry Powell. To make matters worse, this one was barely eight or nine years old.

And she came with a runny nose.

'Let's get you inside,' he said. He glanced down at the discarded bag of food lying on the paving stones. He was loath to leave it there in case someone walked off with it. Stopping to pick it up seemed tactless under the circumstances, but he wasn't a lottery winner. That would come out of his wages.

'You go on inside.' He smiled down at her. 'We'll work out what to do next.'

The tears were still flowing and her lip still quivering but she nodded and dragged herself to the front door as if death really were waiting on the other side.

Harry seized the corner of the dog food bag and carried it at an awkward angle to make as little noise as possible. He didn't want the distraught child to turn around, but he didn't want to be out of pocket either.

Realising he wasn't ranking highly on the moral scoreboard, he had the good grace to leave it inside the hallway at the bottom of the stairs, tucked as far out of sight as he could manage.

Harry was unsure whether he should be in someone else's house alone with their young and frightened child. Still, he was unlikely to be doing the right thing by leaving her running along the road towards traffic and who knew what else.

'Anyone else at home?' he called out after her.

Harry stepped towards the kitchen, where the girl had disappeared.

'What's your name?' he called a little louder this time.

'Her name's Alicia,' a voice said in his ear.

'Good grief!' said Harry, jumping in the air at the stealthy approach of the newcomer. 'For a minute I thought I was having a supernatural episode. You know, voices in my ear type of thing.'

He turned to look at the person who had taken a couple of minutes off his life expectancy.

Harry didn't doubt he was looking deep into the brown eyes of Alicia's mother. At over six feet tall, he usually peered down at people, especially women, but she was only a couple of inches shorter than him. They held each other's stare, Harry in surprise and she more in anger.

'Who are you and why are you in my house?' she said, eyes hardening by the second. When he failed to answer her, she pulled her mobile phone from her pocket.

'That's it, I'm calling the police.'

'Doggie Delight,' said Harry in a voice so meek it took him by surprise.

'What?'

Harry pointed to the bag on the floor.

She looked at the bag and back at Harry.

He pulled back his jacket to show her the logo stitched onto the right breast of his garish red T-shirt.

'See,' Harry said as he pointed at his nipple, still maintaining eye contact. 'It's a cartoon pooch. All happy and healthy. Not to mention pleased with his lunch.'

'Oh,' she said, features softening, slow nodding accompanying her slow speech. 'Yes, they said that the new guy had some… issues.'

'Issues?' Harry said, now acutely aware that his finger was prodding at his nipple. 'I don't have *issues*.'

For the first time, she looked away from his face and moved her gaze to his hand. Harry folded his arms, a movement he knew made him look as if he was on the defensive.

'Alicia,' he said, the real Harry coming back with that one word.

'What's happened to her?'

'She was upset. Something about Colonel.'

The woman's freckled face turned paler than it had been, and she rushed past Harry towards the kitchen.

'Alicia! Colonel! Where are you?' she shouted as she ran across the wooden floor to the back of the house.

She reached the back door and flung it open, only to be knocked off her feet by a bounding Great Dane.

Harry towered over Alicia's mum as she lay on her back, the slavering Great Dane covering her face with kisses.

'Colonel!' she said, trying to move her head from side to side. 'For goodness' sake, get off me!'

'Here, boy,' said Harry, taking a couple of steps back to allow the enormous dog room to move across the kitchen. He crouched down to give the dog a pat on the head and a tickle under his soft, grey chin.

In one swift movement, Colonel was on his back, all four legs in the air.

'Seems he likes you,' the woman said, now upright. 'I'm Dawn Jones, by the way.'

'Nice to meet you,' Harry said as he stood up, knees clicking. He wiped his hand on the back of his trousers and held it out for Dawn to shake. 'I guess Colonel's returned home.'

'Hang on,' Dawn said, placing her fingers against her temple. 'What do you mean returned home? And why does Alicia have all the body language of someone very much in trouble?'

Harry glanced across at Dawn, the sunlight from the open back door lighting up her face. He put her at early to mid-thirties, with shoulder-length brown hair, neither straight nor curly but with a kink that gave her a casual, not-trying-too-hard appeal. Her jacket was vintage and her jeans a little on the worn and faded side. He got the impression the wear and tear were not a fashion statement.

The parts of the house he had seen gave him the impression everything they owned was made to last its natural lifetime, and then a bit longer. The paintwork needed refreshing, two of the kitchen cupboard doors were hanging at a slight angle and the vinyl flooring Dawn had been lying on only seconds ago was stuck down in two places with silver masking tape. As Harry had rushed through the kitchen, a patch of damp in the corner above the sink had caught his attention. Now he was reluctant to steal another glance in case Dawn saw him and thought he was judging her. Alicia and Colonel looked well cared for and the house appeared clean and tidy, simply run-down.

Harry had delivered the dog food and their dog was safe and sound, meaning that was the end of his business here.

'Alicia thought that your dog was gone,' said Harry. 'She was worried you'd be beside yourself when you got back.'

Dawn's head snapped in his direction. There was the fury again.

'I wasn't out,' she said. 'I went next door to hand over a letter that got put through our letterbox by mistake. I wasn't out. I was next door.'

'OK,' he said, 'really not asking you where you were. I was concerned about Alicia but now that I can see she's perfectly fine and your dog's back, I'll be off.'

Stony-faced, Dawn stood where she was.

'Mum,' said Alicia from the garden, hands in the pockets of her pinafore dress, one foot pushing a stone backwards and forwards into the lawn.

'Yes?' said Dawn, hostility not completely gone from her voice, although it had a mellower tone to it than she had used for Harry.

'It's not *his* fault. I think Colonel must have jumped the fence again because he was frightened.' Alicia thumbed at the rear of the garden where several short trees and evergreen bushes did their best to hide the road running alongside the back of the house. Harry saw that there was a green wooden fence amongst the trees made up of four horizontal slats. A couple of the slats were on the ground, leaving an easy escape route for a Great Dane.

Dawn let out a long breath.

'Breathing exercises?' asked Harry. 'I do those too.'

She gave him a withering look. 'I thought you might. No, I'm fed up with everything being broken and in disrepair. There are never enough hours in the day.'

Harry scratched at his stubble. 'I can come over and fix it for you later if you like.'

'Why would you do that?'

'Because I like dogs, don't have one of my own and I'd like to stop yours from running away again.'

Dawn put her head on one side while she thought through Harry's offer. 'OK… What do you expect in return?'

'*Mum!* That's rude. And you're not listening to me.'

Despite the tension Dawn was adding to the situation, Harry laughed.

'Tell you what,' he said, with a wink in Alicia's direction, 'if I fix the fence and you're not a satisfied customer, the next bag of Doggie Delight is on me. If I fix it and you're happy as a pig in the proverbial, you can order an extra bag from me next week and donate it to the local dog shelter. Sound like a deal?'

'Sounds like a deal,' Dawn said, offering her hand to shake Harry's.

'That's still not going to stop them,' said Alicia, mouth turned down and her face solemn.

'Stop who, sweetheart?' asked Dawn.

'The dog robbers. The men in the big black car. I've been trying to tell you!'

CHAPTER FIFTEEN

Satisfied that she had unsettled Sandra to the point of provoking her into action, Belinda found herself at a loose end. Her feet took her to where Harry's car had been parked. She doubted he would still be there, especially as she had told him not to wait. It didn't stop the pang of disappointment she felt as she rounded the corner. He had done as she'd told him; that should have given her a good feeling. But she had no strong desire to go home, and she didn't know how to pass an hour or so in the village.

That feeling caused her more concern than any other, because she knew what it meant: she was getting restless again and needed to get back out into the big wide world, away from the cosiness of Little Challham. Belinda had not experienced the desire to leave her village for some time, so the feeling caught in her chest and stopped her in her tracks as she reached the entrance to the castle grounds.

For a moment, Belinda hesitated. She gave a wistful glimpse at the Gatehouse, a scowl in the direction of the Dog and Duck, before making up her mind to retreat home, up to the sanctity of her attic room.

Before she had taken a step, though, movement from across the green caught her eye, and she saw two Skoda Octavias drive slowly through the centre of the village.

From the way they were driving, Belinda was convinced they weren't locals, and it was too late in the day for market shoppers.

As the first car pulled to a stop outside the New Inn, the other directly behind it, there was no doubt in Belinda's mind that the police were back.

Four plain-clothes detectives strolled towards the pub, two to the front door and two to the side cellar entrance she had used herself only a few hours before. Already that felt like days ago.

As Belinda stared, mesmerised by their silent swoop on the New Inn, the twitch of a curtain in the living room window of Tipper's flat above the pub drew her attention away from the officers.

She dismissed the idea that anyone else was up there. It must have been an open window. And yet, they all seemed to be closed.

She knew full well it wasn't Tipper up there, and Sandra was at the Dog and Duck.

Sandra. That was it. The police were after Sandra.

Belinda considered going over and telling them where she was.

If Sandra was the murderer, then the police would surely catch up with her soon. And if she found out that Belinda had tipped them off *twice*, then Belinda did not relish the idea of bobbing up and down in the bitter barrel.

The very thought turned her stomach over. But she had to tell them about the twitch of the curtain.

She smoothed down her skirt, gave one last quick look at the Dog and Duck and raced over the green to the gathering police officers.

'Excuse me,' she said, slightly out of breath. 'Up there, I think I saw—'

'Out of the way, please, ma'am,' said the older of the two policewomen, mobile phone held to her ear and gesturing wildly towards the Dog and Duck.

'Wait there,' said one of the police officers to Belinda as all four of them headed towards the Dog and Duck and the two people coming out of the front door.

Even allowing for the distance between Belinda and Sandra and Lennie, the surprise on their faces was evident at the sight of two men and two women in trouser suits running towards them full pelt.

Sandra turned to Lennie and said something that made him grab her by the shoulders and lean down towards her ear. It would have been impossible for Belinda – or, indeed, the detectives – to have picked out anything Lennie was saying.

What Belinda could not have failed to miss, however, was the open-mouthed expression on Sandra's face. Nor her attempts to prise herself away from Lennie.

None of her struggling came to much. The four officers surrounded Sandra and Lennie; one of the policewomen placed handcuffs on Sandra and then led her back to one of the waiting police cars.

With all the excitement of watching an arrest take place in her tiny, leafy village, it had slipped Belinda's mind that she was still standing beside the police cars.

'What have you told them?' Sandra screamed at her. 'What have you said? You interfering witch! It's not enough you wouldn't give me a job, but now you're stopping me ever getting another one.'

Flecks of spittle flew in all directions as Sandra continued to shout and rant at Belinda, who stood her ground and stared back, albeit with a lot less wild-eyed craziness about her.

'You wait until I get out of here,' said Sandra as she was placed in the police car, a stern-faced policewoman guiding her head through the open door.

'I don't think you should be making threats,' said Belinda, her temporarily lost composure now regained.

'Step back from the car, ma'am,' said the policewoman to Belinda. 'We've got this.'

Belinda did as she was asked, mainly because she was standing near the open car window and had a sneaking suspicion that Sandra was slight enough to wiggle through the gap. She was not entirely sure that, given half a chance, Sandra would be able to stop herself from launching through the window.

The police drove Sandra away, her shouting still audible and her pale and seething face visible through the car's rear window until the Skoda went around the corner and out of sight.

The only trouble was, now Sandra was in custody, things didn't feel right. Belinda had a sinking feeling that the police had the wrong person in the back of their car. Perhaps it was time she went home and spoke to Marcus about his row with Tipper…

CHAPTER SIXTEEN

Belinda set off for the castle, thinking about Sandra and if she had it in her to be a killer. Perhaps her earlier visit to the Dog and Duck had merely been to ask Lennie if he had any work for her and then they got on to the subject of rambling. If someone else had been watching from the flat as Sandra was taken away in handcuffs, the killer could be someone completely unknown. That would rule out her brother too. With a jolt, she remembered Sandra's sudden arrest had stopped her from telling the police about the curtain she saw moving in Tipper's flat.

Briefly, Belinda thought about the promise she had made Harry that she wouldn't go anywhere without telling him first. He wasn't here and she had left her mobile phone at home. With a shrug, she walked back across the green to the New Inn and around to the side entrance.

The side door was locked so she wandered round the back of the pub, keeping a careful eye out for returning police officers.

As she turned the corner of the pub's solid brick wall, she saw that the rear door that opened onto the recently done up garden was ajar. Belinda walked towards it without any further hesitation: it was a pub she had invested in after all.

A few minutes later, she was back outside in the sunshine, temporarily satisfied that no one was inside now, although they could have slipped out the back while she was watching Sandra being taken away.

Curiosity satisfied, she turned towards home again.

She had always enjoyed the stroll, no matter the weather. Even in the deepest snowfalls, the scenery was always spectacular, and she made the effort to walk the route at least twice a day.

Today, however, was another glorious day, so she tried to push all negative thoughts out of her mind and lose herself in the countryside. She took in so much more of the natural beauty of her surroundings when she was on foot, rather than behind the wheel of her Land Rover. Even late at night, coming back from the pub, she relished the fresh air, exercise and stillness.

Now, the sun was lighting up the clear blue sky, the warmth of the day still lingering despite the lateness of the afternoon. Her feet crunched softly on the gravel as she meandered along, pausing from time to time to appreciate the shrubs and plants either side of the driveway.

Barely a day went by when Belinda failed to pause and appreciate the generous hand that life had dealt her.

Some minutes later, Belinda arrived at the side kitchen entrance, her preferred means of getting inside. As a child she had loved to run straight into the belly of the castle and considered the front door cheating. Where was the challenge in going through something as ordinary as the front door?

Gripping the door handle firmly, Belinda paused, swept her gaze across the garden and opened the door.

She stepped silently inside the kitchen, pleased to be home after the emotional and exhausting day, although aware she desperately needed to speak to her brother.

One very important point she had omitted to tell PC Vince Green was her brother's argument with none other than the murdered landlord. The very least she could do was warn Marcus and give him time to get a story together.

A frown creased her forehead as she considered where her thoughts had taken her. *Should* Marcus need time to get a story together? If she could work out who the murderer was, then Marcus's name wouldn't even have to come into it. Her brother often had daft business ideas but she knew he would never take another's life. That was one thing she didn't have to worry about.

Even so, Belinda had to speak to Marcus before the police got in touch. Who knew where that would end? She certainly was not going to be able to do very much to help him this time. An alibi for murder was a step too far, even with her formidable skills.

This time of day, Marcus was usually on the patio sipping a cold beer. Alcohol might be just the thing to lure him into letting down his guard, if she was going to get the truth about what Tipper had come for.

Steeling herself for what she hoped was not going to be an argument, Belinda went to find her brother.

She congratulated herself as she put her head around the drawing room door and caught sight of Marcus on the patio, exactly where she thought he would be.

The back of his head was visible as he stood facing away from the open patio doors, one hand in his trouser pocket, the other holding a mobile phone to his ear.

'He was here earlier,' said Marcus. 'Truth be told, it all got rather ugly. He was shouting and threatening me. Well, you know that I won't tolerate that, but it's of no concern to us now. I've taken care of it.'

Her brother's words stopped Belinda dead in her tracks. Instinct told her to step out of sight and keep listening, praying her brother was not about to confess to a crime to whoever was on the call, and that anything he had done, she could make go away – anything that wasn't actually murder. That was most definitely a step too far.

Belinda positioned herself to the side of the open door, heavy floral curtains between her and Marcus.

'No, no,' he laughed. 'She doesn't suspect a thing, although I did have to promise her a puppy to throw her off the scent.'

Belinda could not resist a peek outside. Her brother was finding all this extremely amusing.

To say that she was angry was one very big understatement. Still, if she lost her temper now, there would be no helping her brother. There had to be an innocent explanation to this and she knew from previous experience that direct confrontation simply would not work. Subtlety was called for.

She steadied her breathing, gritted her teeth and pressed herself back against the wall.

'Look, as far as I'm concerned,' said Marcus, voice fading a little as he walked towards the far end of the patio, 'we're very much still on track to conclude our deal soon. It's still of benefit to both of us.'

Belinda risked flitting across the open doorway to get a little nearer. Anything she could catch of his conversation would help.

She reached her new hiding place in time to hear his shoes as they scuffed along the paving stones on his way back towards her.

Again, she held her breath and waited.

'So, getting back out of the country won't be an issue?'

Belinda bit her lip.

'OK,' said Marcus. 'I'll leave the rest of it to you. Call me again on this number if you need to. Otherwise, I won't expect to hear from you.'

Aware that the call was about to come to an end, Belinda calmed herself down, smoothed her skirt, plastered a smile on her face and did her utmost to breeze outside to her brother.

'Hello,' she said, hoping her attempt at nonchalance was convincing. 'I've only just got back from the village. You'll never guess what's happened!'

'Hello, sis,' Marcus said, shoving his mobile phone into his back pocket with what Belinda thought was a little too much keenness.

'Something up with your phone?' she asked in a weak attempt to delay asking the bigger questions, her nerve failing her already.

'Oh, that, no. I was thinking of getting a new one. The tariff's gone through the roof.'

He smiled at her and waited for her to continue. Since when was Marcus ever bothered about something like a mobile phone bill? He had so little regard for money, it was almost comical.

'You were saying something about the village? What's happened?'

'There's been a death,' she said.

'Sad, but people do die.'

Belinda watched his face closely. 'When I say death,' she said, 'I mean murder.'

'Good grief,' he said. 'Murder? Well, I'll be. Who's been murdered?'

'Tipper.'

Her brother seemed to sag. His shoulders slumped and his head dropped. 'That's a bit of a blow.'

Marcus pulled out one of the patio chairs and lowered himself onto it. 'Where was he… you know, was it in the pub?'

'What makes you say that?'

'He lived and worked in the pub,' said Marcus, confusion clambering all over his face. 'Where else was he going to get himself done in?'

'Fair point,' she said, pleased that that was a natural assumption to make.

Some of her brother's old self was coming back. He eased himself back in the chair, remembered his mobile phone was still in his pocket, pulled it out and placed it down on the table next to his abandoned beer.

Belinda couldn't help but notice Marcus peering intently at the screen before putting it down.

When she was sure she had his full attention again, she said, 'I found Tipper. Tipper's body.'

Marcus jumped up from his seat, his leg catching on the table and knocking the bottle of Peroni onto its side. Beer poured over his mobile phone and onto the floor.

He grabbed hold of Belinda, swept her into his arms, one hand on her back, the other around her neck.

'Sweet Bel,' he said. 'I'm so sorry you had to see that. It must have been horrific for you.'

Belinda stood rooted to the spot, surprised at the speed with which he'd moved, his strength as he held her tight and, more worryingly, how taken aback she was that he had one hand on her neck.

In fact, it was some time before she stopped shaking.

CHAPTER SEVENTEEN

After pushing herself away from her brother's overenthusiastic embrace, Belinda watched Marcus take a handkerchief from his pocket and dab at the beer on his phone.

She wasn't sure what she found more disturbing – the casual way he patted the phone's screen or what he was patting it with.

It was a bright pink handkerchief, ripped in one corner. The same pink material that was caught on the crate in the New Inn's cellar.

Belinda stood in the early evening sunshine, on the patio of her family home, a place she associated with love and warmth, and felt chilled to the bone.

'I've, er, got to run back down to the village,' she said, staring intently at the spilled beer as it trickled over the side of the metal table edge, the drips splashing against the paving stones.

'I thought you'd only got back this minute?' he asked as he picked the phone up and shook the remaining liquid to the floor. 'I know you enjoy the walk but let me give you a lift.'

'No!' she said, her tone and volume taking them both by surprise. 'I haven't been for a run for a couple of days and could do with the exercise.'

'All right, but give me a call if you need a lift back.'

Belinda nodded and backed away from her brother, a very unusual gesture in itself, especially in her own home.

Belinda Penshurst was not the sort of person who fled from a situation.

*

On her way down, Belinda knew her reason to return to the village – she had to speak to Harry Powell about Marcus. Did the bright pink handkerchief with its ripped corner mean her brother had been in the New Inn's cellar around the time of Tipper's murder? She wrestled with her thoughts over whether that made him a murderer or merely a visitor confronting Tipper.

Perhaps that confrontation had turned into an argument, one that ended in a killing.

Belinda needed advice and the most obvious person to give that was a former detective inspector who had worked more murders than she cared to think about. He would be able to help her prove Marcus's innocence, or at least try to work out what her brother was up to and why he had been rowing with Tipper in the first place. She knew her brother couldn't have killed anyone.

She had already placed her faith in Harry, and even if he did want to bore her senseless with some sort of a flip chart to talk 'investigation strategy', at least he had agreed to help her investigate.

The sun had started to go down by the time Belinda reached the end of the driveway. Dusk was creeping over the village, wrapping up the day until the world was ready to do it all again in the morning.

Belinda was so lost in thought over whether Marcus was in trouble or *was* trouble, that she turned a sharp right towards the Gatehouse without even considering whether Harry would be home.

She had also failed to consider whether anyone else would be at his house.

She was concocting her opening line to Harry in her head when she turned ninety degrees onto the path separating Harry's home from the pavement, only to be struck in the face by an elbow. The blow knocked her off her feet and left her sprawling on the kerb.

Belinda's vision went black.

Whoever had hit her clearly felt that wasn't enough punishment and cracked the side of her head with their knee as a parting shot.

Instinct kicking in, regardless of the temporary blindness, she rolled away, curling into a ball, managing to cover her head with her hands.

Belinda's entire head felt as though it had been slammed against the pavement.

Heavy footsteps rushed towards her, scuffing along the uneven paving slabs.

She would be damned if she'd lie on the floor and take a further beating.

With impressive agility, despite the knocks to her head and impractical footwear, she sprung up from the ground, fists raised and fighting stance adopted.

'Belinda,' said a voice she instantly recognised as being Harry's. 'What on earth? Let me call an ambulance.'

She dropped her hands a few inches lower, regained her posture and smiled at Harry.

'Typical policeman,' she said, 'turning up *after* the crime's been committed.'

Harry stepped forward, took her by the elbow and glanced in the direction the attacker had run off in.

'A man, I'd say,' said Harry. 'Slim build, although I only got the briefest glimpse of him.'

Despite the ringing in her ears and the throb in the side of her head, Belinda was feeling better than she had when she'd left home. It most certainly hadn't been Marcus who had attacked her, so someone else was worried that they were digging around and was feeling threatened. Perhaps it wasn't yet time to tell Harry her concerns about Marcus.

She looked Harry up and down. 'Due to the fact that you were huffing and puffing along behind him, I suppose you didn't see his face?'

Harry scratched his chin. 'Well…'

'And you didn't manage to catch up with him as you ran towards him out of your own front door while he was thrusting his elbow against my cheekbone?'

'I was about to take off after him,' said Harry, flush of red creeping into his cheeks. 'I thought that making sure you were OK came first. I'll call the police,' he added.

'I don't think I want the police here,' said Belinda. 'I'm completely…'

More chin-scratching from Harry, eyes anywhere but on her.

'Oh,' she said. 'You were calling the police because someone was in your house, not because they knocked me to the ground and accidently-on-purpose collided their knee with the side of my head.'

'Please just come inside, at least,' Harry said. 'I think you've got the wrong end of the stick. Of course the call to the police was for you. I'm embarrassed that this happened to you outside my door when I was only feet away.'

'Apology accepted.'

Without another word, Belinda sidestepped him, marched up the pathway and through the front door.

The last thing she wanted was more police officers asking questions, especially before she at least had a chance to mull things over.

Harry followed her into the kitchen, where she had already pulled up a chair and made herself at home.

'I was going to say take a seat,' said Harry, 'but you already have.'

She arched a perfectly plucked eyebrow at him.

'Tea? Coffee?' he said, gesturing at the kettle.

'Do you have anything more interesting? For the shock, you understand.'

Harry opened the cupboard directly opposite Belinda. 'Whisky, brandy or I have beer and wine.' With a frown he added, 'Not too sure about the quality of the vino, to be honest.'

'If you're calling it vino, I'll stick to brandy.' She watched him reach up for a bottle. 'Unless you're going to pour it into a jam jar or an egg cup.'

Harry swung the bottle by its neck.

'I prefer my brandy from a wellie boot, especially as I'm out of crisp packets to quaff it from,' he said, although it was accompanied by the start of a smile.

'That's an excellent start,' said Belinda, shifting in her seat to watch him as he opened another cupboard.

'Will these do?' he asked as he put two brandy glasses on the table, one either side of the bottle of Rémy Martin.

'I approve.'

For the second time that day, Belinda warmed a brandy glass between her hands, palms cupping the bowl.

'Cheers,' said Harry as he took a sip of his.

Belinda did the same, enjoying the familiar feel of the alcohol warming her throat.

'How are you feeling?' he said.

'I'm fine, really. I was on my way here to speak to you, and I'd allowed my mind to wander so far that I wasn't paying much attention. I'm sorry.'

He sat back in his chair, puzzled look on his face. 'Not sure what you've got to be sorry about, Belinda.'

She sighed and said, 'If I'd had my wits about me, I would have seen who was burgling your house. Did he take much?'

Harry frowned. 'That's the thing,' he said, 'I've not had a look round, but I know full well I'd locked the back door, and when I got home it was ajar. I suppose it was the sound of my car pulling up, but I think I disturbed whoever it was before they had a chance to take much.'

He suddenly stopped talking and stared up at the ceiling.

'What?' she asked, following his gaze.

'Someone else may be here,' he said, voice a whisper. 'Stay here and don't get in the way if someone else tries to make a run for it.'

Belinda put a hand up to her cheek, now red and beginning to swell.

'There's ice in the freezer,' he said.

He stood up, reached inside one of the cupboards and pulled out a spatula.

Despite the pain in her cheek and the dull throb in her head, Belinda couldn't help herself.

'What are you going to do?' she said. 'Flip him like an omelette?'

'No,' said Harry. 'I wouldn't use this for an omelette. That would be stupid.'

With that, he was off towards the living room.

CHAPTER EIGHTEEN

Belinda sat in Harry's kitchen, trying to focus on the sound of Harry creeping through the ground floor of the house. She smiled to herself at how stealthy he could be when the need actually arose.

In spite of the throbbing in her head, as well as feeling pretty useless that she had failed to spot a person charging at her, Belinda knew she couldn't sit and wait for his return.

She glanced up at the ceiling, expecting at any moment to hear Harry's size tens stomping above her head as he reached the upstairs.

Belinda was very familiar with the layout of the place, from the front gate all the way up to the attic, plus a couple of parts of the Gatehouse not known to many others. That thought made her smile: she knew a couple of things about the property Harry was living in that he didn't.

With a look around the kitchen, Belinda armed herself with a knife and silently made her way to the stairs. She caught sight of Harry's back as he pushed open the bathroom door, made sure it was clear and rushed across to the next room.

Taking her time, Belinda reached the landing as Harry went through the last door, the one that led to the main bedroom.

Perhaps she should go back downstairs and leave him to it. After all, there was clearly no one else here, or surely she would have heard shouting and crashing by now.

She stood still, listened to the silence. There was definitely no movement.

Belinda used one hand to push the door open, the other she held at chest height.

Harry had his back to the door, unaware Belinda was behind him. He was looking up at the attic hatch, directly above his bed.

'Don't worry—' Belinda began, making Harry holler and jump in the air.

'Are you actually trying to frighten me to death?' he said, one hand flying up to his chest. 'That's twice now you've sneaked up on me and this time, to make sure you're taking actual years off my life, you're threatening me with a knife.'

Belinda stared down at the seven-inch kitchen knife she was pointing at his heart.

'Oh, sorry, Harry.' She smiled, lowering the blade to her side. 'It was either this or an egg-whisk.'

'I need to check out the attic,' said Harry, about to step onto the bed.

'I wouldn't waste your time,' she said, causing him to stare at her with a quizzical look. 'It's sealed off and has been for some years. It was always a strange place to put an attic trapdoor and it's not been opened in a very long time. Pure decoration now.'

'Well, in that case,' said Harry, blush creeping across his cheeks as he tried his best to avoid looking at his bed, 'the place is all clear.'

'Perhaps we could go back downstairs and talk through Tipper's murder,' said Belinda. 'I could really do with getting things straight in my head. Indulge me with a thought: what if it wasn't Sandra? That would mean the murderer is still out there.'

Harry scratched his chin with the spatula, realised what he was doing and threw it onto the bed.

'I came here to ask your advice,' said Belinda. 'The last thing I expected was to end up in your bedroom.'

She waved a hand in the direction of his bed, both instantly mortified that she had made such a flippant comment and a little amused at the full horror on Harry's face.

'The thing is,' he said, 'I've only recently come out of a relationship and—'

'No, no,' said Belinda, the hand not clutching the knife waving away his words. 'I came here to pick your brains about a couple of things, mostly Sandra and Lennie at the Dog and Duck. I wasn't trying to pry into your personal life either.'

At the sign of Harry's shoulders removing themselves from his ears, she carried on talking.

'Here's what I was thinking,' she said. 'How about we go downstairs, talk through our main players and then we go over to the Dog and Duck and… What is it you detectives call it? Make some enquiries.'

He opened his mouth to say something but was instantly stopped by Belinda.

'Only we'll be undercover – deep, deep undercover. And I've got a sneaking suspicion you'll absolutely love it.'

He tried to say something else, but his words were lost as she turned and walked from his bedroom, shouting over her shoulder at him, 'Come on, Harry. Come and help me solve a murder.'

CHAPTER NINETEEN

Belinda made her way back downstairs, aware that Harry was rummaging around in the front box bedroom for something, presumably to help them figure out who had murdered the pub landlord.

She'd known that it wouldn't take much to get Harry swept along in her wake when it came to a dead body. All he had needed was a nudge.

After all, even with decades of cynicism from the police force, Harry still had a sense of decency and civic duty, plus he'd want to satisfy his curiosity.

Belinda replaced the kitchen knife in its rightful place and sat down again.

'So, before we go to the Dog and Duck,' said Harry from the doorway, 'we need to run through who we think is responsible for Tipper's death if we're entertaining the idea that it wasn't Sandra.'

'Murder, surely,' she said.

'Well, I could try to explain to you the difference between manslaughter and murder,' he said, animated expression lighting up his face.

'Strewth, no,' she said. 'Let's run with what we've got so far.'

'OK, then,' said Harry, producing a three foot by three whiteboard and a black marker pen.

She watched with fascination as he leaned it up against the wall on the kitchen worktop, took the cap off the marker and wrote:

TIPPER JOHNSON – What do we know?

Harry stood back to admire his work and glanced over at her. 'I'm not sure what you're finding so funny, Belinda.'

'I'm truly sorry, but is this how you start every murder case?'

'No, it's usually with a team of detectives, dozens of uniform officers, a forensic strategy and senior officers yelling at me to get a result,' said Harry, a mixture of hurt and embarrassment on his face. 'Even then, with a Home Office post-mortem, it would be virtually impossible to come up with an accurate time of death for Tipper, so there are still people we can't rule out. Hence the need for a whiteboard.'

'Forgive me,' said Belinda, wondering quite what it was about Harry that was making her fall for him. 'Let's start with Anthony Cotter. His microbrewery is doing very badly.'

'Good, good,' said Harry, furiously waving the marker pen. 'Anthony Cotter's on the list. I'll add in Sandra Burgess, my money's still on Sandra for now.'

'Lennie Aisling too,' said Belinda, crossing her legs and easing back into the kitchen chair. 'I meant to tell you that when Sandra was arrested, I think there was someone in the New Inn. It looked as though someone was behind the curtain in the flat. I popped back to check the place was empty and—'

'You did what?' Harry's face turned scarlet. 'And you didn't tell me that Sandra was arrested!'

'Oh, calm down,' said Belinda, waving away his reaction. 'With your friends on the force, I thought you'd have heard by now. The pink cotton in the cellar must have been a match with the rip in her blouse, although we still don't have a motive. As for my trip to the pub, there was no one there but I did find the back door open. The police wouldn't have left it like that so it could have been a visit from the same person who mistook my face for a punchbag. I'd say it's probably too much of a coincidence that someone breaks into the pub where someone's been murdered and then tries to break into your home on the same day unless they were connected to this.'

'Hoodie the House-breaker makes it four in that case,' said Harry, standing back to read his list, cheeks returning to their normal shade. 'I'll add in "Unknown Dognappers" as number five, more for completeness than anything else. The daughter of one of my customers said she'd seen a large black car and thought someone was trying to take their family dog. Anyone else?'

'Not right now,' she said. The sense of relief that it couldn't have been Marcus who assaulted her took the sting from her injuries. There was no point in muddying the waters further by bringing in another suspect to add to Harry's growing list. 'You being the ex-detective, I'm sure you'll have thought of this, but either Lennie or Anthony could be Hoodie.'

Harry tapped his temple with the marker.

'We can have a subtle word with both Lennie and Anthony, see what they know about our friendly neighbourhood Hoodie. Shake the tree, see what falls out. Slowly, slowly, catchee monkey.'

With a sigh, Belinda stood up and said, 'Talking about this is all well and good, but how about we go to the pub now and speak to Lennie again?'

'I've only spoken to him a couple of times,' said Harry as he put the cap back on his marker pen. 'What's he like?'

'He's a little odd and frequently quite rude. Some people claim it's the head injury he had some time ago that changed his behaviour but I found him unpleasant long before that happened.'

For a second or two Harry considered what she'd said.

'What sort of injury?'

'He fell off some scaffolding several years back,' said Belinda. 'He was in the building trade and some sort of Health and Safety thing went wrong. Another bash on the head, no matter how small, may finish him off apparently.'

'Was he bald before he fell?' said Harry.

'What's that got to do with it?'

'More hair might have cushioned the blow.'

They walked across the green after making sure the Gatehouse was as secure as it could be, locks clearly not much of a bar to whoever had managed to get inside once already.

Shoulder to shoulder they strode, heading in the direction of the pub. Tonight, it needed no clever marketing or competition to give the New Inn a run for its money. From the throng gathering outside and the crowd visible through the windows, Lennie was taking full advantage of his rival being closed.

'It's a far cry from the empty pub I visited earlier,' said Belinda.

Harry glanced across at her. 'This is hardly deep undercover, is it? Everyone knows you. Also, you still haven't told me what happened here today.'

'I've not exactly had a chance what with the murder mood board you created, the getting knocked to the ground and checking out your bedroom.'

Belinda could almost feel the heat from Harry's face.

He coughed as the couple near them drew level.

'Oh, yes, thanks for helping me out with that, er, problem I had. Couldn't have done it without you.'

Belinda stopped short and threw her head back, laughing until she feared her mascara had run. Dabbing at the corner of her eyes, she said, 'Harry, you really are funny. The only reason that couple took any notice of us at all was because you coughed like you had the plague and then shouted about your bedroom trouble for all to hear.'

She took in the slightly hurt expression on his face and said, 'I am sorry. I won't do it again. I'm tormenting you, and I really am enjoying your company.'

She took him by the arm and drew him away from a group of three people sauntering along in the pleasant evening's warmth.

'Look,' she said, keeping her mouth close to his ear, breathing in his aftershave, 'Sandra was in the Dog and Duck today. She came in, had a whispered conversation with Lennie, about walking by the sound of it, and when they came outside a few minutes later, it looked to me as if Lennie was warning her about something, moments before she got arrested.'

'He was warning her about something? Have you told the police? Are you ever going to tell me anything?'

'Calm down, I'm telling you now, aren't I? And will you stop firing questions at me? When I say warning her, it may have been to keep quiet about something.'

'About what?' said Harry.

'How am I supposed to know? He might have been warning her about prison food for all I know. I was across the street. You're the detective, you tell me.'

'I'm a retired police officer, not a lip-reading time-traveller.'

'There's no need to be sarcastic. And another thing,' said Belinda, her grip tightening on his arm. 'Did you notice that the butcher's shop was closed *after* we found Tipper's body? On market day?'

'So? Perhaps they ran out of meat?' said Harry. 'Where are you going with this?'

'Look,' said Belinda, turning 180 degrees on the spot. 'George Reid was at the front of his shop when I first noticed the crowd outside the New Inn. His butcher's shop is next to the New Inn.'

'I can see that,' said Harry.

'How stupid of me to have forgotten. George and Tipper had a falling out some months ago. Tipper owed him money for supplies that he claimed were faulty, some off meat or something, but anyway, it was fairly hostile at some point and they never really let bygones be bygones.'

'It's unlikely after all this time that George flipped and drowned him. I've been in his shop a couple of times and he seemed pleasant enough.'

'Did you ever complain or take anything back?' she asked, eyebrow arched.

'Well, no,' said Harry, 'but it's food. You'd only take it back if there was actually something wrong with it.'

'He chased someone out of the shop with a meat cleaver once because she said he'd leaned on the scales to make the sirloin weigh more so he could overcharge her.'

'Really?' said Harry. 'I don't like the sound of that.'

'Let's go and have a drink and hope George – or should I say suspect six – pops in for a drink,' she said. 'If he does, you can ask him all about it.'

It took a few minutes before they made it to the bar and got themselves drinks. There were surprisingly few people standing at the bar area, most preferring to spill outside where the temperature was a couple of degrees cooler.

'Evening,' said Lennie when they finally caught his eye in a break between serving thirsty punters. 'Are you feeling better, Belinda?'

'Yes, thank you,' she said.

'Good,' said Lennie, raking a hand through his thinning grey hair. 'Listen, I can't believe I didn't think of this before your visit here earlier today, you know, nosing around. It made me think, so you've done me a favour.'

'Really?' said Belinda, a wave of suspicion washing over her, the recent incident of Sandra's arrest etched very clearly in her mind. None of it more vivid than Lennie's face and the way he'd grabbed Sandra's shoulders.

'Yes,' said Lennie. 'Business like this doesn't come along every day, so I thought it wise to capitalise on it a bit. Strike while the iron's hot type of thing.'

Lennie leaned under the counter and pulled out a handful of flyers, thrusting one at Belinda and one at Harry.

'This is a bit sick, don't you think?' said Harry, scowl on his face as he skimmed over the paper.

'Not in the least,' said Lennie. 'People love all that true-crime stuff, so why not this? Besides, I only thought of it a couple of hours ago and we're almost sold out.'

Belinda held the bright orange flyer by the edges, a frown creasing her forehead as she read the words aloud. 'Murder Mystery Night at the Dog and Duck. Prizes for guessing the murderer and a consolation prize for not getting killed.'

CHAPTER TWENTY

For a couple of minutes, they stood at the bar, staring at the flyer, before Belinda pulled herself together and ordered a round of drinks from a young barman who introduced himself as Freddie.

He was in his late twenties, tall and thin, with short black hair, a goatee and black-framed glasses that made him look like a young Colonel Sanders before he found out he loved chicken more than low cholesterol.

'Been working here long?' asked Harry as the young man concentrated on the till.

'Not really,' said Freddie, voice a lot deeper than seemed to fit his appearance.

'Know much about the murder at the New Inn?' said Belinda.

Freddie gave a shake of his head and was about to answer when Lennie leaned across and said, 'Would you mind leaving my bar staff alone, please? They've got work to do.'

'While you're there, Lennie,' said Belinda, 'what was it you were saying to Sandra moments before she got arrested?'

'Not that it's anything to do with you,' he said, his face inches from Belinda's, 'but I could see what was about to happen and told her that I knew a good solicitor if she needed it. He helped me out when I had my accident. You know I don't like talking about it, even if the pay-out did result in me being able to afford this place. Now, kindly take your drinks away from the bar and stop harassing my staff.'

A little crestfallen, they took themselves off to a corner of the pub and chewed the fat over Tipper's murder. They discussed the black car that Alicia had seen near her house and whether it was the same one Harry had seen outside Ivy White's. They got involved in casual conversations with other pub dwellers – out of Lennie's eyeline – about what cars they owned and who was new to the village who might have been staying with Tipper. Their discreet enquiries brought no return.

Despite spending several hours together, they had to admit that between them they'd worked out hardly anything of merit.

'Sandra was looking very promising,' said Harry, 'until you told me you thought someone was hiding in the New Inn. Now I'm not so convinced.'

'I still don't like Lennie very much,' said Belinda, 'but being rude doesn't usually mean someone's a killer.'

'And he'd have very little reason to kill Tipper,' said Harry. 'They're rival landlords, but no offence to the New Inn, this place is in a league of its own. Just take a look at the décor, the attention to detail, the gorgeous Kent hops giving it that—'

'Thank you, Harry.'

'Sorry, I didn't mean anything. But if we're ruling out Lennie on that basis, we've got to rule out Anthony Cotter too. The micro-brewery could never be a threat because it attracts a completely different sort of customer. The three are worlds apart.'

Belinda stared at him. She was stalling for time and hoped he took her expression as displeasure at his accidental insults towards the pub she'd invested in. All the while she was thinking that a lack of motive from anyone else on their list put her brother very much back in the picture.

'What about Tipper's finances?' said Belinda. 'It could simply be someone he owed money to, like me.'

'True,' said Harry, 'but the police always look into someone's finances as a matter of course for something like this, so I don't think you're a likely suspect.'

'Well, that's something positive to have come out of tonight,' she said.

Towards the end of the evening, with no insight into who was staying with Tipper or how to find Hoodie, Harry said to Belinda, 'I've counted something like twenty times you've picked up that flyer and read it. There are only a couple of sentences on it.'

'It's making me think, that's all,' she said, fingers curling up the corners. 'This would be a good time to gather all the potential killers under one roof.'

A well-dressed couple walked past Belinda and Harry's table on their way outside with their drinks. All four of them exchanged pleasantries, the younger two appearing eager to get outside where the heat was less intense.

'What about them?' said Harry, nodding half-heartedly towards the couple who were now standing on the far side of the doors, staring lovingly into each other's eyes.

'Kulvinder and Steve Parry?' she said. 'Don't be ridiculous. They've not been back from honeymoon long, and if the rumours are true, they've barely let go of each other's hands since they walked down the aisle.'

'Steve looks as though he could take care of himself,' said Harry. 'I wouldn't fancy a clump from him. He could have grabbed one of Tipper's arms while Kulvinder held the other, the two of them still hand in hand, and dunked him in the barrel.'

'Can you hear yourself?' said Belinda. 'We've had exactly the same number of drinks and I'm not talking incoherent nonsense.'

Harry took a mouthful of his pint.

'Anyway,' he said, 'I forgot to ask: who was that woman you were talking to in the WI car park?'

'That was Delia Hawking,' said Belinda, lifting her brandy and taking a minuscule sip. 'She's lived here all her life, knows pretty much everyone and pretty much everything, only on this occasion, she didn't know who found Peter Clayton's dog after he was killed in the hit-and-run.'

Belinda glanced over at Harry.

'You have a smug look about you,' she said. 'What do you know?'

'I made a couple of calls, that's all,' he said. 'Ear to the ground, that sort of thing. It pays to be a retired detective inspector. I asked around, delicately of course, back at the police station. I had an update by text when you were at the bar trying to find out about guests in Tipper's flat.'

'Oh, for the love of Ada, tell me!'

Harry shifted in his seat. 'Well, they couldn't actually give me a name.'

Belinda roared with laughter, earning herself a few strange looks from the people sitting near them.

'Oh, Harry,' she said, biting her lip to stop herself from smiling, 'you are quite the tonic.'

'I did manage to find something out though,' he said, looking into the distance. 'At the risk of sounding dramatic, I shouldn't really have made a phone call to one of my former colleagues. I wanted to be useful, that was all.'

'Please don't sulk,' she said. 'The day has been far too weird for that. I'd love to know what you discovered.'

'Here's the thing,' said Harry, tapping his finger against the side of his nose, 'a young lad took Scooter to the local dog rescue centre in Great Challham. Even though he didn't leave a name, my *contact* told me that they had the impression that Cynthia Walker, the manager at the centre, knew who the lad was but wasn't prepared to tell the police. She may well be prepared to tell us, especially since it's a year on from the crime.'

Belinda sat up straight, her mind firing into action.

'How about we go there first thing in the morning?' she said, feeling that Harry had at least tried to make an effort in helping her solve Tipper's murder and it was time for her to reciprocate. 'I'll walk down to your place and we can head off together.'

'I knew something would turn up eventually,' said Harry.

'I have to hand it to you,' said Belinda, 'you're making more progress with the dognapping side of the investigation than I am with Tipper's murder. About the only thing I've managed to find out this afternoon, other than the odd behaviour between Lennie and Sandra, is that someone's sprayed yellow paint to the side of the Women's Institute front door and Delia is extremely angry about it.'

'Did you say yellow spray paint?' said Harry.

'Yes, I did. Is that significant?' said Belinda, annoyed with herself for thinking her contribution wasn't relevant to solving the mystery.

Harry shrugged. 'It's sparking something with me. When I went to Mrs White's house today, there was a yellow spray-painted mark on the road near the top of her driveway. It could be a coincidence, it could be the local council marking broken paving slabs, only…'

'Only there could also be more to it,' said Belinda. 'That's our plan of action for the day, then: work out what the yellow marks are once we've been to the dog rescue centre. From what you've said, it sounds as though someone there may well know more than they've previously been prepared to tell the police.'

CHAPTER TWENTY-ONE

Harry woke incredibly early the next morning. Even before he opened his eyes, his mind immediately threw up images of walking Belinda home the night before and thoughts of their animated discussions about who could have killed Tipper. They hadn't got any further than they had in the pub, but it made him feel more alive than he had since he'd retired. He wasn't really sure how she had roped him into solving a murder with her. She had played him, there was no doubt about it, only he didn't fully know how. What was more, he didn't seem to care. He liked her more than he was prepared to admit. She was the complete opposite of his ex-girlfriend, but perhaps that was the attraction.

Harry's time investigating murders should have been long behind him. He knew better than this – better to leave it to the professionals, his former colleagues.

Perhaps he could find a breakthrough and pass it to the police, and then they could all get on with their lives. In his heart of hearts, he knew he should leave it well alone.

Since moving in six weeks ago, he had loved to people-watch, especially on market day. He loved to be that little bit removed from the throng but able to observe people, ordinary people, milling around, studying the ingredients of locally produced honey, considering whether they really needed another bottle of cider, or if the lamb and mint pies were worth the risk.

The first week he had moved to the Gatehouse and realised there was a market taking place on Fridays, he had moved a dining room chair into the front garden to watch the world go by. At least, the part of the world that was in Little Challham on market day.

It warmed his heart but had also taught him that villages were a hotbed of scandal and intrigue. Daisy, the local postwoman, always took the special deliveries round the back of the delicatessen and was gone for longer than it took to sign a receipt. Whenever she reappeared, her shirt buttons were often misaligned and her delivery bag over a different shoulder.

Now he wondered whether he had seen something from his vantage point that was relevant to Tipper's murder, only he had had no idea at the time.

All those weeks ago, when he had first got his weekly fix of people-watching, he had sat and idly watched Tipper Johnson cross the green. In Tipper's left hand there was a dog lead and on the end of that lead was a Cavalier King Charles spaniel.

There should have been nothing odd about that, and had it not been for the recent unusual and fatal turn of events, it was probably a memory that Harry would have left undisturbed.

Except Tipper didn't own a dog. He lived alone at the pub so what was he doing with someone else's dog and where had he been taking it that morning?

There was something very strange going on amongst the dog owners of the village.

Feeling he was on to something, Harry got dressed then took a chair and placed it outside the house. He positioned it as best as he could remember in the same spot where he had been that morning, coffee in hand while he took in the sights and sounds of his village.

Harry closed his eyes to try and recall where Tipper had first appeared. It had been from the direction of the New Inn, but it could have been the post office or the delicatessen, possibly even from the new estate.

It could even have been from the far side of the green, from the Dog and Duck. Yes, that could have been it.

Harry sat upright and opened his eyes.

Someone was staring at him from the other side of his fence, leaning against it with one hand curled around the metal railings.

'I wondered yesterday where I'd seen you before,' said Dawn. 'Now I've watched you slumbering on your front doorstep, it reminds me that I've walked past you on several occasions.'

'Have you?' said Harry as he put a hand up to shield his eyes from the sun. 'For a minute there, I didn't recognise you without your Great Dane. Hang on...' He stood up and glanced up and down the green.

'What?' she said, attempting to work out what had grabbed Harry's attention.

He stepped towards Dawn, said, 'No, it's the sunlight. It wouldn't have been directly in my eyes then. He wasn't coming from the pub at all. I can't believe I missed it. He was—'

'Morning, Harry,' said Belinda as she bowled into view, purple shift dress brightening up the street. 'Morning to you too, Dawn. Sorry, I can come back later if you're in the middle of something.'

She turned her attention to Harry. 'You look odd. Are you all right?'

'That's exactly what I was going to ask him,' said Dawn. 'He got all strange and started looking up and down the green. Are you OK?'

'Fine, course I'm fine,' said Harry. 'I just thought of something, that was all.'

Both women laughed. As he stared at them, confused, they pressed their lips together and adopted full empathy poses.

'It's probably better if we don't discuss the case in public,' Belinda said, casting her eyes at Dawn.

'Oh, I, well, we are in the middle of something,' said Harry, looking at Dawn apologetically.

'But you're on different sides of the fence,' Belinda said. 'What were you in the middle of? Some sort of protest with plans to chain yourselves there?'

'We don't have any chains?' said Harry.

Belinda did the head tilt again.

'It's nice they've given him a job, isn't it?' said Dawn.

'Oh, yes, it is,' agreed Belinda.

'How about you stop that sympathy head thing, and come inside,' Harry said, remembering now why people got his goat so much.

He turned and walked back into his house, hoping he had enough clean coffee cups to offer them drinks before remembering that he hadn't wanted guests in the first place. He and Belinda were supposed to be going to the dog rescue centre, something that had slipped his mind once he'd started thinking about Tipper's appearance with a dog he clearly hadn't owned.

'Tea or coffee?' said Harry when Dawn and Belinda joined him.

'Coffee, please,' said Dawn, making a complete 360-degree turn in the centre of the room. 'Nice kitchen. How long have you been here?'

'Only about six weeks,' he said as he busied himself with the freshly ground coffee and percolator.

'Instant will do for me,' said Dawn. 'Don't go to too much bother.'

'Personally, I prefer proper coffee,' said Belinda, from the doorway, 'if it's not too much trouble.'

Both Harry and Dawn turned in her direction.

'That's settled then,' said Harry, a frown creasing his forehead as he spooned coffee into the machine.

Now Harry had their attention, he was toying with the idea of confiding in them both. Surely the three of them would turn up more than he and Belinda alone. He hadn't had time to run it by

Belinda, but he was sure Dawn couldn't have murdered Tipper. She had been nowhere on Belinda's list of likely suspects, after all.

'Listen,' said Harry, 'can I talk to you two about something?'

'Do you mean about Tipper drowning in his own cellar?' said Belinda.

'Or coming round to fix my fence?' said Dawn.

Her face reddened as the other two glanced at her, surprised.

'No, sorry, I wasn't trying to make out that my fence was in any way more important,' said Dawn, face aglow. 'It's only the small matter of the…' She gave a wary look in Belinda's direction. 'The dognappers. What if they come back?'

'What makes you think there are dognappers in Little Challham?' said Belinda.

Harry broke off from the coffee to concentrate on what Dawn was saying.

'I think they're trying to take my dog,' said Dawn. She looked up at the ceiling. 'The only reason I felt OK about leaving Colonel today was because he's with my neighbour. I don't even like leaving him in the house alone right now. And the only reason I got a Great Dane in the first place was because Tipper put me in touch with the breeder. I love that dog so much, the thought of losing him is terrifying.'

'I promise I'll be over later to sort that fence out,' said Harry, feeling a little annoyed with himself that it had slipped his mind, especially since he had decided to take on the dognapping investigation.

'OK, then,' said Belinda, 'we need to find out as much as we can about what's happening and then Harry will be over to mend the fence, won't you?'

Harry wasn't entirely sure how something he had offered as a good deed had turned into a task he was being ordered to complete.

'I've heard that Ivy White's terrified to come out of her house,' said Dawn. 'What with it coming up to the anniversary of Peter Clayton's death and someone stopping to stroke Bonnie when they were out on a walk last week, the poor soul will be frightened to death.'

'Please don't worry too much, Dawn,' said Belinda. 'Harry's got that one covered too. Whether it be Cavalier King Charles spaniel or Great Dane, no pooch too small or too big, he'll be there.'

He wasn't sure if he appeared as annoyed as he felt.

'Thanks for the reassurance,' said Dawn, 'but once Alicia explained she'd seen a large black car hanging around, both in the street and at the back of the house, I couldn't see what else they could have possibly wanted.'

'There's absolutely no one else who could have any reason for hanging around your house?' said Belinda, eyebrows almost touching her hairline.

'I don't know anyone with a car like that,' said Dawn.

One glance at Dawn's face, her mouth twitching, meant Harry felt obliged to help her out. He hadn't wanted to share his latest revelation about Tipper and the Cavalier King Charles spaniel until he was alone with Belinda, but thought it was worth sacrificing a little bit of news in exchange for rescuing Dawn.

'There's something else,' he said, moving over to the coffee maker. 'The reason I was sitting outside earlier was because I'd remembered something from market day during my first week here.'

Harry filled the nearest and cleanest three mugs he could find with the freshly brewed coffee, plonked them on the table next to the sugar bowl and reached across to the fridge to grab a pint of milk.

'It didn't strike me as odd at the time,' he said. 'The fact that I'd seen someone walking their dog across the village green… But then with all this talk of dogs and dognapping, I remembered that I'd seen Tipper with a Cavalier King Charles spaniel and he didn't own a dog. So, what was he doing with one?'

'That not such a big mystery really,' said Dawn, adding milk to her coffee. 'From time to time, Tipper walked Mrs White's dog,

Bonnie. He might have been a heavy drinker, but still he helped out his regulars.'

'Regulars?' said Harry. 'Mrs White drinks in the New Inn?'

'She used to,' said Dawn, 'but I haven't seen her in there for years.'

Belinda glanced at her watch. 'I can't believe Saturday morning's galloping away from us. Sorry, Dawn, I really don't mean to be short with you, but Harry and I have a couple of places we have to get to this morning.'

'OK, then,' said Dawn, getting up and pushing her untouched drink away from her. 'We can forget about my fence.'

'Not at all, Dawn, not at all,' Harry said, embarrassed that Belinda was all but throwing someone out of his house. 'I've got your number, so I'll give you a call and sort out a convenient time.'

'There was one other thing,' said Dawn, looking embarrassed.

'Go on,' he said.

'It's probably not the time but Alicia was very taken with you and wondered what it's like to be a detective,' said Dawn, fiddling with a bangle on her wrist. 'Is there any chance that you'll speak to her about it?'

'Nothing would give me more pleasure,' said Harry, enjoying the feeling of being wanted.

'Thanks,' she said. 'I'll leave you both to it.'

Harry and Belinda stood in silence until the slam of the front door spurred Harry to speak.

'That was a bit odd,' said Harry.

'Yes, I thought so too,' said Belinda.

'Actually, Belinda, I meant you – your behaviour was a bit odd.'

Belinda tucked her hair behind her ears, black tendrils framing her face.

'Are you telling me that you didn't notice?' said Belinda.

For a moment, Harry was stunned. He had no idea what he was supposed to have spotted. 'Give me a clue,' he said.

'Dawn got her dog through Tipper,' said Belinda. 'That's not a coincidence, surely. I'm very surprised and a little disappointed that you gave so much away in front of Dawn. How do we know we can trust her? Or who she may tell? You've told me that two people in the village are frightened of dognappers – one of them got their dog via Tipper, the other used to have Tipper walk their dog, and now the man's been murdered.'

'When you put it like that, there may be something in it,' said Harry.

'For goodness' sake, wake up and smell the coffee,' said Belinda.

'I would, except you've just poured it down the sink.'

'You know what I mean,' said Belinda. 'Dogs have gone missing in the village, people are in fear of their dogs being taken, and the one man who seemed to be some sort of dog dealer, or breeder go-between, or whatever you want to call him, has been murdered.'

'So,' said Harry, 'we crack the dognapping, we solve the murder. It's lucky I thought of that.'

If Harry wasn't mistaken, Belinda seemed a little annoyed with his observation.

CHAPTER TWENTY-TWO

Belinda felt she should go easy on Harry as he drove them towards the dog rescue centre in Great Challham. It was obvious he knew the roads and his driving was very good for an impatient man. It didn't stop her having to tell him the shortcuts, where to avoid the horses and their riders, where the laybys would be full of lorries parking up for their journeys across to France, and what times the trains were due so he could change route and make sure he didn't get caught up in the traffic queues when the lights turned red.

It struck her as odd that Harry had stopped talking and seemed to be blocking her out.

The sign for Great Challham's dog rescue centre told them it was the next turning on the left. Harry indicated and slowed down before turning the car into the long entrance to the dogs' home.

The centre was set back from the road, the driveway leading up to it taking them several hundred yards further away from any other signs of life. On one side was a large field, a six-foot-high metal fence running all the way around it, and on the other side, acting as a buffer between the dogs' home and any of the local residents, was a dense copse of trees and shrubs.

'Before we go in,' said Belinda as Harry released his seat belt and made to open the door, 'we need a plan.'

'We go in and ask her questions,' said Harry. 'It's the basis of detective work. I need to find out what's happened to the dogs in Little Challham, and if we find out who dropped Scooter here, it may lead to who killed Peter Clayton.'

Belinda reached out a hand and placed it on his arm.

'As you so astutely pointed out before we left the Gatehouse,' she said, tone neutral, '*if* we find out more about the hit-and-run accident and *if* the purpose was to steal Peter Clayton's dog, it *may* connect to Tipper's murder. We still don't really know what the motive was for his death.'

'Perhaps Tipper knew more about the hit-and-run than he was letting on,' said Harry. 'There's always the possibility he was blackmailing whoever killed Peter.'

The words had the effect of turning Belinda's spine to ice. Tipper had been in her home hours before he was murdered, threatening her brother with blackmail. Marcus was getting dogs from somewhere. There was no way he could be involved in stealing dogs, could he? He was certainly involved in odd-sounding deals and he had a ripped pink hankie made out of similar material to Sandra's top, and that had been enough to get her arrested for Tipper's murder. Right now they had work to do, but Belinda knew that, sooner or later, she either had to confront Marcus or tell Harry her fears.

'Let's go and find out who was driving the car that killed Peter Clayton,' said Belinda. 'Anything we can do to solve this tragedy will help us all sleep easier in our beds.'

The sound of barking only reached their ears when they were much nearer to the main reception. A large sign told them they were on CCTV, and sure enough, high up on the wall was a camera pointing straight at them.

'Hello, how can I help you?' said a cheerful woman of approximately forty years of age, plump build and shockingly white-blond cropped hair, as they came inside. She was wearing a pale blue sweatshirt with the name of the rescue centre emblazoned across the front and a smiling cartoon dog underneath. The charity had seemingly commissioned the same designer as Doggie Delight, and it appeared the designer hadn't seen an actual dog when he drew this piece of fine artwork either.

'Good morning,' said Belinda. 'My name is Belinda, and this is my friend Harry. From your name badge, I see you're Cynthia.'

A smile accompanied by, 'Morning, yes, that's me.'

Belinda glanced around the empty reception area. Both rows of plastic seats were empty, including the 'Quiet Zone' for nervous and shy dogs. A corridor ran to the left-hand side of the reception desk, its dividing wall a combination of brick and glass panels. Belinda could see half a dozen kennels the other side of that. Three were empty; three housed canine occupants.

'You're not full then?' said Harry, looking through one of the windows. 'You have a number of empty kennels.'

Cynthia smiled again, as if well versed in the art of conversations with simpletons. She came out from behind the reception desk and said, 'We only put the dogs out here who aren't going to be too disturbed by seeing people, and dare I say it, the cutest ones, so they have a bigger chance of getting rehomed.'

'We came to ask you about a particular dog,' said Belinda, who had walked over to gain a better view of the centre's pin-up pups.

'What sort of dog were you looking to adopt?' said Cynthia, rubbing her hands together, an act that she was probably unaware of.

Belinda and Harry exchanged a glance.

'I have to be honest with you,' said Belinda, 'it's more about the person who dropped it off.'

Crestfallen didn't come close to describing the expression on Cynthia's face.

'Oh, I see,' she said, and walked back around the other side of the reception desk. 'If you're the police,' she went on, 'I can't help you.'

'We're not the police,' laughed Belinda. 'We look nothing like police officers. Not in the slightest.'

She ignored the coughing from Harry and said, 'A year ago, a man called Peter Clayton was run over and someone found his dog Scooter and brought him here.' Belinda spoke softly, all the time scrutinising Cynthia's face. It didn't take very much effort to pick up on the nervous laugh and uncrossing of her arms.

'I'm sorry,' said Cynthia. 'I don't want to come across as unhelpful, but you see we often get people leaving dogs with us in dubious circumstances, and we have a no-questions-asked policy. If we don't adhere to that, people won't leave the dogs with us. The dogs come first, every single time.'

'So you're saying you can't help us,' said Harry.

Cynthia tidied some papers in front of her. 'It's not that I can't help you, it's that if I do, I risk losing a lot,' she said. 'We guarantee anonymity.'

Belinda looked over the edge of the reception desk at the A4 forms Cynthia was pushing into neat piles.

'If we were to sign up by direct debit to one of your sponsorship schemes there,' said Belinda, 'could you perhaps give us a description of the young lad who dropped Scooter off?'

At least Cynthia had the good grace to stare ruefully out of the window and mutter, 'Oh my,' before sliding the forms across the counter.

With a smile, Belinda picked them up, helped herself to a pen and handed them to Harry.

'Be as generous as you'd like,' she said to him before returning her attention to Cynthia. 'I appreciate it was a year ago, but anything you can recall would be a great help.'

'Now, let me see,' said Cynthia as she pursed her lips and stared thoughtfully across the corridor at one of the dogs in his kennel.

'Anything at all,' said Belinda.

'He was young, fairly young,' said Cynthia, reaffirming her words with a nod. 'Fairish blond hair, I think. I remember being surprised he brought the dog right up to reception. A lot of them, they tie the dog to the gatepost and run away. He didn't do that.'

Cynthia turned to face Belinda, one chubby hand on the pendant around her neck chain, sliding it back and forth. 'He was wearing a hoodie, but then, aren't they all?'

'Mostly, yes,' said Belinda. Out of the corner of her eye, she saw Harry's head pop up, briefly pausing from filling out his bank details.

'The youngster sounded like he was from nearby,' said Cynthia. 'I definitely didn't see a car.' She threw in the last bit as a hurried afterthought. 'That's why I think he was local.'

'Was there anything else at all?' said Belinda.

The question was answered with a shake of the head.

'Would you recognise him if you saw him again?' said Harry as he examined his bank card and checked his details against the form.

'My, now you sound like a policeman,' said Cynthia, nervous laugh back again. 'I would if he walked in here now, yes, certainly.' She turned back towards Belinda. 'I've got a good recall for faces. They say I've got a memory like an elephant, Bella.'

'That's comforting,' said Belinda. 'Well, you've got Harry's contact details on his sponsorship form here, so would you call if you think of anything else?'

'Of course.'

The three of them said their goodbyes. Belinda and Harry headed outside while Cynthia went back to some paperwork, no doubt starting the process of Harry bankrolling the charity.

As the two of them walked across the car park, Harry said, 'Now I'm twenty quid a month down. Not forgetting the raffle tickets I'm bound to end up buying.'

'It's for a good cause,' said Belinda, looking down at her hand as she reached for the car door. 'Bother. I didn't realise I'd picked up Cynthia's pen again. I'd better take it back before she ups your direct debit and puts you down for an entire pack of dogs.'

'You're hilarious, do you know that?' he called after her.

Belinda raced towards the reception area. She and Harry still had plenty to do and she didn't want to waste a minute by dawdling. Her approach was so speedy, all Cynthia had time to do was look up, phone still to her ear, her words mumbled yet their urgent tone fully evident.

Despite not being able to hear the conversation, it was as clear as day that the friendly dog rescue centre manager looked like a startled rabbit in the headlights. Belinda could almost feel the heat from the other woman's cheeks.

'Thanks for the call,' said Cynthia. 'I'll, I'll call you back. Goodbye.'

'Your pen,' said Belinda, popping it back on the reception desk. 'I left with it. Apologies. And one other thing I forgot to ask earlier, if I may?'

'Yes, of course,' said the red-faced Cynthia.

'Is Scooter still here?'

'No, no,' said Cynthia, picking up the pen and clicking the top a few times. 'A sweet boy like that, he was snapped up within a couple of days by a lovely elderly couple.'

'Thanks,' said Belinda. 'Goodbye again.'

With that, Belinda made her way back to the car to tell Harry she was certain Cynthia had been untruthful with them from her very first to her very last word.

CHAPTER TWENTY-THREE

'Well, that was interesting,' said Belinda as she got back into Harry's car.

Harry looked across at her. 'Go on, then,' he said. 'I thought we were in this together, so spill the beans. What I know, you know, and what you know, I know. That's how it works.'

Belinda took slightly longer than necessary buckling up the belt so she could compose herself without him seeing her expression. She hadn't mentioned her brother and the thought was crippling her. It wasn't that she didn't trust Harry, just that she didn't want to say the words out loud. Not yet.

'As I went back into the reception, Cynthia was on the phone talking to someone in a very urgent voice. I couldn't hear what she was saying, but from her behaviour, I'd bet it had something to do with our visit.'

'I knew it,' said Harry and slapped his hand on the steering wheel. 'I've a good mind to cancel that direct debit.'

'You know you won't do that, Harry,' she said, laying her hand on his, a firm and gentle touch. 'It's dogs, so you won't. You're more likely to go back and take one of the shelter pups home.'

She watched his jaw clench and unclench, suspecting she was right and that an adoption was on the cards. So much about Harry reminded her of Ivan, someone she had thought of as the love of her life. Until he'd broken her heart.

Harry drove them back along the same country roads and lanes, needing no direction from Belinda this time about where to avoid the bottlenecks or tractors.

'Stop the car,' said Belinda, pointing at a passing spot ahead to the side of the road.

'What have you seen?' said Harry, pulling the Audi over.

'See the rudbeckias over there, the ones planted in the long grass?' she said, leaning across Harry and pointing out of his window. 'Peter's family planted them after his death. That's the spot where he was killed.'

'Where was Scooter found?' said Harry, seemingly mulling over the year-old crime scene.

'Over there.' She pointed out of her window. 'He was found on the far side of that field, either caught on a branch or tied to a post,' said Belinda, 'depending on which version's correct.'

The sound of Harry scratching his chin focused her attention back to him.

'What are you thinking?'

'A dog the size of a West Highland terrier would struggle to get up the bank,' he said as he opened his car door.

Belinda watched him check both ways for traffic and run to the other side of the road. He stopped by the rudbeckias and peered up and down before looking across to the area where Scooter had been found after his owner's death.

Realising that Harry might be on to something, and wanting to be in on the action, Belinda got out of the car and crossed the road.

'I understand your point,' she said, squinting towards the field, 'but there easily might have been a gap in the bank further along. Besides, don't forget how petrified Scooter would have been. Dogs can, well, scoot for incredible distances when alarmed or the mood takes them. It only takes an interesting whiff on the breeze and they're lost in the moment. Add in being scared witless, and who knows where he might have ended up?'

'Mmm,' said Harry. 'I have a feeling, that's all. And over in the direction where he was found are the outskirts of Little Challham.'

'Perhaps he was running home.'

'Or perhaps someone was taking him to Little Challham and had second thoughts, so left him with plans to come back later,' said Harry.

'Talking of Little Challham,' said Belinda, 'next stop the Women's Institute. Let's see if we can find Delia. If she's not there, I know her address. We'll speak to her and see what she's managed to find out about who took Scooter to the dog rescue centre.'

'The problem we have,' said Harry, 'is that the suspects we've come up with for Tipper's murder so far are Lennie the pub landlord, Anthony from the microbrewery, Sandra the angry barmaid whose involvement we're now doubting, George the even angrier butcher and an unknown in a hoodie. None of them seem to have strong enough motives. And if the dognapping and the murder are linked, the only one who could possibly fit the bill for dropping Scooter at a rescue centre is the hoodie, and we've no idea who he is.'

'With any luck,' said Belinda, 'Delia has the answer we're looking for.'

'If not,' said Harry, 'it's back to mine for another session with the whiteboard.'

Belinda could feel a headache coming on.

For the next few minutes of the journey, Belinda watched Harry from the corner of her eye as he navigated the country roads. Fortunately, he was concentrating so was unaware he was being examined, or at least that was the impression Belinda got. She had a sense of dread that, at any moment, he would add her brother to the list of suspects. If he had overheard the row between Tipper and Marcus, he was doing a very fine job of pretending he hadn't.

Belinda had to work out who the murderer was before the spotlight fell on Marcus. He had frightened her when he'd put his hand on the back of her neck. No, not frightened, unnerved her. She stared out of the passenger window so Harry wouldn't notice any expression of anguish that might creep across her face.

Belinda had to be wrong about Marcus; he simply wasn't capable of taking another's life. She must have misinterpreted his mood and his behaviour, that must be it. She had overreacted because he was clearly stressed about his business deals, and after the last debacle, it was little wonder.

Harry drove into the village and straight to the Women's Institute car park. He had no trouble finding a space amongst the dozen or so bays, only two of which were occupied.

'The door's open,' said Belinda, nodding towards the hall: a one-storey building, painted white, 'Women's Institute 1922' proudly emblazoned above the porch entrance. The car park was to the left-hand side of the hall and set back a few feet to allow for a generous path to the front door.

Once out of the car, they walked towards the spot Delia had indicated to Belinda, near the porch.

While Belinda headed to the front door itself, Harry stood on the edge of the pavement, scrutinising the road.

'Harry,' called Belinda. 'I've found it. It's on the pavement beside the door, not the road.'

He walked back towards her and bent down to look at a yellow spray-painted mark.

'It's faded a little,' said Belinda, 'but that looks like the letter "D" to me.'

'What are you both doing down there?' asked a voice from the front door.

'Oh, hello, Kulvinder,' said Belinda. 'We're just looking at this graffiti; Delia mentioned it to me the other day.'

Belinda and Harry stood up, Belinda taking a second to smooth down her dress.

'Wow,' said Kulvinder, sweeping her long black hair over one shoulder. 'Is there so little going on in your lives you've popped over to look at our tarmac?'

'It's important to keep active at our age,' said Harry.

'Speak for yourself,' said Belinda. 'You're older than me.'

Kulvinder smiled politely. 'Have you dropped by to help out with the sewing bee?'

'Er, possibly?' said Belinda, knowing it was something she wouldn't have the first clue about but that it might help get them in the door.

'You as well?' said Kulvinder to Harry.

'Men can sew,' said Harry.

'Yes, I know,' Kulvinder said. 'But can you?'

'Well, no,' said Harry, 'but that's not—'

'Belinda, how lovely to see you again,' said Delia, appearing in the doorway behind Kulvinder. 'Come on in, although Pilates is filling up, so you'll have to book.'

Harry shot Belinda a look of pure terror as Kulvinder stood aside to let them in. Stifling a laugh, Belinda made her way inside, followed by a mortified Harry.

'Could we speak to you in private?' said Harry when the four of them were inside the main hall.

'Yes, of course,' said Delia, glancing around at the dozen or so women busy at work around the hall, each at a large table with sewing machines, piles of fabric and brightly coloured bags in front of them. 'I'm afraid I got nowhere with Belinda's request to find out more about the unfortunate happenings of last year.'

Belinda's heart sank.

Kulvinder had already returned to her table and was engrossed in what she was doing. A pair of small gold-framed glasses was perched on her nose, her almond eyes were alert to the needlework in front of her, and her petite, pixie-like face the picture of concentration.

'Come through to the small hall,' said Delia. 'It's where we're keeping the rest of the stock.'

They followed Delia through another door in a folding partition wall to the smaller of the halls, this one about a third the size. As Delia closed the door behind them, Belinda started to say something, but words momentarily failed her. She stood, hand to her mouth, and gazed at dozens of fifty-yard rolls of bright pink fabric stacked next to the wall.

'Yes, I know,' said Delia. 'It is very, very pink, isn't it?'

'What's this for?' said Belinda, unable to resist walking up to the nearest roll and caressing the material.

'We asked for donations from the local business community,' said Delia. 'Be careful what you wish for, I suppose. We can use it, of course, but the entire village and all the local parishes are going to be, well, dare I say it, a little gaudy.'

'What are you going to do with it all?' said Harry.

'We've already made some T-shirts and tops,' said Delia, walking over to a chair and taking a seat. 'The trouble is that the quality of the fabric isn't that great. The ladies have tried their best, but it tears easily. We tried making handkerchiefs, but we've had little success.'

'Who have you sold them to?' said Belinda, praying she'd get the right answer.

'Poor Tipper bought some,' said Delia. 'The dear sweet man even bought a top for Sandra – pink's her favourite colour. He was thinking of making them staff uniform. He was always so supportive of the WI and our charity events. Of course, that wasn't going to happen with the edges fraying so easily,' she added with another sigh.

'Anyone else?' said Belinda.

'Let me think,' said Delia. 'Tipper had the idea of turning them into dog bandanas and was toying with the idea of going into business with someone, although he didn't tell me who.'

'Dog bandanas?' said Harry, taking a seat opposite Delia.

'Yes, dear,' she said. 'Bandanas for dogs.'

'Did Tipper happen to give you any idea who he was proposing to work with?' said Belinda, sitting down next to Harry.

'No,' said Delia. 'He wouldn't tell me, but I had a strong feeling it might have been your brother Marcus.'

'What makes you say that?' said Belinda.

'I saw your brother come out of the New Inn one day a couple of weeks ago with a stack of the bright pink squares we'd been sewing through there.' Delia pointed towards the adjacent hall. 'They weren't fit for much, so we had the idea of using them for handkerchiefs, but as it turned out, one good blow and they were in shreds.'

For some reason – whether it was relief that her brother was one of about a hundred people who had stacks of the hideously coloured, unfit for purpose cloth that had been found at the scene of Tipper's murder, or the thought of people sneezing straight through the bright pink material – Belinda laughed like a blocked drain.

When she finally got herself together, she said, 'I am extremely sorry about that. I don't know what came over me.'

'Anyway,' said Harry, giving her a strange look, 'is there anything else you can tell us about the yellow marking by the door?'

'Sorry, I really can't,' said Delia. 'I'll check in the diary for the day I first noticed it.'

She pulled an A4 hardback black notebook across the table and took her spectacles from her pocket. Glasses on, she ran her hand down the page and said, 'I know I'm getting older when I have to rely on my glasses for reading. I used to have perfect vision, but after seventy-five, it started to go— oh, here it is.'

Delia turned the book around for Harry and Belinda to look at.

'Here,' she said, 'Thursday twenty-first.'

'One yellow spray-painted mark by the front door of the main hall,' Harry read out.

Belinda gasped.

'What's the matter?' said Harry.

'The next entry,' said Belinda. 'Friday twenty-second: Dog Grooming Made Easy in the main hall.'

'Oh, that's right,' said Delia. 'It was a very popular talk with lots of outside interest. It was supposed to take place at the village hall but at the last minute it was switched to our hall. It was all very dramatic, now I think about it. We almost had to call the police after one of the ladies left her schnauzer in her car and popped back inside to get her jacket. She was only gone for a moment but it was long enough for someone to try pinching her dog from the back seat.'

'I think we've worked out what the D stands for,' said Belinda.

CHAPTER TWENTY-FOUR

Back outside in the car park, Harry had something he needed to get off his chest, but it seemed that Belinda had her own agenda.

'So, let's see,' she said, turning towards him, her face almost luminous. ''D clearly stands for dog. The mark was put there by someone to distinguish the WI hall from the village hall just down the road, and placed at houses with names rather than numbers with unsuspecting dogs of interest inside, such as the schnauzer. We know how stupidly difficult it is to find a house with a name in a five-mile-long country lane like Ivy White's if you don't know where you're going.'

Harry didn't say anything.

'What's the matter?' said Belinda when they were back in the car, Harry silent and motionless in the driver's seat.

'Your reaction to the nose-blowing thing was, at best, over the top,' said Harry. 'Something you want to tell me?'

It was Belinda's turn to keep quiet.

Harry was determined he wasn't moving a muscle until she told him the truth.

After some time, Belinda said, 'I didn't tell you the concerns I had about my brother.'

'Your brother?'

'Yes,' she said. 'The whole thing about the dogs at the castle and the falling out he had with Tipper.'

'OK,' said Harry slowly. 'When did they have a row?'

'Shortly before he was killed.'

Harry closed his eyes and let out a slow breath. 'And you didn't think to tell me this? You didn't think this was at all important?'

'I knew it might have been important, but Marcus couldn't have done anything like that!'

'So you're telling me, Belinda, that there is no way you thought he could have been responsible, yet you gave me absolutely no clue whatsoever he had had a row with a murder victim hours before his death.'

Belinda mumbled something that Harry didn't catch.

'Pardon?'

She pushed her head back against the car seat. 'I said it wasn't hours, probably half an hour or so beforehand.'

'Wait a minute,' said Harry. 'If it was half an hour or so…'

He stared at her face, where sadness and shame were jockeying for first place.

'Tipper was rowing with Marcus yesterday afternoon, around the time you arrived to talk to him about the Doggie Delight order.'

Harry got out of the car, slowly shut the door and leaned back against it.

He heard her open her door and walk around the car towards him.

'Please don't be angry with me,' she said. 'I can't begin to tell you how sorry I am that I didn't tell you, but you'd have done the same if it was your brother. Yesterday, I went home to speak to Marcus, and he had a bright pink handkerchief in his pocket with a rip on the corner. I thought the worst when I saw that. Now we've spoken to Delia, I know half the village probably has them, including Tipper. That's as likely to explain the cotton on the edge of the crate as anything else.'

Harry ran his hand across his face, not really sure whether Belinda couldn't see it herself or whether she just didn't want to.

After a leaden pause, he said, 'Do you understand that even though Tipper, Sandra, Delia, Kulvinder, every other inhabitant of the county *could* have had a ripped pink handkerchief, it doesn't rule any of them out? That means it doesn't rule Marcus out either.'

'He couldn't have done it,' said Belinda.

'Out of all of the people in this village,' said Harry, 'Marcus was the only one to have a row with Tipper half an hour before he died.'

'No,' said Belinda, shaking her head so hard that her black hair flew in her face, 'he's the only one we *know* had a row with him shortly before his death.'

'What exactly were they rowing about? Anything to do with why Marcus was ordering bag after bag of dog food for dogs he doesn't have?'

'I honestly don't know what they were rowing about,' she said. 'I was going to speak to him about the dog food but the murder got in the way.'

'Again, we come back to the fact that you didn't tell the police about their barney, or else he'd have been arrested by now.'

Belinda pointed at Harry and said, 'Excellent point, but here's another one. You have a lot of insight into the police and how deeply they investigate every angle of a murder. So far, they've only arrested Sandra, meaning they currently don't suspect anyone else. And besides, they clearly need a little help. How about you come to the Murder Mystery with me tonight, we'll put this to bed once and for all, work out who the murderer actually is, and if we can't, you can drive me to the police station yourself.'

Against all his better judgement, with a heavy heart, Harry said, 'You've got until last orders.'

CHAPTER TWENTY-FIVE

At six thirty that evening, Belinda rapped on Harry's front door. She was a little on edge, so instead of standing and waiting, she walked back down the path, trying to use her pent-up energy.

He opened the door, an annoyed expression on his face.

'What?' she said. 'You are coming with me to the pub?'

She stood with one hand on her hip, sky-blue knee-length jersey dress clinging in all the right places. She had aimed for smart-casual but wasn't about to lose her grip on dressing for the occasion. After all, they had a murder to solve.

She watched Harry glance back over his shoulder, one hand on the door frame.

'I've got the tickets,' she said with more certainty than she felt. 'I hope you haven't changed your mind. This is our chance to get the low-down on the suspects.'

Harry made what sounded like a groaning noise. 'We don't have any suspects, don't you see? We have a dead landlord who was found in a barrel of stale beer.'

'As it currently stands,' she said, 'we have one fewer suspect to worry about.'

'Meaning?' said Harry, folding his arms across his chest.

'I called the police station and told them about the glut of eyewatering pink material that Little Challham is awash with,' she said. 'They've probably let Sandra go by now.'

'So we're back to square one,' said Harry, puffing out his cheeks.

'All the more reason to come to the pub,' she said, unable to resist giving her best smile. 'Oh, come on,' she went on when it looked as though Harry's hesitation might take him back inside the house. 'I'll only wear you down with my personality otherwise.'

At last, Harry gave a laugh, checked his pockets for his wallet and keys – a sure sign, as far as Belinda was concerned, that he had been ready all along but was merely making her anxious – and slammed the door behind him.

The short walk to the Dog and Duck was never going to be enough time for Belinda to say everything she had been hoping to say. She momentarily regretted not hurling herself through Harry's front door and speaking to him again in private. Another apology would be futile: she had said as much as she was going to at this point about Marcus and any fears she had.

More pressing at the moment was a chance to mull over Tipper's murder, the dognappers and who else was a likely candidate as the killer. But as they were almost at the pub, that window of opportunity had slammed firmly shut.

Harry turned to face her as they reached the pavement in front of the Dog and Duck.

'OK,' he said. 'Let's get a drink and mingle.'

'That's it?' She threw her hands up in the air. 'It's a pub, it's what one does in a pub.'

'Then we won't look suspicious, will we?'

Harry reached out and opened the door for Belinda.

She winked at him, stepped into the pub and ran an eye over the clientele.

The first person Belinda saw standing at the bar was Sandra, very much free from police custody.

Belinda felt the tension in the air. 'It's now or never,' she said to Harry and surged off into the sea of customers.

'What's now or—' said Harry, mouth agape as Belinda pulled out a chair from one of the nearby tables and dragged it across the pub carpet.

'Whatever you're about to do,' he said, 'please don't.'

Barely registering that he had spoken, let alone what he had said, Belinda was up and on the chair, much to the astonishment of the entire establishment.

'Ladies and gents,' she shouted. 'Can I have your attention, please?'

An uneasy hush fell, a few people gaping at her, a number nudging each other, some peeking through their fingers as they dropped their heads into their hands.

'We all love this village,' she said, scanning the crowd for any signs of obvious guilt, 'but one of us is a murderer.'

Several people muttered and murmured, and someone called out, 'Not me, love.'

'Please think about where you were yesterday around the time when Tipper was killed and about anything you saw or heard. It could be important.'

With a sinking feeling, Belinda was aware that her speech had lost momentum and people were talking amongst themselves, many looking at her as though she were delusional, including the startled tea room manager Angie and her date for the evening, Max the delivery driver.

She looked down at Harry as he offered her his hand to help her step down from her beer-stained soapbox.

'It was worth a try,' he said before leading her away towards the bar, 'but I'm not sure what you hoped to gain from that display.'

Unfortunately, there was even less room to manoeuvre by this time. Although Belinda tried not to stand next to the obviously seething, hate-filled Sandra, there weren't many places to go. Every table except one was full.

With a well-hidden measure of relief, Belinda sensed Harry join her and stand between her and Sandra. Still, never one to let someone else fight her battles, least of all a man, Belinda moved closer to Sandra.

'I'm glad to see you here,' Belinda said. 'Good to see that the police didn't have enough evidence to keep you.'

'Really?' said Sandra, eyebrows all but disappearing up under her fringe. 'Then why did you tell the police I was in the Dog and Duck yesterday?'

'Look, it wouldn't have taken them long to find you anyway, but I didn't tell them.'

'That's not what it looked like to me.' Sandra's face clouded over as she looked away, focused on the glass of lager she was holding.

'I promise you that I didn't,' said Belinda. 'How about when there's a break in this Murder Mystery evening, you and I catch up and you tell me what's been going on? I can help.'

Belinda heard Harry clear his throat.

'I mean, *we* can help,' she said, eyes flitting in Harry's direction before she added with a sweet smile, 'A large Sauvignon Blanc, please. And get Sandra one, would you?'

She couldn't help but notice the eye roll from Harry as he flagged down a member of the bar staff.

'I can't accept a drink from you,' said Sandra, 'because I can't afford to buy you one back. You see, Tipper never paid me.'

'Listen, let me sort that out. I'd like to,' said Belinda.

'I don't know why you'd do that; you've always had it in for me,' said Sandra with more of a sulky tone than a bitter one.

'What on earth makes you think that?' said Belinda.

'You were always coming into the pub moaning about everything I did, whether it was my hours or cling-filming the stupid sandwiches. What is it with you and cling film? And I really wanted that job running your tea room, but who did you give it to? That

Angie over there with her new fella and her tiny skirts. What chance did I stand?'

Completely exasperated, Belinda slowly blew the air from her cheeks. 'Sandra, seriously. Angie had previously run a coffee shop and worked in two cafes and a roadside diner as a student. You had none of that experience.'

Belinda watched as Sandra's eyes softened and she bit her lip.

'I-I didn't know that.'

'Because you've never given me a chance to explain,' said Belinda. 'Let's put this behind us and, tell you what, Angie is soon going to be taking on another member of staff. I can put in a good word.'

'You'd do that?' Sandra beamed.

'Of course I would,' said Belinda, her own face breaking into a smile. 'In the meantime, you can tell me what this Murder Mystery business is all about.'

'Lennie's spent most of today planning it,' said Sandra, 'and he's organised it really well. Everyone's got a seat at a table. You'll easily find yours. It's probably the only free one and it'll have your name on it. Lennie should be about somewhere. He's got a revolver – fake, of course – some rope, a dagger, wrench, candlestick and—'

A scream pierced the air, bringing instant silence to the pub.

'It's Lennie,' sobbed a woman from the kitchen door. 'Someone's hit him on the head with the lead piping. He's dead.'

CHAPTER TWENTY-SIX

'Lead piping,' said Belinda, finishing Sandra's sentence and, of course, repeating the murder weapon.

Sandra stared first at her and then at Harry, who was peering over Belinda's shoulder at the newly released murder suspect.

'Now, listen,' said Sandra, banging her glass down on the bar. 'Don't look at me. I've hardly spoken to—'

'Never mind that now,' said Harry, making a move towards the kitchen. 'Just don't leave before the police arrive.'

'You're not going anywhere without me,' said Belinda, putting a hand out to stop him brushing past her. 'We're a team, and don't you forget it.'

In spite of the seriousness of another murder, she saw Harry attempt a smile. He put a hand on her arm, and a shiver ran through her on this warmest of evenings.

'You're right,' he said.

'I usually am,' she said, and added, 'Oh, about what?'

'We're a team, so come on.'

The pair of them forged a path through the gawking drinkers, Harry pausing to check if anyone had called the police and an ambulance.

Belinda left Harry talking to the slightly hysterical woman who had screamed out from the kitchen door. On her way past, she overheard the woman tell Harry that she was a new member of staff and had only started that morning.

Making a mental note of the sobbed conversation, Belinda rushed over to where Lennie lay beside the industrial-sized glass washer, which had recently come to a stop and was in drying mode.

Lennie was on his front, left side of his face to the floor, right side now being inspected by Belinda as she crouched down next to him.

The lead piping was a couple of feet from his head, blood on one end of it.

'Police are on their way,' said Harry, coming over to her. 'We should check for a pulse.'

'No need,' said Belinda. 'I can see he's breathing. Look, he's got saliva coming out of his mouth. I can see air bubbles. He's very much alive.'

Harry took Belinda's word for it and said, 'We should get him in the recovery position.'

'Should we?' she said. 'I was looking forward to you giving him mouth to mouth.'

'If he's still breathing, that's not only unnecessary but some sort of assault.'

'Some sort of assault?' she said, standing back up. 'That doesn't sound very police-ish.'

Harry shrugged. 'I mostly dealt with murders. If there wasn't a corpse at the end of it, the finer points were largely forgotten.'

'Reassuring,' she said. 'Here come the paramedics.'

They stood aside to allow the crew to do their work, checking on the patient and making sure he had a pulse. There was little that Harry and Belinda could do, except stand back and hope that Lennie pulled through.

It wasn't long before the police arrived. Belinda earned herself a chastising look from Harry when she cooeed at PC Vince Green. The tired, worn-out-looking police officer clearly couldn't quite believe his eyes. Here he was once again in a pub with Belinda, who for the second time in two days had found herself a witness in the midst of a serious criminal investigation.

Belinda watched with a kind of morbid fascination as a paramedic, a young woman who looked no more than twenty-five years old, deftly took charge.

The paramedic busied herself checking Lennie's vital signs and getting him onto a stretcher, all the while continuing to talk to him. Of course, Belinda was really watching for any further clues she could glean. She tried her best to blank Harry, who was giving her some very hard stares from across the room.

'Lennie, can you tell me what happened?' said the paramedic.

Belinda held her breath. The background noise in the pub was growing louder and louder. Belinda leaned in closer to the patient, now strapped to a trolley. It didn't escape her notice that Harry did the same.

'I, err, what happened?' whispered Lennie.

'Take your time, Lennie,' said Belinda.

He was about to say something when PC Green surged forward through the ever-growing crowd forming in the kitchen.

'I'm going to have to ask you to come outside,' he said to Belinda, one hand firmly on her arm.

'But wait,' she said, resisting the officer's pull away from the latest of Little Challham's victims. 'He was about to tell me something.'

Realising this might be her last chance, Belinda wriggled free of the police officer's hold and moved closer to Lennie.

He barely opened his eyes but managed to say, 'I was hit from behind. But please, don't blame Sandra.'

Belinda watched his eyelids flutter closed and then he stopped talking.

'OK, folks!' shouted the paramedic. 'Everyone out of here, please. Now!'

Harry and the two police officers worked to usher as many people out of the kitchen as they could. Belinda looked round the room for any sign of things that were out of place.

While past and present law enforcement officers were busy shepherding the nosy public back into the bar, she took the opportunity to riffle through the kitchen.

Completely unaware of what she was looking for, Belinda opened cupboards and drawers, all of them disappointingly empty of clues. Her attention was drawn to the large walk-in freezer at the back of the kitchen. Surely nothing sinister lay inside. It would be too obvious, too clichéd. Even so, she steeled herself to open the door. A quick check to make sure that no one was watching her confirmed they were all busy trying to clear the room and take care of Lennie.

With a grim determination, she pulled the handle to open it and peered inside.

It was stocked with meat, bread and the general contents of a busy pub's freezer.

Disappointed, but sure there was something she had missed, Belinda closed the door and stood with her back against it.

She glanced towards where Harry was trying to bond with the police officers again. It was quite sweet really, if a bit sad.

When will he realise that he isn't an officer any more? she thought to herself as she perused the rest of the room.

Something jumped out at her. There, high up on a shelf near the main door of the kitchen, impossible to see on entering the room, was a large bag of dog food.

Lennie's dog had died some time ago and he had told her himself that he wasn't looking to get another one, so what exactly was he doing with a huge bag of kibble?

'Belinda and I were just...' she heard Harry say to PC Green, causing the officer to scan the room for her, ill-disguised anger on his face.

'I've asked you once, ma'am,' PC Green said, taking a step towards her.

'All right, all right,' she said, holding her palms out towards him in a placatory manner. 'I'm coming.'

As she drew level with Harry, unable to resist, she whispered, 'Back to the drawing board, or should I say whiteboard, Harry. Looks like we can cross Lennie off the list of suspects. Two down, three to go.'

CHAPTER TWENTY-SEVEN

Forced to leave the kitchen by the police, but also told they couldn't yet leave the pub, Belinda and Harry went and found their allocated table. Lennie had thoughtfully placed name cards at each setting before someone had tried to kill him.

The spare seat at the table had a name card in front of it. Belinda picked it up and read it: *Sandra Burgess*.

'Awkward,' Belinda said and showed the card to Harry.

'I thought you'd cleared the air.'

'We had,' she whispered to him. 'You were distracted by PC Green at the time, but Lennie regained consciousness enough to tell me he was hit from behind and that we shouldn't blame Sandra.'

'That doesn't mean anything,' said Harry, leaning closer to Belinda. 'That could have meant any number of—'

'Oh, hello, Sandra,' said Belinda, a tad too loud to masquerade as natural. 'Are you joining us?'

'We're not supposed to leave,' said Sandra, sitting down next to Harry. 'What do they expect us to do to pass the time? We're not even allowed to get another drink.'

'I've an idea,' said Belinda.

'I know I'm not going to like this,' said Harry, elbows on the table and his head in his hands.

'We came here for a Murder Mystery night, so let's have one,' she said, getting to her feet.

'Oh, strewth,' said Harry. 'Here we go again.'

'There's George Reid, the angry, knife-wielding butcher,' said Belinda. 'Let's go and talk to him.'

With the body language of the extremely weary, Harry stood up. 'I suppose he won't be tooled up on a nice night out with his family, at least.'

'Look on the bright side,' said Belinda, 'the police have sealed the kitchen off too, so he's got no chance of arming himself with the equipment.'

'Things are looking up already,' said Harry. 'For a minute, I was worried this might go awry.'

Ignoring the negativity from her teammate, Belinda walked over to the Reid family's table.

'Good evening, George and Anita,' said Belinda. 'I see you have your two lovely sons here tonight too.'

She smiled at the four of them. George and Anita smiled back and returned her greeting. The two teenagers scowled and ignored her.

'I also hear you had some problems with Tipper before he was murdered?' said Belinda.

'Subtle,' muttered Harry.

'What are you saying?' said George, now on his feet.

'From what I know, you've got a bit of a temper,' said Belinda, standing her ground.

'Who hasn't?' said George, vein popping out of the side of his shaved head. 'Especially when someone accuses them of murder.'

'She didn't actually accuse you of murder,' said Harry, stepping forwards.

'Didn't she?' said George.

'Didn't I?' said Belinda. 'I meant to.'

'That's what it sounded like to me,' said Anita.

'Thank you, Anita, at least someone was paying attention,' said Belinda, a triumphant look on her face.

Harry put a hand on Belinda's shoulder and said, 'I think we should go back to our seats.'

'Not until I find out where George was at the time Tipper was killed,' said Belinda.

George looked down at his wife, then over at his two teenage sons, who had put down their mobile phones and were looking thrilled at the drama of their quiet night out in the local pub.

'Do you have an alibi?' said Belinda.

'Yes,' said George. He pursed his lips together, took another look down at his wife and said to her, 'Sorry, love, but I was in the pub.'

'Aha,' said Belinda. 'So, you were in the New Inn at the time of the murder.'

'No, not the New Inn, the Dog and Duck. I was in here.'

'George, you promised me no more lunchtime drinking,' said Anita. 'Family nights out and birthdays, that's it.'

'Thanks very much, Belinda,' said George, 'now the missus is going to give me the cold shoulder for the rest of the night.'

'It's convenient that you were in here when the landlord, the only person who could vouch for you, is on his way to hospital with the back of his head bashed in,' said Belinda, her feeling of elation restored.

'That would be true if I hadn't been in here drinking with your brother,' said George.

'My brother?' said Belinda. She felt relieved her brother had an alibi although she was surprised it was someone so surly. 'Why were you drinking with Marcus?'

'He called me in the shop, asked me to close for half an hour and meet him in the Dog and Duck,' said George with a shrug of such speed, the tattoos on his arms blurred. 'We had a quick pint and he asked me about scraps from the shop for some dogs he's getting. It's a charity thing apparently – well, you'll know more about it than I do.'

'The charity thing,' said Belinda, a smile hiding her annoyance that she still had no idea what Marcus was up to. 'That slipped my mind. Thanks for clearing that up. I'll let you get back to your family now.'

'OK,' said a voice behind Belinda, 'that's enough, Ms Penshurst. Will you please leave the questions to us unless you want to get yourself arrested?'

PC Vince Green was standing next to Harry, who didn't know where to look.

'I tried to tell her it wasn't a good idea,' said Harry, earning himself a narrow-eyed glare from Belinda.

'I expected this much from her,' said PC Green, 'but not you.'

'No one was doing anything,' said Belinda. 'I couldn't just sit there and watch.'

'We're gathering everyone's contact details,' said PC Green. 'There are far too many people to get statements from them all tonight, so as I've already got yours from yesterday's murder you found yourself involved in, I won't need them again.'

'I know a lot of the villagers,' said Belinda. 'I like to use the local facilities. Is that a crime?'

'No, it's not a crime, but interfering with witnesses is, as well as perverting the course of justice,' said PC Green.

'And don't forget wasting police time,' said Harry.

His remark earned him a stare from both PC Green and Belinda.

'Take her home, please, sir,' said PC Green. 'And please make sure you stay there. I'll need to come and speak to you, rule out where you were at the time of the attempted murder.'

Belinda took a step backwards, aware that the Reid family, as well as many of the other locals, were watching.

'Are you saying I'm a suspect now?' she asked, hand flying up to her chest. 'What about Sandra Burgess? Strange she gets released from custody and immediately Lennie's bopped on the head. You were there when Lennie said not to blame Sandra. What do you make of that?'

PC Green's face had the world-weary look of a police officer who had dealt with imbeciles and their idiotic questions for far too long to be mentally or physically healthy for him.

'We've already checked, and Lennie was behind the bar serving drinks while Sandra stood on the other side of the counter supping a pint,' said PC Green. 'Lennie left and got hit on the head while Sandra stayed put in the bar. It could not have been her.'

'So we're all in danger if you haven't found the culprit,' said Belinda.

Harry was hopping from foot to foot and looking horrified that she would say such a thing to a man with a warrant card and an oath to the queen.

'Ms Penshurst, do not leave Little Challham before I've had a chance to take a formal statement from you,' said PC Vince Green. 'We need to rule you and your family out.'

For the first time since stepping foot inside the pub, Belinda wondered if she should have stayed home that evening.

CHAPTER TWENTY-EIGHT

Following a fitful night's sleep, Harry had barely been out of bed for half an hour but had already managed to shower, drink two cups of coffee, munch his way through two burnt slices of toast and get dressed for work.

It was fortunate he was ready so punctually, as Belinda was rapping on his front door by the time he had his car keys in his hand.

'Morning, Harry,' she said, brushing her way past him and heading towards his kitchen.

'I was on my way out,' he said, momentarily puzzled as to whether, in all of the hullabaloo last night, they had arranged to meet up this morning.

'Oh, good,' she said. 'I'll come with you.'

'You don't even know where I'm going,' said Harry, feeling forced to follow her back inside his own house.

'Of course I do,' said Belinda.

'Where am I going?'

Belinda turned and gave him a look that he thought conveyed smugness, mixed with a liberal sprinkling of sympathy.

She pointed at his T-shirt, where the Doggie Delight logo was barking joyfully.

Harry glanced down at his chest.

'Anyone could have worked that out,' he said, trying not to redden. What was it with this woman and her uncanny ability to make him feel like a fool?

'I gather being a detective doesn't take all that much training?' she said. This morning she was wearing a cream, long-sleeved wrap-over top, which made her skin glow, and pale blue trousers.

'I think you should leave,' he said, a little more abruptly than he'd anticipated.

By the look of surprise on Belinda's face, it had sounded as harsh to her ears as it had to Harry's own.

'Sorry,' he said. 'That was rude. What I meant was, I'm off to see a customer soon and I don't think she'll take all that kindly to you turning up.'

After what seemed like an eternity, yet was probably only three or four seconds, Belinda said, 'If you tell me who the customer is, I'll decide whether I should go with you or not.'

Harry considered his options. He liked Belinda's company – in fact, anyone's company was comforting. Since his last relationship had ended a little abruptly, he sometimes felt lonely, and after his outburst, it would seem that his social skills were on the fritz.

While he thought this over, Belinda, no doubt sensing his quandary, said, 'I'll tell you what I discovered in the pub's kitchen last night before PC Green threw me out if you let me come along with you.'

'You found something else out last night and didn't tell me?' said Harry, throwing his hands up in the air. 'Belinda, you know full well that you shouldn't be snooping around in a crime scene. You got us into enough trouble interrogating the other drinkers, without doing that too.'

'Yes, yes,' she said, 'but there was so much to soak up last night, so much opportunity to run a detailed eye over the crime scene, and besides, no one even knew, including you.'

'What you were doing,' said Harry, 'was interfering when you should have left things to the professionals. Now there's been a second attack, we really should leave this to the police.'

'The name of the person you're about to visit on this fine Sunday morning and I'll tell you what I saw,' she said.

He weighed up his options carefully. Curiosity was getting the better of him; he was no longer a police officer, but a little bit of interference by the well-intentioned Belinda surely couldn't do anybody any harm.

'OK,' he said, 'I'm on my way to see Mrs White.'

'Oh, Ivy,' she said. 'How lovely! I haven't seen her or Bonnie for an age and we can see if she's remembered any more about Peter Clayton's accident and Scooter. Now wait a moment.' Belinda paused, one painted fingernail to her bottom lip. 'You said that you'd seen Tipper walking a Cavalier King Charles spaniel some weeks before his death. Let's assume it was Bonnie. If so, Ivy must have heard by now about Tipper and she'll be beside herself. Come on, let's get going.'

'Now, hang on,' he said. 'You had something you were going to tell me, remember? In exchange for telling you who I was about to visit, on the off-chance I *allowed* you to come along.'

'Absolutely,' she said, 'although, let's be fair, now I know it's Ivy, I don't need to go with you, I could drive myself.'

'What did you see in the pub last night?'

'Dog food!'

'What?' said Harry, feeling his face morph into a mask of utter confusion.

'Dog food,' she repeated. 'You know, like the stuff you sell, as advertised by your amusing T-shirt.'

'What's so strange about seeing dog food in a pub?' Harry said, doubting his own words.

'In the kitchen?' she said, hands clasped together as she leaned towards him. 'What would Lennie be using dog food for in the kitchen?'

'Perhaps he was swapping it for croutons in the soup?'

'Don't be stupid, Harry. There was an enormous bag of dry dog food on a shelf in the kitchen. His dog's been dead for some time, and when I went in there on the day of Tipper's murder, I asked him if he was going to get another dog, and he said no.'

'I'll grant you,' said Harry, 'it does seem strange, but not beyond the realms of possibility.'

'Yes, but throw in that Lennie's injuries aren't fatal,' said Belinda, 'and he'll be home in a day or so – doesn't that make you wonder?'

'Wonder about what?' said Harry, arms flapping around now in an effort to keep up. 'Wonder why he'll make it home or why he's not dead?'

'Both. I've been thinking a lot about this and it must have been a warning shot for Lennie, especially with his previous head injury. It's a wonder he wasn't killed outright. Maybe the murderer was disturbed and didn't get a chance to finish the job. Now let's get over to Ivy's before the day runs away from us. We can talk about who had it in for Lennie and Tipper on the way.'

With a sigh of resignation, Harry indicated that Belinda should make her exit via the kitchen door.

'My car's parked at the back,' he said. 'Let's get going.'

Belinda grinned at him and trotted over towards the door.

He stopped to lock the door behind him, paused and said, 'How do you know Lennie's coming home in a day or so?'

'I called the hospital and asked.'

'And they told you?'

'When the ward sister is an old friend,' she said, opening the car door, 'finding things out is never a problem.'

With an exasperated shake of his head and a mumble about data protection laws, Harry resigned himself to being drawn into Belinda's plans, started the engine and drove towards Mrs White's house.

CHAPTER TWENTY-NINE

Within seconds of getting in the car, Belinda felt that Harry was very much regretting her coming along. As if reading her mind, as they drove from the rear of the Gatehouse towards the centre of the village, Harry said, 'I really don't want to get fired. I'd planned to go and see Mrs White, check she was doing OK, and give her a couple of my rapidly dwindling free samples, you know, so as not to cause her any further alarm.'

'Then that's what we'll do,' said Belinda. 'Obviously, what you'll do, as they're your free samples.'

'Thanks for noticing.'

'From what you've told me,' continued Belinda, 'she was very shaken up, and that was before Tipper was killed. Who knows how she'll react if she hasn't already heard the news?'

'Mrs White was clearly rattled by whatever was going on, and if Tipper sometimes walked Bonnie, it's certainly going to put the wind up her.'

Belinda picked up the small cardboard box of a dozen chicken and beef flavoured biscuits and turned it over.

'You really think these will do the trick?' said Belinda.

'All that promise of extra calcium and wet noses?' said Harry. 'I'll have her eating out of my hand.'

When Harry had finished laughing at his own joke, Belinda said, 'We'll have to get this right: if Ivy thinks someone's trying to take Bonnie and this is the first time anyone's told her about Tipper, she's going to be very frightened indeed.'

Belinda ran an eye over the green as they passed by. She couldn't help a peek towards the New Inn, still closed, then made a futile attempt to work out if anyone was yet inside the microbrewery. Its frontage was so narrow, the window of opportunity to see who was inside was literally small. However, what she saw when she glanced over at the Dog and Duck forced her to turn in her seat.

'What is it?' said Harry.

'That looked very much like Sandra about to go into the pub,' said Belinda. 'Only someone's stopped to talk to her. A man in a red jacket.'

'Perhaps they're checking on the place,' said Harry, attention back on the road.

'I suppose you're right,' said Belinda. 'She and Lennie seem to be in cahoots, only that can't have been Lennie. He won't be released from the hospital yet.'

She settled back and said, 'I'm thinking out loud here, but the one thing that connects both the landlords of the New Inn and the Dog and Duck is Sandra. Other than her, I'm struggling to think of anyone who has it in for the pair of them. Tipper because he was, after all, not the best boss, and Lennie looked as though he was warning her about something. Lennie's denied that and I never got a chance to clarify it with her in the pub last night.'

'Sandra was in the New Inn at the time Tipper's body was found,' said Harry. 'The only problem with that theory is that she was also standing at the bar talking to us when Lennie was found with head injuries and the lead piping next to him on the floor.'

'Yes,' said Belinda slowly, 'I know what PC Green said about Sandra being in the bar, but don't forget I was attracting a bit of attention at one point. Sandra could have sneaked away and attacked him. We don't know exactly how long it was between someone knocking Lennie out and him being found. The kitchen was shut last night so there shouldn't have been many people going in and out.'

'Perhaps Sandra's in league with someone else,' said Harry. 'You're not the only one who found a couple of things out last night, you know.'

After a short silence, Belinda said, 'Tell me. We're supposed to share *all* information.'

'You have some neck, you know that? Last night, Anthony Cotter didn't open the microbrewery. It was closed all evening.'

'Interesting, interesting,' said Belinda. 'OK, then, Ivy's house and then the microbrewery. I get the feeling that we'll have some questions for Anthony, especially about where he was when someone tried to kill the village's only other landlord.'

'Talking of landlords,' said Harry, 'perhaps Marcus can help us out by telling us what he and Tipper were rowing about.'

'Marcus was in the pub with George Reid at the time of the murder,' said Belinda, without pausing for breath.

'Yes, we know,' said Harry. 'But we still haven't got to the bottom of what he rowed with Tipper about and exactly what he's up to with butcher shop scraps and hundreds of kilos of dog food for dogs he doesn't have.'

'All right,' she said. 'Marcus is bound to be home this evening. We'll take care of this, drop by the microbrewery and then speak to my brother.'

Belinda knew it was something she would have to do sooner or later. It might as well be with Harry by her side.

It wasn't long before they arrived at Mrs White's house. Harry pulled into the driveway and told Belinda how he had found his customer cowering inside last time he'd visited her.

'The curtains are open,' said Belinda, 'so that's a positive sign.'

'So is this,' said Harry as he nodded towards the front door, where Mrs White stood on the threshold, waving weakly at them as they got out of the car.

'Were you expecting someone else?' he said, unable to hide the surprise in his tone.

'I wasn't expecting anyone at all, least of all the both of you,' she said. 'I got home only a couple of minutes ago and can't settle. I couldn't ask for two nicer visitors.'

Belinda beamed a triumphant smile in Harry's direction and forged a path towards the septuagenarian.

Ivy gave them both a wan smile.

'What's wrong?' said Harry, the few metres between them covered in as many strides.

'Why is it that every time you see me, I'm crying?' said Mrs White, through her tears.

'I'll begin to take it personally if you don't at least invite us in.'

She smiled and stepped out of the way, allowing Belinda to head inside first.

'And I've something lovely for Bonnie too,' said Harry, holding aloft the chicken-flavoured snack as he stepped inside.

Her sobbing stopped him in his tracks.

'Where's Bonnie?' said Harry, a hand over Mrs White's as he glanced down, expecting to see the little dog bounding around their feet, jumping excitedly.

This didn't bode well.

'Where is she?' said Belinda.

'She's, she's – oh, I can't…'

'It's OK, it's OK,' said Belinda, taking Mrs White by the elbow and leading her back inside the living room.

'Has someone taken her?' said Harry, his gentle manner belying his true feelings.

'Bonnie is… She's… Come and see.'

Wondering what could have happened, sick at the thought of animal cruelty, Belinda walked beside Mrs White for support, Harry following behind at a respectful distance.

Mrs White stood to the side of the kitchen entrance and pushed open the door.

With heavy hearts, the two gazed inside.

There, on her bed, sat Bonnie.

As far as Belinda could tell, she was perfectly content, and even got up in what she supposed was an attempt to wander over to the visitors.

'No, Bonnie,' said Mrs White. 'Stay.'

They stood next to one another, both peering at what appeared to be a perfectly healthy hound.

'What's wrong with her?' said Harry after an uncomfortable silence, broken only by the noise Bonnie's tail made as it wagged against her cushion.

'I couldn't tell at first,' said Mrs White. 'She didn't have as much energy as usual, then she seemed to be putting on weight, and she didn't always fancy her Doggie Delight.'

'I'm sure the food's fine—'

An elbow in the ribs from Belinda stopped him.

'I can't believe what the vet has told me this morning. It's so awful. She's not even been out of my sight.'

'What's wrong with her?'

'Somehow, Bonnie's pregnant.'

CHAPTER THIRTY

For a moment, Belinda and Harry stood staring down at the angelic face of the small dog. Handling the next part about Tipper was going to be very tricky indeed.

'Can we sit down?' said Belinda. 'Harry's got something awkward he needs to ask you.'

Belinda felt the heat of Harry's glare as they moved to the kitchen chairs, Mrs White seemingly so dazed by the news, she failed to notice the tension between her guests.

Once seated, Harry gave her a smile and said, 'You said Bonnie hasn't been out of your sight.'

A nod.

'Does anyone else ever walk her or look after her?' said Harry.

He watched Mrs White's face as she weighed up what she should say, her attention on her wedding ring as she fiddled with it, pushing it round and round.

Finally, Mrs White said, 'It was after my Arthur died. I started venturing out a little bit more. We usually kept ourselves to ourselves – it was always more about us and our family. Well, I was lonely, so I started visiting the tea room, got to know a few more people in the village.'

She stopped and looked up at Belinda, who sat in silence, listening to a story that, for some reason, Mrs White seemed embarrassed to share.

'One day, I walked to the village, realised that the tea room was shut and couldn't face going home again and sitting all alone. It was before Bonnie came into my life,' she said, smile spreading to the corners of her eyes. 'I needed to go to the post office and saw a sign outside the New Inn that said, "Freshly brewed coffee served here." I can't pretend I wasn't nervous as anything walking into a pub when it was barely open for the day! The last thing I wanted was for people to think I was a lush.'

Harry erupted in laughter, earning a less than encouraging frown from Belinda.

'Mrs White, I cannot think of anyone less lush-like than your good self.'

'Please, Harry, call me Ivy.'

'Ivy,' he said. 'How well did you get to know Tipper?'

Her face softened. 'He's always been so kind to me. The first time I walked through the pub door, my heart was hammering in my chest. It probably sounds stupid to you.' She nodded towards Belinda. 'You young girls think nothing of going out by yourselves, but I rarely went anywhere on my own that wasn't the shops or to friends' houses before Arthur died. Younger women these days would find it odd or even ridiculous that I didn't go out more by myself, but I simply didn't.'

She shrugged her shoulders and glanced across to where Bonnie was now slumbering in her bed, gentle snores barely audible.

'As I walked in the door, I almost changed my mind, and turned to go back out again. Tipper saw me from behind the bar and shouted a warm and lovely, "Good morning to you. Thanks for coming in today. Can I get you a menu, soft drink, tea or something stronger? We have everything you'd like." His warmth stopped me from walking back out, you know what he's like. Do you know how much difference it can make to have a friendly greeting? All I wanted was someone to chat to, a coffee and a seat amongst people. I didn't even need to talk to them, or for them to talk to me. I only wanted to be around other folk. Loneliness is a killer.'

Mrs White fiddled with her wedding ring again.

'I can say with a fair degree of certainty, being isolated would have killed me by now.'

Once again, Harry reached out a hand and placed his over Mrs White's.

It was a gesture so simple and kind, Belinda felt the need to look away, as if by being there she was intruding. Harry had his faults but caring too much was not one of them.

Harry sat passively, the lightest of touches to Mrs White's hand, making no attempt to rush or interrupt her.

'Thank you for listening to me, Harry. Both of you, really. Many people don't, you know. When someone else is talking, all they're doing is thinking about what they're going to say next rather than actually hearing what the other person is saying. You're hearing me, and I'm grateful for that.'

'And Tipper listened to you?' Harry said.

'To be honest, not really,' she laughed. 'I know that doesn't make sense, but he welcomed me and introduced me to the locals, other staff. He even tried to get me to work behind the bar. Now that would have been funny. No, he's just simply… decent.'

Harry opened his mouth to say something. He closed it again, steeling himself for the bad news.

Belinda came to his aid: she couldn't sit still and hear Mrs White wax lyrical about her newly discovered best friend, not knowing he had drowned in a barrel of flat, oily beer.

'Ivy, I—' said Belinda.

'I know what you're going to say,' Mrs White said, half-heartedly holding her palm up.

'I'm not entirely sure you do,' said Belinda, her tone as hushed as she could muster.

'Tipper drinks a lot, and he owes many people money,' said Mrs White with a sad smile. 'You won't shock me with that.'

'Both of those things are true,' agreed Belinda, herself being one of the creditors.

'I once heard him talking when I'd got to the pub and he didn't realise I was there,' said Mrs White, moving back in her chair slowly. 'I tended to go in early, a little after opening time. I'd sit with a coffee and the morning paper, peruse the menu and order before midday. I was the only one they allowed to do that.'

Mrs White gave a small smile.

'The chef, Temi, didn't seem to mind. At least, he told me that he didn't mind and would get my order ready early. I didn't like to be there when it was too crowded.'

Harry leaned across towards Mrs White. 'You heard Tipper saying what?'

'Oh, sorry, Harry, I've gone off on a tangent. So sorry. Yes, Tipper was talking about money he owed. Some was to the brewery and some was to… What's the owner of the microbrewery's name? Is it Anthony something?'

'The microbrewery?' said Harry. 'Anthony Cotter, I think his name is.'

A nod from Belinda encouraged Mrs White to keep talking.

'Tipper was hardly keeping his voice down when he was on the phone, and I remember wondering why they didn't speak face to face; they were only across the green from each other. The noise Tipper was making, he might as well have opened the door and shouted.

'Anyway, after I stood there for a while, he turned around and saw me. Well, the look on his face was complete embarrassment. He's ridiculously kind to me, so I never mentioned it again, but he definitely said, "Anthony, you're bleeding me dry over here. I've told you: you'll get your money as soon as the deal is sorted." Of course, I've no idea what the deal was or whether the money was ever sorted. I had my lunch and left not long after that.'

Harry scratched at his chin, gave Belinda a solemn look.

'Ivy,' said Belinda as she placed a hand next to Mrs White's, unsure whether to touch her, not wanting to crowd her, 'there's no easy way to tell you this, I'm afraid. Tipper's dead.'

Mrs White let out a gasp.

'What?' she whispered. 'When? How do you know? Are you sure?'

'I'm certain. I found him two days ago. We came here thinking you'd already know, to be honest. I wasn't expecting to have to break this to you. He was… in the pub cellar. There had been an accident.'

Belinda read shock and disbelief, but there were no shifty looks, no avoidance of her gaze. A seventy-seven-year-old woman was unlikely to have had the strength to force a man of Tipper's size and age into a barrel of beer and hold him there until he drowned.

Probably.

'Does anyone ever walk or look after Bonnie?' said Harry again, not having got an answer the first time around.

Mrs White's forehead wrinkled and her reddening eyes narrowed.

'Yes, Tipper does, did, but… I trusted him with Bonnie. He liked to walk her. He said the exercise was good for him as it got him out of the pub and gave me a break some mornings. Do you think he did this to her?'

All three of them sat back in their seats at this question.

'Obviously, I don't mean he… Oh, you know what I mean. But do you think he allowed her to be taken advantage of by another dog? He wouldn't have done that, surely. Tipper loved dogs, all dogs.'

'Possibly… We won't know what happened, Ivy,' said Harry. 'What I do know is that you wouldn't have left Bonnie with anyone you didn't completely trust.'

Her face relaxed a little.

'I completely trusted him,' said Mrs White. 'After all, why wouldn't I? He was the one who arranged for me to get Bonnie in the first place. He knew the breeder.'

CHAPTER THIRTY-ONE

Both Belinda and Harry sat and stared at Mrs White, unsure exactly what to say.

Eventually Harry said, 'We should tell the police.'

This earned a stare from Belinda, who said, 'Tell them what? Ivy's dog is pregnant? You're always telling me how overstretched the police are, so what part of CID are we going to report it to?'

Belinda knew that she and Harry needed to get their heads together and discover whether there was merit in digging a little deeper. There was nothing to actually tell the police as far as unwanted dog pregnancies went, and yet a local landlord who knew most of the village had put two women in touch with two dog breeders. It was hardly vital information, but add to it a murder and Belinda's own brother talking about getting her a puppy and there was far too much here to be a coincidence. The last bit was the part she hadn't told Harry.

Perhaps it was about time she did.

'What are you going to do about Bonnie?' asked Harry.

'Look after her and keep her as comfortable as she can be,' Mrs White replied with a sigh.

'You know where we are if you need us,' said Harry as he stood up, Belinda doing the same.

Harry briefly placed a hand on Mrs White's shoulder as he walked towards the door, while Belinda scribbled her phone number on a piece of paper.

'Here's my number if you need anything at all,' said Belinda, handing it to her, and wondering whether hugging the distraught woman would be too much.

As if reading her mind, Mrs White threw her arms around her and said, 'You've no idea what that means to me. Thank you.'

'Ivy didn't seem to take that at all well,' said Harry as he drove away from her house. 'It sounds as though Tipper was involved in the dognapping and was making money from breeding pedigree pups. Perhaps it was a disgruntled owner that killed him.'

After a pause, he glanced across at Belinda.

'Sorry, Harry. What was that?' she said.

'Ivy,' he repeated. 'She was very upset by the news about Tipper's death, so I didn't want to spell it out to her that he might have been behind the entire dognapping crime wave, together with her dog being pregnant. Are you OK? You look a bit tearful.'

'Hay fever.' Belinda wiped the corner of her eye with a tissue before regaining her composure. 'What shall we do now?' she said, almost bouncing in her seat.

'I've got work to do, so I'm dropping you home,' said Harry. 'We can visit the microbrewery another time. Like I keep saying, we should leave this to the police. Only you won't listen.'

'Let me come with you?' She shifted towards him. 'I don't want to go home. Besides, we can talk on the way about the dognappers. And I still say we should go to the microbrewery, and speak to Sandra again.'

Belinda watched Harry sigh, something he attempted to hide by pretending to mumble to himself, but then he said, 'I need to go to the depot to see my boss and pick up a delivery, but then I'm definitely taking you home.'

She grinned and then made herself look serious. 'You won't know I'm there,' she said, pleased to get a little more time with him.

'I very much doubt that,' said Harry, although she thought she saw a flash of a smile break out on his face.

'I'm very sure I wouldn't have known the place was here,' said Belinda as Harry drove them towards the remote access road leading to the Doggie Delight depot, signage complete with cute cartoon dogs seemingly pleased with the paw life had dealt them. 'And I didn't know it pretty much backs onto the outskirts of our land. It must be in a dip or I'd have seen it from the grounds.'

'Eric Whitley, my manager, likes to try and keep things a bit off the grid,' said Harry as he bumped the car along the track. 'For some reason, he thinks that keeping everything low-key will stop people finding out where he is and pilfering his supplies. Truth be known, the security is dreadful, and someone keeps snapping the padlock off the gates. Snacks have gone missing several times, but having said that, I'm sure the ones I have at home keep disappearing too.'

'Is the food that good?' asked Belinda.

'I wouldn't know,' said Harry, 'I've never tried it.'

'Next time we go to the Dog and Duck, you can order the soup.'

The depot was a single-storey building, around the size of two football pitches, with huge electronic metal shutters at the entrance where Harry was heading.

Harry pulled his Audi into a space close to the area marked out for the loading bays. He paused before he got out.

'For a moment there, I thought you were suggesting we go and carry out enquires in the pub again,' he said.

'Perhaps after we've finished here,' she said, leaving the thought hanging.

A shout from the inside of the building distracted Harry from giving her an answer, which at that moment was probably a no.

Harry waved at someone and shouted, 'Hi, Eric,' before walking off inside the warehouse.

Keen to satisfy her curiosity about the depot while Harry was occupied, Belinda took her time following him.

She wandered past row upon row of piled-high bags of dry dog food, numerous boxes of dog treats, biscuits and a mountain of packeted wet food.

'It's our new range,' said a voice behind her.

She turned to see Harry and another man, aged about forty, with short wavy brown hair, greying at the sides. He was sporting a shirt, tie and lightweight blue jacket.

'I'm Eric,' he said, holding out his hand.

'Belinda Penshurst,' she said, taking his hand, surprised at the firm grip.

'Ah, yes,' he said, with the briefest of glances at Harry, 'Marcus's sister. I see the resemblance now. I didn't notice when I saw you a few nights ago in the New Inn with the Ed Sheernanigans fella singing away.'

'You've met my brother,' she said, trying her level best to make it sound like a statement rather than a question, and managing to keep the astonishment from her voice that he had taken any notice of her in the pub. She certainly hadn't noticed him.

'Your brother is potentially one of our best customers, so yes,' enthused Eric.

'I know he's placed a large order with Harry here,' she said.

'We couldn't be more pleased,' said Eric, 'and with what he's planning, long may it continue.'

'Has he given you any idea of timescale?' she said.

'Let me think,' said Eric, scratching his head absentmindedly. 'He mentioned something about a six-month minimum contract. That'll be good for old Harry here.'

Eric delivered a slap to Harry's shoulder which caught him off guard and almost knocked him over.

'Sorry about that,' said Eric. 'All those years of lifting huge sack after huge sack of dog food. I don't always know my own strength.'

'No harm done,' said Harry, rubbing at the spot where Eric had clouted him.

'Let me show you the rest of the warehouse,' said Eric, rubbing his hands together, 'including the new doggy day care crèche at the back, for the staff to bring their own dogs in for the day.'

'Oh, I'm not sure that Belinda would be—' said Harry.

'I'd be delighted,' said Belinda, with a sweet smile at Eric and a glare at Harry. 'Nothing would make me happier.'

Harry fell into step beside them as Eric led them into the depths of the storage unit.

'Harry, didn't you say something about a delivery you had to pick up?' said Belinda.

'That's settled then,' said Eric, so happy to have someone to show his empire to that he spun in a complete circle and stretched his arms wide. 'I'll show Ms Penshurst here the whole operation, and you can pick up the bags you need. They're by the entrance but you'll have to do it yourself as the rest of the Sunday lads are out doing drop-offs. The place is completely dead.'

'Please, call me Belinda,' she said, waggling her fingers goodbye in Harry's direction, never taking her gaze from Eric's.

'This way, Belinda,' he said. 'We'll start with the office. It's here towards the back and it's where we keep all of our customer files.'

'No computer?' she asked.

'Some of the basics are on the computer,' he said, pushing open the office door for her. 'The thing with pen and paper is that they can't be hacked, files can't get deleted and they won't float away in "the Cloud".'

Belinda gave him a kind smile as she made her way into the office.

The room was about twelve feet by twelve, with shelves lining two of the walls, a window covering most of the far wall and a desk to the left of the door.

'Compact,' said Belinda in lieu of anything more positive to say.

'The customers' details are safe as houses here,' said Eric.

'Impressive. If, for example, you were going to run through my brother's order, would you immediately be able to put your hands on it?'

'Ah, I see what you're doing,' said Eric, leaning back to perch on the edge of the desk, arms crossed.

'What do you mean?' said Belinda.

'You're going to report back to your brother about how good our customer confidentiality is.'

She pointed a finger at him and said, 'Nothing gets past you, Eric, does it?'

'Aye, aye,' he said, tapping the side of his nose. 'I knew immediately what you were up to.'

'You can clearly read me like a book,' she said, moving back to get a better look at how the files along the wall were organised. Her eyes flitted over something she wasn't at first convinced was real, it was so unexpected.

'I certainly can,' said Eric with a self-satisfied nod. 'You were going to report back to your brother anything I'd left lying around, but you see, I've got a system, a very complex system.'

'Wow,' she said, fortunately with less sarcasm than it merited, trying as surreptitiously as she could to gaze over his shoulder.

'And I could tell you my system,' said Eric, pushing himself away from the desk and stepping across the office towards her, blocking her view, 'but then I'd have to kill you.'

Belinda flinched as he shot a hand up behind her head.

'Only joking,' he laughed as he took down a folder from one of the shelves. 'Here's what I'm after.'

Eric opened the folder to show her lists and lists of names.

'See, what I've done here is a catalogue, or should I say dog-alogue, of the customers with a unique number next to their names, and then I've stored the folders with their unique reference on it. Clever, eh?'

'Extremely.' She smiled. 'Alan Turing, eat your heart out.'

'Did he sell dog food?'

'Not that I know of,' said Belinda, beginning to wonder if there was a secret ingredient in the kibble that seeped through the packaging and sent the salespeople slightly mad.

'I'd love to show you more about the business,' said Eric. 'Perhaps we could spend a little more time together at some point.'

Now this wasn't something Belinda had foreseen.

The last thing she wanted was to spend an evening with Eric and his dog-alogues. Still, needs must.

'That sounds like a very good idea,' she said, turning to face him.

'It does?' he said. 'I wasn't actually expecting you to agree.'

'Life is full of surprises,' she said.

The sound of Harry stomping towards them brought Belinda some respite and, it would appear, a little relief to Eric.

'I'm done now,' said Harry, face somewhat flushed from hauling bags of dog food into the boot of his car.

'Good,' said Belinda, giving him a wide-eyed stare when she was sure Eric couldn't see. 'We've taken enough of this gent's time, we really should be off.'

'I'll call you,' said Eric.

'OK then,' said Belinda and Harry in unison, then exchanged puzzled glances with one another.

'What was that about?' said Harry as they walked back through the warehouse to his car.

'Eric promised to show me his filing system,' she said.

Belinda took another couple of steps before she realised that Harry was no longer walking along beside her. She glanced back over her shoulder to see him doubled over, hands on his knees and unable to stand.

'Are you quite all right?' she said, running back to his side and bending down.

'Apart from my sides about to split from laughing,' he eventually guffawed. 'That is really funny.'

'Come on, you imbecile,' said Belinda, feigning annoyance. 'You can make up for it by taking me to the pub. I've got something important to tell you.'

'It's ten thirty in the morning,' said Harry as he wiped a tear from his eye.

'It won't be busy then, will it?' she said. 'I can tell you all about Eric's filing and, more importantly, about the aerosol of spray paint he has in his office.'

CHAPTER THIRTY-TWO

Their journey took them back along country roads, flanked by trees and hedgerows, the sun still glaring down. They were some minutes clear of the depot and Eric's special filing system before Belinda had a chance to fully recount their conversation. Harry was still so amused at the thought of Eric flirting with Belinda that the snorts of laughter briefly silenced her.

'I thought it was a bit odd that he rushed out of the warehouse to check we'd actually left,' said Belinda.

'He can be slightly off the wall,' said Harry, wiping a tear from his eye, 'but I'm not sure your suspicions are well founded. Eric was recommended to me by an old police colleague. I can't see for one minute why he'd be involved in spraying yellow paint on the road outside people's houses, let alone have anything to do with dognapping. Did you see what colour paint it was?'

'Of course I didn't. I was too busy trying to distract him enough to look over his shoulder.'

Belinda was silent again while she gave it some further thought.

'It seems too much of a coincidence that he's got a can of spray paint in his office, works in a dog food distribution centre in a village where dogs are going missing, and he has nothing to do with it. He'd know all your customers' addresses for a start.'

It was Harry's turn to be silent for a moment.

'Belinda,' he said, 'there's one person we need to talk about again.'

She felt the bile rise in her throat. She was aware of a shooting pain in the palms of her hands and then realised that she had her hands curled into the tightest of balls, her fingernails cutting into her own skin.

'On the way here,' she said, changing the subject, 'remember we saw Sandra outside the Dog and Duck talking to a man in a red jacket?'

Harry gave out a gentle sigh before he said, 'If I recall correctly, you saw what you thought was Sandra going into the pub, talking to an unknown man. I wasn't looking and you weren't totally certain.'

'Stop splitting hairs,' said Belinda. 'We should get over there, find out who he is and what Sandra's involvement is. Was she in league with Tipper?'

Harry stopped the car at the next junction and said, 'We know that Lennie and Tipper like dogs. Tipper used to put local people in touch with breeders and Lennie's own dog died. I can see why someone would have it in for Tipper if, for example, their dog wasn't the pedigree they thought it was, something like that, but enough to murder him? I don't think so.'

'But what if he and Lennie were in the business of snatching the dogs back and selling them on again?' said Belinda. 'That's big business. Thoroughbred dogs are worth an absolute mint. Not forgetting Lennie had dog food in the kitchen. Let's not overlook that when Tipper arranged for Ivy to get her dog through a breeder he knew, Ivy didn't know any of the details. And Tipper used to walk Ivy's dog and now she's pregnant. Something that Ivy knew nothing about and was certainly not a party to.'

'I get that,' said Harry, bringing the car to a stop at a T-junction and giving Belinda his full attention, 'but Tipper's dead.'

'I know that. Unless your memory has given up on you, you'll remember I was the one who found him bobbing up and down.'

'So, Tipper can't tell us anything, and Bonnie is unlikely to pick anyone out in a line-up.' Harry laughed despite the gravity of the situation.

'Any chance you can stop making yourself laugh at your own jokes?' said Belinda. 'What we should do next is go and see Sandra, ask her if she knows anything about Lennie and Tipper being involved in dognappings and what she knew about Tipper walking Bonnie. Where he used to take her, that sort of thing. Remember I heard her saying something to Lennie in the Dog and Duck about walking. Perhaps she meant dogs.'

Harry chewed over Belinda's suggestion.

'Then I take you home,' he said, 'and we have that chat with your brother.'

'Would you please let it go about Marcus?' she said, at the end of her tether with him. 'There are so many other leads for us to follow, what with the microbrewery, Sandra, the black SUV Alicia saw, yet you continually harp on about my brother.'

'OK,' said Harry after several seconds. 'If you're not going to take this seriously, I think it's probably best if we see who that was at the Dog and Duck, I'll drop you home and perhaps see you in passing at some point in the village.'

'Agreed.'

'Agreed.'

Harry drove them straight to the Dog and Duck and pulled up directly outside. As it was before opening hours, the street was empty of parked cars and there weren't many people around, though a few were walking between the post office, general store and delicatessen with one or two heading towards the tea room, one of the few places open for Sunday trading.

For once, Belinda paid no heed to who was using her inaugural Little Challham business. Nothing could have been further from her mind as she pressed her face up against the pub window, trying to see who was inside.

Belinda watched Harry push at the front door, knowing full well he would find it locked but allowing him to try nonetheless. They hadn't exchanged a word in the last few minutes of the journey so she wasn't going to waste her breath on him now.

While he was occupied, she looked over the front of the pub. There were two upstairs windows open, but no chance of her scaling the wall to get to them. Instead, she walked around the side of the pub to the garden, wanting to get away from Harry's futile banging on the window. It was clear that no one was going to be opening the door to them any time soon.

She reached the rear garden, saw that one of the kitchen windows was open and let herself in through the latched gate and across the small patch of lawn, edges browning in the relentless summer sun. A row of raised wooden planters ran around the perimeter of the garden against the fence, all heavy with blossoms, a cascade of yellows, whites and pinks.

Her curiosity got the better of her. Belinda dragged a wooden garden chair towards the window and climbed up. With both hands on the peeling paint covering the windowsill, she pulled herself up in one effortless movement and was halfway inside the kitchen when she heard Harry clattering towards her across the pub garden.

'Belinda, you can't go and let yourself in like that.'

'I can, and I have,' she replied as she manoeuvred herself onto the enormous stainless-steel draining board, the clatter of cutlery giving away not only her entrance but her lack of dexterity when it came to breaking into someone else's property.

'Come out of there,' he said, standing on the chair and peering in after her. 'You'll get us both into so much trouble.'

'That makes you sound a touch, well, wet,' she said, brushing down her trousers, glad that when she'd got dressed that morning she had decided against a dress or skirt.

Belinda put her fingers up to her lips to silence a clearly furious Harry. His expression really was too comedic at times. As she moved across the dimly lit pub kitchen, Belinda decided that whatever happened, despite their very recent row, her life would always be better with Harry Powell in it. Fate had decreed it would take her over twenty years to meet him again, so Belinda prayed to all the gods that he would be around for a very long time to come.

She was snapped from her reverie by Harry's urgent tone and much gesticulating at something behind her.

Now regretting getting lost in the moment, Belinda spun on her heels to see what Harry had been trying to warn her about.

The walk-in freezer was open.

The door had been left ajar, meaning someone was either in there at that exact moment, or they weren't too far away.

'Could you give me a hand?' said Harry, heaving himself up to the edge of the window, which was barely bigger than him.

But Belinda couldn't stop herself from being drawn towards the freezer and the thing on the floor keeping the door propped open.

It was one of her pet hates: a roll of cling film. This was an industrial-sized catering pack, the type that Belinda hated with its single-use, river-polluting, bird-strangling, ocean-clogging nastiness.

Edging closer to the inside of the gigantic freezer, it was all too clear to Belinda that someone had used this very roll to wrap Sandra's entire body, head and face, preserving her like an old-fashioned cheese and pickle pub sandwich before propping her lifeless body up next to the pork pies and Scotch eggs.

CHAPTER THIRTY-THREE

'Oh, good grief!' shouted Harry as he clambered towards Belinda, having fallen through the window and made enough noise to alert anyone else in the building of his presence. Seemingly not satisfied in the noise department, he then knocked virtually everything from the draining board into the stainless-steel sink.

'We should call the police,' said Belinda as Harry managed to disentangle himself from the taps and join her in staring at Sandra.

'My mobile's in the car,' said Harry. 'I'll use the one in the bar. Will you be OK if I leave you?'

'Of course,' said Belinda, stepping closer to the lifeless, staring corpse.

'And don't touch anything,' said Harry as he ran towards the bar.

Belinda crouched down in front of Sandra, searching for any sign that might give her at least a hint of who would have done this. All to no avail.

There was nothing on the floor, nothing around her, nothing to point to anyone who could have done this.

'Why cling film?' muttered Belinda to herself. 'And why poor Sandra?'

Suddenly aware that she was alone and in a lockable walk-in freezer with a corpse, Belinda stood up and moved towards the main part of the pub where she could hear Harry making a call to the emergency services.

Her eyes sought out the bag of dog food she had seen last night.

There was a large space where the bag of dog food should have been.

Harry burst back through the door, phone still to his ear, to find her standing with her hands on her hips, staring up at the empty shelf.

With a look of puzzlement, he tried to see what she was seeing, but of course, she was looking at a gap.

Harry finished the call and stood in front of her, forcing her to turn her attention to him.

'I take it,' he said, 'from your frown and pursed lips, the dog food you told me about has gone too?'

'Yes,' she said with a slow nod. 'It's gone and the cling film…' Belinda pointed behind her to Sandra's body.

'What about the cling film?' said Harry, a frown now weighing down his own features.

'Oh, er, nothing, really,' she said, forcing a smile to her lips. 'It's only that someone went to a lot of effort to use so much of it.'

'Now's not the time to worry about single-use plastic,' said Harry. 'We should go and wait in the bar for the police, keep out of the crime scene. Again.'

She walked towards the kitchen door, the one they had rushed through only the night before after an attempt on the landlord's life.

'Harry,' she said, 'it's going to be very difficult to attract bar staff around here over the next few weeks.' The nastiness of the whole situation was getting to her now.

'Come on,' he said, putting an arm around her shaking shoulder. 'They shouldn't be too long.'

'Why would someone kill Sandra?' said Belinda. 'I know we had our differences, but she was a good person.'

'Let's wait for them in the bar,' said Harry. 'There's nothing we can do for her now.'

*

This time when PC Vince Green set eyes on Belinda, he seemed less surprised and more resigned to seeing her.

'You're either extremely unlucky,' he said, 'or one very slick assassin.'

'Are you sure you should be cracking jokes like that?' said Belinda, smiling shakily.

'Who said I'm joking?' said PC Green.

His crew mate gave a snort of laughter.

Belinda, Harry and PC Green all stared at the older officer.

'I'll, er, wait outside for the paramedics,' he said, taking his cue to leave them to it.

'Can I have a word with you, please, Ms Penshurst?' said PC Green. He shot a glimpse at Harry.

'Oh, certainly,' she said.

He led her to a corner of the bar as more police officers, crime scene investigators and ambulance staff arrived, took over the bar and started to search the upstairs.

'We've got someone who tells us that you had a thing about cling film,' said the police officer, arms crossed over his stab vest.

'What, like a fetish?' said Belinda, still slightly reeling from the shock. 'Not that it's any of your business, but I don't think this is really the time—'

Vince Green uncrossed his arms and held his palms up.

'Not that sort of thing about cling film,' he said, a tinge of red creeping across his youthful cheeks. 'You rowed with Sandra and you'd also rowed with Tipper about wrapping sandwiches in cling film and leaving them behind the bar.'

Belinda cocked her head to one side, wondering who could have told him this, especially considering that both people she had fallen out with over it were now dead.

That didn't bode well for her.

'I'm sure Harry's already told you,' said Belinda, panicking at the thought of getting arrested, 'that I've been with him all morning, so I couldn't have been involved in Sandra's death in any way.'

'After our last meeting,' said PC Green, 'I carried out some checks on you and your family.'

'Naturally.'

'You've invested in a lot of local businesses.'

Belinda stared at him. 'I am aware, officer,' she said when he was silent for longer than made her comfortable.

'And then there's your previous arrest.'

She let out a long sigh. 'Seriously?' she said, temper beginning to flare. 'For something I did over twenty years ago. And now you think that makes me a murderer? What am I supposed to be? Some sort of Rip Van Winkle sleeper agent?'

PC Green put his hands up in mock defence. 'Ma'am, all I'm letting you know is that I've done some research on you and I've—'

'Can I step in there, officer?' said Harry, who Belinda had seen inching his way across the room behind the uniformed officer's back.

Belinda and PC Green glanced up at him, one more pleased at his intervention than the other.

'Depending on how well you did your research,' said Harry, towering over the PC, 'you may also know that I was the arresting officer.'

The total shock all over PC Green's face as he glanced open-mouthed from one to the other was quite the picture.

'What I'm sure you won't know,' continued Harry, 'is that Belinda could have walked away with a caution for what she did, and a caution would have dropped off her criminal record by now, in fact many, many years ago.'

Harry stepped forward, his size-ten loafers toe to toe with Vince's size-seven Magnum boots.

'And what you also won't know,' said Harry, face a blotch of red patches, 'is that I tried to talk her and her friends into taking the easiest route out and avoid going to court. As you well know, son, if she'd admitted her guilt and accepted a caution, that would have meant the end of it. Belinda was the only one who went to court. She stood up for what she believed in and still believes in.'

Harry bowed his head towards PC Green until their foreheads were inches apart. The PC's Adam's apple bobbing up and down fascinated Belinda briefly, until she was drawn back to Harry.

'What you will undoubtedly know,' said Harry, 'is exactly what that arrest was for.'

'She was protesting,' said PC Green.

'Pardon?' said Harry.

'I said she was protesting,' said PC Green with a little more assertion.

'Mm,' said Harry. 'She was protesting, but let's try not to make it sound more sinister than it was. It was forty or so young women standing in Dover docks on a freezing cold January day wearing little more than a smile because they were disgusted and outraged at the treatment of live animals being exported to the Continent. That's all, nothing more.'

'I'm a vegetarian,' said PC Green.

'What?' said Harry, with a quick glance in Belinda's direction as her shoulders started to shake with laughter.

'Bordering on a vegan, sir,' said PC Green.

'Then best you go and get yourself a carrot,' said Harry, at last stepping back and allowing the officer an escape route.

'Harry,' Belinda said, fingers curling around his arm, earlier row forgotten, 'you never fail to surprise me.'

CHAPTER THIRTY-FOUR

After some considerable time giving statements to the police, Belinda and Harry made good their escape from the Dog and Duck. They decided to get as far away from PC Green's angry stare as they could.

Perhaps it's the lack of vitamin B that makes him so cranky, thought Belinda as they crossed the road towards the tea room.

'Honestly, Harry, I'm fine,' she said as he glanced back to check on her for the third time.

'What you need is a nice sweet cup of tea and a bun,' said Harry.

Belinda let out a giggle, placed a hand over her mouth and said, 'A bun? Are you ninety? We only serve the finest pastries, desserts and cupcakes at the Little Challham Tea Room.'

'What about the cinnamon buns?' said Harry. 'Many a morning I've watched that letch of a lorry driver, Max, try it on with Angie and make inappropriate bun jokes.'

'Really?' said Belinda. 'I'd better keep an eye on him then. I don't want my staff harassed.'

Belinda was eyed suspiciously by more than one of the patrons already settled at their tables as she and Harry made their entrance. Even the usually affable Angie appeared a little out of sorts at seeing her.

'Hello, Angie,' said Belinda. 'I see it's a bit quieter in here today.'

Angie stood in front of them in her standard unofficial uniform of tight T-shirt, skirt consisting of a hem, and Birkenstock sandals. She fidgeted as if unsure what to do or say, her mouth contorting.

'It may have something to do with the fact that people keep getting killed, Belinda,' said Angie, seemingly a little taken aback at her own words.

'No one's been murdered in the tea room, have they?' said Belinda, looking round at the half-dozen or so customers who were failing to meet her eye and concentrating on their tea and cakes. Not a bun in sight.

'I heard that someone else was found dead in the pub,' said Angie. 'Is it true?'

'Yes,' said Belinda, indicating that she and Harry were going to take a table at the back.

When Belinda and Harry were seated, Belinda pushed out a chair for Angie and said, 'Take a seat for a moment.'

Once the young woman had done as asked, she said, 'Who was it?'

'I'm sorry to say it was Sandra,' said Belinda. 'It's shocking enough to find anyone like that, but I genuinely liked her as well.'

'Oh my goodness,' said Angie, the usual colour to her cheeks a distant memory considering the news. 'Didn't she apply for the job here before I was given it?'

'Yes, yes, she did,' said Belinda, 'and I would have hired her in a heartbeat if you hadn't come along with your formidable skills and experience. It's all too horrible for words. Rest assured, we'll find out who did this.'

They were momentarily distracted by the sound of four of the customers getting up and leaving the tea room.

'It's not good for business either,' said Angie with a scowl at Belinda, who was busy watching her income file out of the door.

'Never mind that now,' said Belinda. 'Any chance you've heard anything in here from customers? Like snippets about Sandra and any problems she may have had?'

Angie gave it some thought and said, 'She was in here a couple of times with a man I hadn't seen before. He used to park his black

SUV around the corner and walk across the green. I've seen him when I've been out the back but I was often dealing with a delivery at the same time. I never paid any attention to what they were saying.'

'What did he look like?' said Harry.

Angie shrugged and said, 'Average. Not as old as you but older than me. Short brown hair, five foot ten or something. There was nothing about him that made him stick in my mind.'

'Anyone else?' said Harry.

The young woman shook her head, mousy hair shaking loose over her shoulders. 'No, but she was on her phone a week or so ago and said something like, "I'll meet you around closing hours." There's nothing strange about that, is there? After all, she worked in a pub so she'd hardly meet someone in the middle of her shift, would she?'

'That's very true, Angie,' said Belinda, 'but what made you remember it?'

Angie's brow furrowed in concentration and her pink-glossed lips formed a tiny 'O' as she racked her brains to recall what she had overheard.

'Yes, that's right,' said Angie after a lengthy pause, 'Sandra laughed a couple of times and said, "As if that's going to stop me."'

The sound of the door opening and customers coming in distracted Angie. She called, 'Hello, won't be a moment,' to a young couple with a toddler who were searching for a clean, empty table.

'Sorry, Belinda,' she said. 'I have to get on. I'm very sorry about Sandra.'

When Angie was out of earshot, Belinda leaned across to Harry and said, 'Black SUV? This has to have something to do with the dognappers. I can't believe I was coming round to the idea of liking Sandra so much. Any clue who she was meeting?'

'Not a clue,' said Harry, attention caught by Angie carrying two plates laden with cherry Bakewell tarts towards two women waiting patiently.

'You sure I can't get you a bun, or cake or whatever?' he said.

'No, I'm fine, but don't let two murders and one attempt stop you from having one,' said Belinda. 'Were you always this unfocused in the police?'

'Well, we ate, for a start,' he said, bottom lip sticking out.

'Harry,' she said, 'I think we need to go and warn Lennie that someone suspects him of stealing dogs and whoever hit him on the head may be back to finish the job. From the description, it wasn't him Sandra met in here. As soon as they let Lennie out of hospital, I say we go and speak to him.'

'Good idea,' said Harry. 'I'll get my tart to go.'

Belinda sighed.

CHAPTER THIRTY-FIVE

Harry finally managed to get some time by himself after Belinda insisted she would go and speak to Marcus without him. Trouble was, it wasn't all that long before he was bored. On more than one occasion, he either glanced across at the passenger seat to say something to Belinda or thought about phoning her.

They had agreed to leave speaking to Anthony until later in the day, and a visit to Lennie would follow whenever he was out of the hospital. Harry still had his doubts that they should be getting involved in a murder investigation at all but it gave him an excuse to look out for Belinda. He worried about her getting herself hurt, and above all, he enjoyed her company.

The truth of it was he liked Belinda. Quite a lot when he thought about it.

'Simply won't do,' he mumbled, all the time aware that he was now talking to himself.

He had to admit, the last couple of days had been good fun, if he didn't stop to dwell on the dead bodies. It was a little like having his old job back, except without all the responsibility, not to mention the paperwork.

Before long, Harry pulled up outside Dawn's house and realised he had been singing along to the radio. That wasn't something that happened every day.

He took his toolbox from the boot of the car, along with a couple of dog treats, which were disappearing at an alarming rate, and walked up the path.

Ferocious barking greeted him until Dawn opened the door and ushered him inside.

'You're in a good mood,' she said, once the lively Great Dane had calmed down enough to allow them to speak, placated by a Doggie Delight freebie.

'What makes you say that?' said Harry as he picked up his toolbox from where he'd left it to fend off Colonel's affection.

'You've smiled twice and I'm pretty sure you were humming when I opened the door,' she said, walking back towards the kitchen.

'Was I?' said Harry as he followed her. 'I didn't mean to.'

'Don't apologise,' said Dawn. 'You must have had a pretty good start to your Sunday, that's all.'

That made Harry freeze on the spot.

'Have I said something I shouldn't have?' said Dawn, one hand holding the kettle, the other on the kitchen tap.

Harry shrugged and said, 'For a normal person, it was an unpleasant one, only I'm not normal.'

He sensed she was inching back towards the sink.

How could he have forgotten that a couple of hours ago, he and Belinda had found the cling-filmed body of a human being? A trifle unusual even for a retired detective inspector; plain bizarre for the ordinary folk of this world.

'This morning,' he said, smile gone now, 'Belinda and I found a body.'

A gasp from Dawn.

'It was Sandra, the barmaid from the New Inn,' he said, trying to read her face for signs of anguish or surprise.

'What happened?' Dawn had abandoned her idea of putting the kettle on, her full attention on Harry.

'It's probably best not to go into details,' he said, looking round for Alicia.

'Don't worry,' said Dawn, 'she's at her dad's. Where did you find Sandra? Was it, you know, an accident?'

'No sort of accident I've ever encountered or think humanly possible,' said Harry, now eager just to get the fence fixed and do something useful, something practical.

'Wow,' Dawn said. 'I was only at the microbrewery a couple of weeks ago and she stopped by to have a drink. We got chatting, like you do, and...'

'Did you know her well?'

'No, not really. I'd said hello a couple of times when I was in the New Inn or saw her in the village. She usually kept herself to herself. It was only that on this occasion, I had Colonel with me. Alicia was at her dad's; I'd fancied a walk and my feet led me to the village.'

Dawn seemed to remember that she had meant to put the kettle on and picked it back up to hold it under the tap.

'Now I come to think of it,' she said, staring out of the window in the direction of the broken fence, 'Sandra came over and made a fuss of Colonel before she started speaking to me.'

'Did she like dogs then?'

Dawn shook her head. 'I assume she did, she all but got down on the floor with Colonel. You know what he's like for lying on the floor with his legs in the air when anyone makes a fuss of him! She asked why I hadn't had him neutered and was I going to breed from him. She asked more than once if she could look after him for me, walk him, that kind of thing. It was a bit strange. I never thought to say anything the other day when you were talking about Ivy White because we were concentrating on Tipper.'

'Sandra was most likely making polite conversation,' said Harry, all the while thinking the exact opposite. He guessed that Sandra was probably thinking of borrowing Colonel for some alone time with a potential mate and making a litter of tiny yet profitable Colonels.

'She may have been, but then she kept asking me if he had any illnesses or whether he had heart or hip issues.'

'Dawn,' said Harry, not wanting to alarm her too much with her current concerns over dognapping, 'it sounds as though she was probably being a touch too nosy, especially as you'd only popped in for a drink at the end of a dog walk.'

'Exactly. The thing is, the owner of the microbrewery, Anthony, clearly thought she was asking too many questions as well. I thought he was going to chuck her out at one point. He took her over to the bar and gave her a good telling-off. It's only because it's compact and quiet in there that I heard him say he was going to mention her behaviour to Tipper if she stepped out of line again. I thought it was a bit over the top for making a fuss of my dog, if you ask me. Poor Sandra. She was only trying to be friendly, what with Tipper being the one who got me Colonel in the first place.'

That was what was bothering Harry. With Tipper and Sandra dead, and Lennie in hospital, the only other person who seemed to show any interest in the villagers' dogs was the owner of the microbrewery.

As soon as Harry was finished fixing Dawn's fence, he'd be off to visit Anthony Cotter in the last remaining licensed premises in Little Challham that wasn't sealed off as a murder scene. If they were all involved in dognappings, so far Anthony was the only one not in hospital or in the morgue.

Belinda was bound to forgive him for going without her. She had her own problems to deal with.

CHAPTER THIRTY-SIX

Belinda was glad that she'd declined Harry's offer to drive her home. She had truly meant what she had told her brother about enjoying the walk along the driveway, aside from the bit about needing more exercise. Perhaps a dog would be good for her. She could take him or her running. That would benefit both of them.

She took her time walking across the green, caught up in a crowd of adults with young pre-school-age children who were taking advantage of another glorious summer's day and the fresh air of the countryside.

She was so entranced watching a young girl in a pink helmet furiously peddling her tricycle, her father quick-stepping beside her, that she almost didn't notice the van leaving through the front gates of the castle.

With a start, Belinda stared at the driver, a woman of about forty who she didn't know, plus the passenger, who she knew very well.

Marcus was in the front seat of the van, whose sides were covered in a language she didn't recognise. Belinda was so stunned that she almost missed the foreign number plates as it turned out of the driveway and away from her.

One thing she couldn't have failed to see were the painted silhouettes of happy dogs along the side of the van, a sure indication that this was part of her brother's plan. What the plan was, she was yet to fathom, but she had no doubt it would involve a plethora of problems, problems that would be left to her to solve. At least even Marcus wouldn't be stupid enough to take part in a dognapping ring and be seen in a van with such obvious signage. That was encouraging.

Exasperated at not knowing what her brother was up to, and fearing the worst, Belinda's eyes were drawn to the Gatehouse. She really shouldn't rely on Harry: she had managed perfectly well without him, but now he was in her life, she truly valued his opinion, as infuriating as he sometimes was.

No, this won't do, she told herself. It was time to go home and find out what Marcus was up to. She had planned to talk to him or risk another telling-off from Harry. Now she would have to snoop around in his office, somewhere she had never pried before. If he got angry with her, what was the worst he could do? Drown her in a barrel of beer? Hit her on the head? Suffocate her with cling film?

Belinda continued her walk back home, at the slowest pace she had probably ever taken in her life. She forced herself to look at the views, the abundance of trees, the bounty of colours and the marvellous bees furiously working their eternal shifts.

She tried not to dwell on her brother's argument with Tipper just before she found his body. Besides, Marcus had an alibi for his murder. She tried not to think about how Marcus was one of the few people on the planet who knew of her hatred of cling film and single-use plastics. But if Marcus wasn't involved in dognapping, he had no reason to kill Sandra either.

Lennie! That was right, there was the unfortunate attempt to cave in the back of Lennie's skull. Her brother had absolutely no reason to do that.

Except… hadn't Lennie barred Marcus once after a row about ordering a drink as the last bell rang and then not drinking up quick enough?

Who in their right mind would try to kill another person because they had had their drink taken off them in a crowded pub? A crowded pub full of their friends, family and contemporaries.

This wasn't good at all.

Once she got home and cleared her head, this would all fade into insignificance.

If Marcus was part of the dognapping gang and it was falling apart, who knew who might be next? The man in the SUV could be coming for Marcus. A thought that made her shudder despite the afternoon sun.

It didn't take long before Belinda was home again, striding through the kitchen door at the side entrance, on a mission to head straight to her brother's study.

Belinda paused at the coffee machine.

It had been hours since she'd had a caffeine fix, something she should put right without further ado, but now was not the time.

On the front of the coffee machine was a handwritten sticky note.

Sis, be an angel and see the Doggie Delight chap, would you? He has some food on order, and I could do with it soon for the imminent new arrivals! Love you, M x

For a second, Belinda held the note between her fingers, let out a low breath and slapped it down on the worktop.

There was nothing else for it, she had to speak to Harry Powell.

She had already postponed talking as freely and openly to Harry about Marcus as she should have, but it could wait no longer.

The dogs were coming, and anything Marcus got involved in was bound to be ridiculous on a grand scale.

Belinda reached up to the rack and grabbed the Land Rover's keys.

Not wanting to wait now she'd made up her mind, she raced to the garage, jumped into the driver's seat and headed back towards the village, hoping Harry was at home.

At the bottom of the driveway, Belinda glanced left and right to check for traffic, and for any signs of Harry, even though she knew that his car would be parked at the back and out of sight.

As luck would have it, her recce didn't disappoint. Instead of seeing Harry, Belinda stared straight into the eyes of a youth in a hoodie, who looked suspiciously familiar.

There was no way she would have been anywhere near certain that it was the same person who'd unceremoniously elbowed her in the face, but on seeing her, he ran as if he was guilty.

That was enough for Belinda. She hit the accelerator and drove around the green as if her very life depended on it. The gunning of the engine attracted more unsavoury looks than she would have liked. However, needs must, and she thought the wonderful local people would understand that, if only they would get out of her way.

Belinda avoided the cute little girl on her tricycle, slightly annoyed that she hadn't mastered it yet and that her father thought the road was the place for her to try. Despite the obstacles in her way, Belinda circumnavigated the pedestrians and roadside furniture that appeared to jump into her path.

She was desperate to keep up with the hoodie man and find out who he was.

Just as she thought she was gaining on him, Belinda turned a sharp right and brought the car to an abrupt halt when she saw the dark blue hoodie disappear down an alleyway.

'That's done it,' she said to herself as she watched him vault over a six-foot-high fence to another garden.

There were few things that Belinda refused to try but this was certainly setting herself up for a fall. Her fence-jumping days were most definitely behind her.

Belinda knew that Harry would have an absolute field day when he found out she had allowed her attacker to escape when she'd had him within her sights.

Still, not one to be dispirited, Belinda drove back towards Harry's home.

'I only hope he has some spare dog food,' she said to herself as she made the journey back across Little Challham. Whatever daft thing Marcus was up to, the dogs at least needed to be fed.

CHAPTER THIRTY-SEVEN

Harry parked his car in the small car park beside the Women's Institute, always empty at this time of day, and walked around the corner towards the green. He stood studying the facade of the microbrewery with its small tinted windows. It was welcoming enough but the limited space inside, and its inability to offer food, meant that it had remained the least used of Little Challham's licensed premises. Still, Harry was happy to sacrifice food and pay it a visit to see if Anthony was around. It had been a while since he had crossed its threshold, and besides, he didn't fancy heading to an empty house just yet.

Harry crossed the road to the microbrewery, glanced up at the sign above the door, smiled at the name and went inside.

Luck was with him: Anthony was behind the bar, mobile phone in one hand, coffee mug in the other.

At least, that was what it looked like as Harry walked into the compact space: wooden bar running along the back wall, line of matching high benches and stools along the wall to the right-hand side, wooden ledge running along the opposite wall. The sunlight didn't reach far enough into the room for Harry to fully make out Anthony's expression, although he saw him look up.

'Harry,' said Anthony, a warmth in his voice. 'You're welcome to sit anywhere you'd like, what with you having the place all to yourself.'

Harry made his way to the bar and pulled out one of the six stools neatly lined up there, which looked like they hadn't been moved for some time.

'Anthony,' said Harry. 'Slow day?'

'Not too bad, not too bad. Lunchtime was busy, but it's died off since then. What can I get you?'

'One of those coffees wouldn't go amiss.'

'Course.'

Anthony sauntered over to the percolator, poured some into a mug and reached to the chiller cabinet for the milk.

'I thought business would be booming, given both pubs were shut recently,' said Harry.

'Yeah,' said Anthony with a sigh. 'It's been a bit strange: people popped in for a drink and a chat, but as soon as the temporary manager opened up the New Inn, the regulars were back in there, and now the bar area of the Dog and Duck's open again after the terrible business with Sandra, it's the same story. Not sure why the punters don't make more use of this place.'

Harry stirred the milk into his mug, picked it up with two hands and said, 'Bit dark in here, Anthony. You heard of lights?'

'It's all part of the ambience.'

'I'll give you this, mate,' said Harry, mug to his mouth, 'it certainly lives up to its name.'

'What I'm selling here, you see, is a drinking experience. People like the dark: they can hide and feel safe. Not to mention it's cosy. The customers know I'm not afraid to put the heating on when it gets nippy out.'

Harry put his mug down on the counter.

'Did you come up with the name yourself?'

'Yeah,' said Anthony, leaning across the bar towards his only customer. 'Tipper, rest his soul, came over a week or two before opening and we poured some brandy, talked a bit, drank a lot, chewed the fat. When I described what kind of atmosphere I was trying to create, plus the idea of saving a few quid on window cleaning, the name simply came to me.'

'Did Tipper actually come up with the name though?' Harry drank most of his coffee in one gulp, relishing the taste. 'You know, did he think he was entitled to some sort of credit for it?'

'I suppose he might have helped a bit, but he's not here now, so only I can really say whose idea it was to call the place the Dark Side of the Room.'

Harry remembered Ivy White telling him that Tipper had been on the phone to Anthony stalling him over money. There must have been more to this than Anthony was telling him, but would he kill someone over the name of a bar? A terrible name at that.

Anthony took some time purveying his domain, dark walnut walls and all. His chest heaved with pride and he was only woken from his reverie by the sound of Harry's muffled snort of laughter.

'Something funny, Harry?'

'No, no. Only the shock of the last couple of days catching up with me,' said Harry. 'Getting back to Tipper – who did he know in the dog trade?'

The change in demeanour was unmistakable. It wouldn't have taken police training to tell that Harry had touched a nerve.

Anthony straightened up to his six feet four inches, folded his arms and, with the start of a twitch to his left eye, said, 'Dogs? No. Tipper had nothing to do with dogs.'

'Oh, OK,' said Harry. 'I must have been mistaken. I was up at the castle the other day sorting out a dog food order and got the impression that Tipper had had some involvement in dog breeding.'

Anthony gave a slow, deliberate nod of his head, stared at Harry and said, 'I don't have much to do with them up there. That Belinda is particularly irksome. She never comes in here for a start.'

With no hint of sarcasm, Harry ran an eye over the dark interior and lifeless atmosphere of the microbrewery, unsure what to say that wouldn't cause offence.

Realising that there was little more to be gleaned from Anthony today, Harry drained his drink, put some coins on the bar and stood up.

'Thanks for the chat,' said Harry. 'I'll see you later.'

Harry made to go and then paused. 'Just one more thing,' he added, knowing he would probably not get anywhere but willing to try. 'I was talking to Dawn Jones the other day. She was in here with her dog Colonel and poor Sandra was in here making a fuss of him.'

'I don't remember,' said Anthony, the twitch in his eye saying otherwise.

As Harry turned around, he was momentarily blinded by the sunlight trying its hardest to breach the leaded glass windows and infiltrate the microbrewery's interior. Despite the opaque glass, Harry's attention was drawn across the green to the windows above the New Inn, where he was certain he had seen someone behind the dirty white net curtains.

By the time he reached the door and stopped to concentrate fully, Anthony was behind him.

'Any idea if the temporary manager is staying at the New Inn?' said Harry.

'No, not as far as I know,' said Anthony as his hand reached past Harry's arm to grab hold of the door.

'May as well take the opportunity to post a couple of letters,' he said in Harry's ear. 'You wouldn't mind waiting for a moment while I run across the street, would you?'

Before Harry had a chance to answer, Anthony was off, shrugging on a lightweight jacket the same bright red colour as the post box he was now heading towards, letters in hand.

According to Belinda, the last person seen talking to Sandra before her murder had worn a jacket just like that.

Harry really should tell the police, but not before he told Belinda. He felt he owed her a peace offering after thinking Marcus was anything but above board.

CHAPTER THIRTY-EIGHT

Still annoyed that she had failed to get a good look at the fence-jumping hooded man, as well as her irritation at running her brother's errands, Belinda pulled up next to Harry's empty garage.

'Bother,' she said and slapped her hands on the Land Rover's steering wheel. She'd only thought Harry would be at home because he wasn't with her, and that made no sense. He was a fully grown man who was very capable of leaving home when he wanted and without telling her where he was going. The truth was, she liked him, she liked him a lot.

For a moment, Belinda sat strumming her fingertips on the dashboard before deciding she would stretch her legs for a bit – or, more accurately, nose around the shed, garage and garden. It was her property after all.

Fortunately, Belinda had only got as far as peering inside the garage when she heard the sound of a car slowing as the driver made the turn into the track running behind the Gatehouse.

Appearing nonchalant was hardly ever Belinda's thing, but she gave it her best shot.

Her attempt at hiding her surprise was undoubtedly unimpressive when instead of Harry's car coming into view, she found herself staring rather gormlessly at Dawn's Ford Fiesta.

Belinda's expression soon changed to merriment when she saw Colonel stand up on the back seat. It was as if a giant grey inflatable had popped into view, overshadowing the rest of the vehicle and Dawn's head.

Colonel let out the loudest bark of excitement, making Dawn flinch in shock and Belinda laugh out loud.

'He's certainly one very vocal hound,' said Belinda as Dawn got out of the car.

'I know,' said Dawn, opening the back door so Colonel could jump out and run happily around the garden. 'He's a wonderful dog, but my ears could do without it sometimes.'

'Harry's not home at the moment,' said Belinda, intrigued by what Dawn wanted with him.

'That's a shame,' said Dawn. She bit her bottom lip and peered over at Colonel, who was sniffing at the bottom of a cypress tree as if his life depended on it.

'I don't think he'll be long,' said Belinda, hoping it was true rather than having any knowledge of Harry's timetable.

'It's a bit cheeky of me really,' said Dawn. 'I shouldn't take advantage of his generosity, except I've got to pick Alicia up from her dad's and then I need to take her into town and get some new shoes and other school stuff for the new term, and…'

Belinda saw the way that Dawn was watching Colonel before turning her attention back to her.

'I don't suppose…' Dawn pursed her lips, shook her head and said, 'Sorry, it's wrong of me to ask.'

'You want me to watch Colonel?' said Belinda, pushing herself up straight from where she'd been leaning against her Land Rover.

'I know, I know,' said Dawn, backing away towards her Fiesta. 'It's very cheeky of me and I should never have even thought it.'

'Why not?'

'You don't have time to look after my dog.'

'Sadly,' said Belinda, 'I've got more time on my hands at the moment than Harry does.'

'You've already done enough for me,' said Dawn, 'with the, well, you know, helping me out.'

Belinda waved away Dawn's comments. 'It's all water under the bridge, and besides, we women should stick together.'

'When Alicia's dad walked out, if it hadn't been for you putting some work my way and helping out like that, I don't know what we'd have done.'

'Relationships sometimes go wrong,' said Belinda. 'When it happens, it's tough, really tough. You both belong here in Little Challham and I couldn't have stood the thought of you not being a part of the village, especially now I hear Alicia is a detective constable in training.'

Dawn opened her mouth to say something, but the sound of Harry's car distracted her. Belinda couldn't fail to notice a sharpening in Dawn's features, and something bordering on panic.

'And Dawn,' said Belinda, 'I haven't and won't mention any of this to Harry. He's completely in the dark about you working for me and it'll stay that way.'

Dawn gave her the smallest of smiles.

They both stood still awaiting Harry's arrival, unlike Colonel, who barrelled straight into him the minute he got out. This was swiftly followed by a shout from Dawn telling him to 'get down and give the poor man a minute'. Words which, naturally, the overexcited dog completely ignored, leaning his entire weight against Harry's knees.

'I can't move,' said Harry, 'not without him toppling over. Never fear, I have one last emergency goodie bar in my pocket for Great Dane emergencies. I really have no idea where my stash of bars and treats has disappeared to. Strange.'

Harry managed to remove the treat from his pocket and throw it on the ground a foot or so away. Once Colonel was suitably distracted, for all of the two seconds it took to inhale the chewie bar, Harry greeted his guests.

'What have I done to deserve a visit from two of my favourite people?' he said, looking from one to the other.

Belinda indicted that Dawn should speak first, more because what Belinda had to say was private than because she was being polite.

Dawn said, 'I was wondering if you could look after Colonel for a couple of hours. You know I don't like leaving him at home at the moment. Not until the dognapping business is cleared up once and for all.'

'We're still looking into the dognapping,' said Belinda.

Harry shot her a look that she couldn't interpret: was it a warning not to say more?

'Have you managed to find anything out?' said Dawn, which was a reasonable question.

Harry scratched his chin and looked away; Belinda inspected her fingernails. 'Not at present, no,' said Belinda, 'but we're working on it.'

Dawn took a step nearer to Harry, who was now bending down, rubbing Colonel's tummy. 'I understand if you can't look after him, but I do need to go into town and only a complete fool would leave their dog in the car when they go shopping, especially as the weather has been so warm lately.'

'I'd love to have him for a couple of hours,' said Harry.

'Thank you so much,' said Dawn. 'I'll get his lead and a couple of bits from the boot and leave you to it.'

Belinda and Harry waved her off a couple of minutes later, Belinda with a feeling of dread that she would now have to speak frankly after stalling for so long.

'I wasn't expecting to see you so soon,' he said as the Fiesta disappeared from sight. 'Everything all right?'

Belinda took a deep breath and said, 'Marcus has sent me to pick up some dog food; he needs a couple of bags for some dogs that are due in soon.'

She felt the weight of Harry's stare as he looked down at her.

'And we're still looking into the dognapping, are we?' he said.

'You can't think for one minute that my brother would have anything to do with stealing other people's *pets*, would you?'

'Would you?'

'Don't be absurd,' she said with something akin to a sneer, then she remembered how much she valued Harry's opinion, not to mention his help.

'Harry, can I talk to you? In private.'

They both looked down to where Colonel was sitting, staring up at both of them.

'I don't think he's a grass,' said Harry. 'It's probably OK to speak in front of him.'

'All right, but can we move the dog food at the same time?' she said with a glance at her watch. 'I'm not sure when Marcus needs the food for, but I'd rather get this done and then we can speak to him properly.'

Harry stood still. 'I noticed your use of the word "we".'

Belinda gave him her best smile, the one she reserved for special favours.

'I have to be honest with you,' she said, 'things have gotten a bit out of hand and I could do with your take on it. In fact, if Dawn hadn't been here last time I dropped by, I might have been more upfront with you then.'

She had the decency to look away.

'Seriously?' he said. 'You were worried about what your brother was up to and Dawn being here stopped you from speaking to me?'

When Belinda next dared to steal a look in his direction, Harry's attention seemed drawn to a spot in the distance.

'You're annoyed and that's understandable,' she said, 'but I'm asking for your help. I've only known Dawn for about ten years, but I've known you for twice as long.'

Harry said, 'I think we'd, er, better shift this dog food. How much does he want?'

Exasperated but not entirely sure what to say, Belinda followed him to the garage where the bags were stored.

'Three should do it, I suppose,' she said. 'I expect you'll be able to drop more off tomorrow?'

'Not a problem,' he said. 'I seem to be running out of everything, so I'll drive over to the depot to pick some more up later on.'

Belinda opened the back of the Land Rover as Harry went to grab the first bag of food.

As he leaned past her to put the bag in the space she had cleared, she put her hand on his shoulder.

'About that,' she said. 'Any chance I could come with you? I still think there's something about your boss Eric that doesn't quite add up.'

Momentarily distracted, Harry caught the corner of the bag on a gardening fork lurking in the back of the Land Rover. The expression on Harry's face as he suddenly moved away from Belinda made her think she had alarmed him by getting so close. Though perhaps he was merely surprised at her comment about his boss.

'Eric?' he said. 'I really don't think so. We've already talked about this. The man's as straight as a die. I've been giving the whole spray paint thing a lot of thought. You weren't sure what colour it was; he often sprays numbers on the pallets so we know which ones are which; and anyway, he's not the only one in the whole village who owns aerosol cans.'

'I see,' was all Belinda could manage to utter. To say she was disappointed over Harry's lack of enthusiasm was underplaying matters by some distance.

For another minute or so Belinda watched Harry go to his garage and rifle through his stash of Doggie Delight snacks and treats. He stopped on a couple of occasions and muttered something about where they had all gone and were all the strays in the county helping themselves. Eventually he realised that Belinda was watching him.

'What?' he said. 'Can't I ponder where all of my dog snacks have disappeared to without getting myself *the look*?'

'I am most definitely not giving you *the look*,' she said, angry that he had caught her doing exactly that. 'All I want to know is why you don't want to talk about the tiniest possibility that your boss, a man you barely know, may be embroiled in something untoward?'

'I'll get the rest of the bags,' said Harry, flush to his cheeks as he turned from her. 'Eric gave me a job and a new lease of life. After thirty years as a police officer, don't you think I'd have noticed if he were a dog thief?'

Belinda stood back from the car, out of his way as he worked.

'We've still got so much to talk about,' she said, earning a startled look from Harry as he made his way back to the car. 'About these murders, I mean.'

He put the final bag in the boot and stood with his arms dangling awkwardly.

'Well, one thing I found out today,' said Harry, 'is that Anthony Cotter is the proud owner of a red jacket.'

'He must have been the person I saw talking to Sandra before she was killed,' said Belinda.

'So,' said Harry, 'that may allay any fears that Eric's involved in murder.'

'And surely Marcus,' said Belinda, somewhat haughtily.

Colonel, who had finished inspecting the shrubbery, nosed between the two of them and jumped into the back of the Land Rover. Immediately he started to demolish the kibble spilling out of the bag Harry had ripped.

'It seems the dog's decided he's coming with us,' said Belinda.

'Let's settle this once and for all,' said Harry with a glance at his watch. 'If we leave it too long, we'll be pushing it to get to the depot to see Eric before he shuts up for the day. How about we go there first, talk to Eric, work out a plan for Anthony Cotter and then we'll visit your brother, and he can explain to us exactly why he isn't caught up in dognapping and possibly murder.'

'Just what I was going to suggest,' said Belinda, glad to have Harry back by her side. Things were looking up already.

CHAPTER THIRTY-NINE

Belinda was glad that she was driving; she was able to avoid Harry's stare. She pulled away from the Gatehouse and, knowing she would be unable to stand the intensity of his gaze for the entire journey, paused at the junction and took a deep breath. It seemed that Harry was keener to eliminate Eric as a suspect than he was to deal with Anthony or Marcus.

'Before we talk about Eric,' she said, 'please let me explain some more about Tipper and my brother.'

Harry settled back into his seat and crossed his arms. 'Go on.'

'The day Tipper came to the castle – you know, when you first spoke to Marcus about his order of dog food.'

A soft laugh from Harry, then, 'The day he put an order in for dogs he didn't have.'

'Please,' she said, 'hear me out. Marcus isn't like that. He's daft and he's sometimes reckless, but he's not a crook.'

A car stopped to let Belinda out, so she pulled away and began to drive towards the depot. For some reason, her stomach lurched as she glimpsed the castle in her rear-view mirror.

'Tipper was very angry that day, I've told you that. What I didn't tell you was that he told Marcus that he knew things, as if he was planning to blackmail him.'

'Belinda,' said Harry, 'I hate to be the one to tell you, but that doesn't make it any better. It's a motive for murder.'

'I know that! I'm getting to the point. Marcus's reply to him was along the lines of, "This is what I do and what I've been doing for years." Don't you see that if he's been doing it for years, it can't be the dognapping, because we'd have noticed it?'

'That does make a sort of illogical sense, I suppose,' agreed Harry, tone matching his unconvinced words.

'Please, help me. More importantly, help Marcus. He couldn't have murdered anyone; he simply doesn't have it in him.'

'Really hate to break it to you,' said Harry, 'but I've worked on many a murder where the killer's family has said exactly that.'

'OK,' said Belinda, 'but what if Eric and Tipper were in on this together? Eric was identifying potential dogs for breeding – so, those that weren't spayed or neutered – by simply asking the question when owners placed dog food orders, and then he'd put Tipper in touch with them.'

'No, not possible,' said Harry with a shake of his head that Belinda could make out in her peripheral vision. 'I would have noticed.'

'Except you've only been working for Doggie Delight for a few weeks,' said Belinda, exasperation tinging her tone. 'Think about it: is it something you'd have noticed in such a short space of time?'

'I was a police—'

Belinda held her left palm up to silence Harry.

'You've got to face facts here,' she said. 'I know there's something amiss at Doggie Delight, what with Eric knowing so many of the dog owners, plus the spray paint in his office. And we're about to find out what.'

Belinda pulled her Land Rover up and they walked inside the large warehouse, Colonel trotting along beside them. Their footsteps echoed as they made their way towards Eric's office at the back of the building, Colonel's approach more stealthy, although his nails clipped happily on the concrete floor.

They were less than thirty feet from Eric's office door when a noise from behind a stack of pallets to their right-hand side froze them on the spot.

Harry indicated that she should stay where she was while he went to take a look.

'Eric,' said Harry, 'are you hiding in the dog food aisles?'

'No, I was just… Oh, hello again, Belinda,' said Eric, slightly manic smile on his face. 'I'll start to wonder if you simply can't keep away from me.'

'Eric,' she said, 'we've been wondering if we could have another word with you.'

Whether it was her tone or the unexpected visit that made the blood rush to his head, Belinda didn't know. Whatever it was, it made him reel slightly and lean back against the nearest tower of food bags.

Eric put both hands up to rub his face.

Since their earlier visit, Eric had shed his jacket, and now that his bare forearms were visible in his short-sleeved shirt, it was abundantly clear that he had perhaps been very modest about not knowing his own strength.

'What did you need to talk to me about?' he said.

'Tipper Johnson,' said Belinda, wondering if she was bad cop, how easily Harry would fill the good cop role.

The two words were met with a shrug, a minuscule shake of his head and a sigh. 'Tragic,' said Eric. 'Such a waste of life.'

'Did you kill him?' said Belinda.

'No! I—'

'Take it easy, Belinda,' said Harry. 'I'm sure Eric didn't have anything to do with his death.'

'To be honest, I did,' said Eric.

'What?' said Harry.

'Pardon?' said Belinda, unable to believe their roleplay had worked so easily.

'I'll come clean: I feel as if I may have played a part in it,' said Eric, leaning over to get his jacket from the corner of a six-foot-high cage on wheels.

Slightly unnerved, Belinda edged away, aware Harry had stood his ground. He was either feeling more confident in his ability to tackle Eric, or was still unconvinced he had anything to do with the recent spate of deaths.

'I can't help noticing that you've got those packets of dog treats in cling film,' said Belinda.

Eric glanced to the metal cage. 'It's shrink-wrap. They arrive from the manufacturer's like that,' he said, frowning. 'What's that got to do with Tipper's murder?'

Temporarily satisfied, Belinda said, 'Nothing. Yet.'

'You were talking about how you feel you played a part in his death,' said Harry.

'Where do I start?' said Eric. 'Come to the office and I'll tell you from the beginning.'

He headed for the office door, struggling into his jacket as he walked.

Belinda and Harry exchanged wary glances as they followed him.

Inside the cramped space, door ajar, Eric chivalrously offered Belinda the chair and Harry perched on the desk, standing between Eric and the only way out.

'I was doing well here,' said Eric, his attention flitting from Harry to Belinda and back again. 'The business was expanding, and our reputation was beating all of our competitors. I couldn't believe how well things were going and then, about three months ago, I got a visit from Tipper out of the blue. I feel partly responsible for his death because I should have stopped him. Perhaps if I had, he'd still be alive.'

Eric shifted from one foot to the other, the smallest of movements towards the door.

'Don't look so worried, Harry,' he said. 'I know your reputation when you were in the force: the last thing I'd try to do is rush past you.'

If Belinda were a gambling woman, she would have placed all her money on Harry feeling a swell of pride.

Despite the gravity of the situation, she resisted a smile when Harry puffed his chest out and waved the compliment away.

'Anyway,' said Eric, 'Tipper said he had a proposal for me, a way that we could both make money, serious money. Well, I do all right here on the financial front. I've saved a bit of money with a part-time night security guard, a limited use of computers, that sort of thing, so I wasn't in the least interested.'

Keen to get on with it, at Eric's dramatic pause, Belinda said, 'What did Tipper suggest?'

'Oh, sorry, sorry. He asked me to let him know what thorough-bred dogs we had on the round in exchange for a fee. Of course, I asked him if fee meant a bung, because I am not that sort of person. It got a little heated when he thought I was accusing him of something illegal, which I obviously was.'

Eric paused again and loosened his tie, then started to take his jacket off but thought twice when it was obvious that he would either end up punching Harry straight in the face or one of them would have to leave the room.

'I asked him outright what he wanted the information for, and he told me it was to breed dogs,' said Eric. 'It made absolutely no sense to me. After all, they weren't his dogs.'

'Did he say how he was going to breed from them?' said Harry.

'Fortunately, we never got that far,' said Eric. 'He wanted to get his hands on my client list, but it's something I share with few people. If it hadn't been for his boy, there's a chance it could have turned a bit nasty. You see, Tipper had been drinking, but fortunately, his boy had driven him here and so—'

'Back up there for a minute,' said Belinda. 'His boy? Are you saying he has a son?'

'Yes, Joe, his son,' said Eric. 'He used to live with Tipper but now mostly stays with his mum in Upper Wallop.'

'Where's his boy now?' said Harry.

'Probably at his mum's, I guess,' said Eric. 'He was very interested in the dog snacks. I gave him a couple for his dog to see if he liked them. I'd have thought about offering the young lad a job if it hadn't been for the way Tipper was carrying on. He got quite nasty at one point.'

'So, Tipper's son's got a dog,' said Harry. 'That puts a different slant on the dog I saw Tipper walking on market day.'

'Yes, I think he took the dog to his dad's with him from time to time,' said Eric.

'This is all very interesting,' said Belinda, peeved that the terms of Tipper's lease in the New Inn's flat did not include his son or a dog. What else had happened in the time she had spent away from Little Challham? 'Would you have an address for Joe?'

'No,' said Eric with a shake of his head, and a slight look of relief when Belinda stood up as if to take her leave.

'Any idea if he's still in Little Challham?' said Harry.

'No,' said Eric.

'Are you able to help us with a description?' said Belinda, reluctant to squeeze past him but seeing no other option.

'Tall, young, fair to blond hair,' said Eric, 'not that you see it very often. He's always got a hoodie pulled up over his face.'

CHAPTER FORTY

'It could be a coincidence,' said Harry when they were in the Land Rover, Colonel stowed on the back seat, Belinda with her foot to the floor to try to get back to the village in a new personal best.

'It could be,' she said through gritted teeth. 'Something tells me it's not.'

'We can't be jumping to the conclusion that he murdered his own dad, can we?' said Harry. 'It's a bit of a leap, even if he was the one who broke into my house and attacked you in the street.'

'Especially if the only reason for killing his own father was to stop Tipper breeding their Cavalier King Charles spaniel with Ivy White's dog,' said Belinda, relieved this time to catch sight of the castle. 'It doesn't sound very likely. However, if he's the one who took Scooter to the rescue centre, he must be involved somehow. If Tipper's son is the killer, I'm wrong about Eric, you're wrong about Marcus, and Tipper was killed by his own flesh and blood because of their family pet. We're missing something.'

Hanging on to his seat belt in an effort to stop himself being thrown against the dashboard, Harry said, 'That's if it was their dog I saw Tipper walking. It could have been someone else's.'

'What? After all of your earlier protestations, you think Eric lied to us?' said Belinda as she turned into the castle's entrance.

'There's always that possibility,' said Harry. 'Besides, we don't know who killed Sandra. Joe could have followed her to the Dog and Duck and killed her too if she saw something at the New Inn and threatened to go to the police.'

'Except the way she was killed was personal,' said Belinda, goosebumps along her arms, even though the breeze coming in through the open window of the rapidly moving vehicle was still warm on her skin.

'Personal?' said Harry. 'Personal to whom?'

'Me.'

For a moment, she felt the weight of his stare.

'Do you want to tell me why?' he said.

'I have this thing about cling film,' she said. 'Tipper knew it, Sandra knew it. But I suppose if Joe were there in the flat when I confronted Tipper about it, he could have heard.'

'That's settled,' said Harry. 'We talk to Marcus, and whatever he says, we're calling the police and telling them everything we've found out. Agreed?'

'Agreed,' she said, after the briefest of pauses. 'It doesn't look as though Marcus is back yet,' she added as she drove the Land Rover past the garages and towards the barn. 'This is where he wants us to put the dog food.'

They had driven around the back of the castle, with the immaculate gardens in the distance blocking the view of the three-acre lake and boathouse. The historic parkland stretched as far as the eye could see and the buildings had been skilfully constructed, so although visible from the rear of the castle, their presence was very much in keeping with the setting.

'All of these cars,' said Harry, with an admiring glance towards the fleet of gleaming vehicles lined up in the open-fronted garage. 'How would you ever know if he was still out?'

Belinda ground the Land Rover to a stop, drummed her fingers on the steering wheel and said, 'Here's another thing...'

Harry gave a short harrumph.

'Here's another thing,' she said. 'When I saw Marcus going out a little earlier, before I came to see you, he was in a van with foreign writing on the side. The van isn't here, and Marcus rarely walks anywhere.'

'You said something about him being in Madrid, or he *said* he was in Madrid. Could the writing have been in Spanish?'

'No, definitely not,' said Belinda, her dark hair shaking free over her shoulders. 'I can speak some Spanish. This was more Cyrillic. I didn't have time to get a good look at the number plates, but I'm convinced I saw a European badge on it as it drove off.'

'Do you think there's a chance he left the country?'

It was something that had crossed her mind, yet she hadn't wanted to hear the words out loud.

'I don't think he would do that, and besides,' she said, her tone brightening, 'why would he leave me a note asking me to get dog food?'

Harry thought that one through and said, 'I'd better get this food out of here before Colonel eats the entire bag. Point me in the direction of where you want it stacked.'

The Doggie Delight was unloaded, Colonel had checked out the barn for corners and crannies to sniff, and Belinda was still explaining to Harry why Marcus couldn't have committed Tipper's murder.

'OK,' said Harry as he stood up to stretch his back, 'even if you could convince me that he wouldn't hurt Tipper, let's take a look at what we know.'

Harry counted on his fingers. 'First, we have the row they had just before Tipper was found drowned in a beer barrel in his cellar. Second, we have Marcus smelling of beer just after the murder, although I'll accept it means little if George Reid said they were in the Dog and Duck having a pint. Third, *you* saw Marcus with a bright pink handkerchief that was tattered and torn, just like the material *you* saw caught on a nail in the same cellar.

'And I haven't forgotten that the Women's Institute seems to have cornered the global market in tatty, migraine-inducing pink material. Not to mention poor Sandra, and I suppose that your brother knows about your hatred of cling film.'

'Ah, yes,' said Belinda, 'but Lennie was hit on the head when most of the village was in the pub where everyone could see them, except Anthony Cotter, who happens to have a red jacket as worn by the last person I saw talking to Sandra. We know that the microbrewery was shut that night.'

'Owning a red jacket won't get him arrested, let alone charged with murder,' said Harry. 'Take it from me, that's never going to be enough on its own. But Marcus wasn't in the pub either. Following your line of thinking, Marcus could have sneaked in through the kitchen and bashed Lennie on the head if you're saying Anthony had the opportunity.'

Belinda opened her mouth to say something but was cut short by loud barking from Colonel as he raced from out of the shadows and stood staring along the driveway.

'Here comes Marcus,' said Belinda. 'That looks like the same van.'

As the van got closer, Belinda and Harry saw Marcus in the front passenger seat waving at them and grinning like a maniac.

'Tell me that he looks like a crazy murderer?' she said with a modest waggle of her fingers at her brother.

'He does look slightly unhinged, like a classic crazy murderer, yes.'

'You can't say that,' said Belinda. 'Didn't you have to learn to be more politically correct than that when you were a police officer?'

'You said it first.'

'That doesn't make it all right, and besides, he's my brother.'

As Belinda stepped forward to speak to Marcus, she was fairly sure she heard Harry mutter something about her crazy murderer brother but thought now was not the time for further conflict. There would be enough of that any moment.

'Belinda, Harry,' said Marcus as he rushed towards them, kissed his sister and shook Harry's hand. 'Let me introduce you to Emma Smith.'

He stood back and pointed completely unnecessarily at the only other person present. A slim woman in her mid-forties, with shoulder-length brown hair and a warm smile, had stepped down from the van to join them.

'Hello,' said Emma, 'very nice to meet you all.'

Harry peered past her at the van's number plates.

'You sound more Yorkshire than Bulgarian,' said Harry.

'He used to be a detective,' said Belinda.

'I see you're still top of your game,' said Emma. 'The name Emma Smith isn't very Bulgarian for a start.'

'This is lovely,' said Marcus. 'We're all getting on so well. I can see that this business venture is going to be a win-win for all of us.'

'Hang on a moment,' said Emma. 'The words business venture aren't quite what we discussed on the phone. Or on the three visits I've made here to run an eye over your premises.'

'Oh, it was your van I heard at night coming up the driveway,' said Belinda.

Emma nodded at Belinda and returned her focus to Marcus, her foot tapping in irritation.

'Business, charity, you know what I mean,' said Marcus.

'I'm not sure I do,' said Emma. 'Please tell me you haven't changed your mind about short-term housing of our rescue dogs?'

'No, no,' said Marcus, taking a tentative step back towards his sister.

'Rescue dogs?' said Belinda. 'From Bulgaria?'

'Yes,' said Marcus. 'I've been planning it for quite some time.'

'We've only been in touch for a couple of months,' said Emma. 'So, what exactly have you been planning? Whatever it is, it isn't with me.'

Marcus had begun to wring his hands and was casting furtive looks towards Belinda, something he did when he had messed up. Again.

'Marcus,' said Harry. 'I think you'd better start from the beginning and tell us exactly what you had planned with these dogs.'

'Well, it was somewhere for them to stay short-term when Emma brings them across from Bulgaria,' said Marcus. 'It was to be a sort of halfway house, or should I say halfway doghouse?'

No one laughed.

'Erm, anyway,' he continued, 'I thought I could help out until they were ready to go to their, what is it you call it? Their *fur*-ever home.'

He appeared pleased with himself, but Belinda was still not convinced she was hearing the full story.

'As gracious as it is, brother, for you to help this charity, what's in it for you?' she said.

'Why, it's to make up for what I did all those years ago,' he said, turning to face her, and gently placing a hand on her shoulder. 'You know, when I encouraged you to go to the docks and lead the protest. I've always felt guilty about that. I've wracked my brains for years for a way to make it up to you, and I thought of this.'

For one moment, Belinda's heart softened, came close to melting. Then she remembered her brother's earlier comment.

'What was the business opportunity?' she said.

'I'd be interested in that too,' said Emma.

'There was to be a sideline in dog bandanas,' said Marcus.

'I notice your use of the word "was",' said Harry. 'Would it have anything to do with the material not being fit for purpose?'

'It's clear to me that your detective skills are still sharp as a pin,' said Marcus.

'I haven't driven all the way here from Bulgaria for dog bandanas,' said Emma.

'What's your business idea, Marcus?' said Belinda, rubbing her temples at the first signs of a sibling-generated headache.

'There's something remarkable I've discovered,' said Marcus, excitement lighting up his features. 'It's the Bulgarian weasel retriever.'

'The what now?' said Harry.

Colonel growled.

All four of them looked at him where he stood beside Belinda, like he was guarding her.

'What's the matter with him?' said Marcus, moving behind Emma.

'Nothing's the matter with him,' said Harry. 'It was when you said Bulgarian weasel retriever.'

Colonel growled again.

'Anyway,' said Marcus, stepping a little further away from Colonel, 'as I was saying, the Bulg… those dogs are quite remarkable.'

'They are lovely dogs,' agreed Emma. 'They need a lot of exercise and crave company, but they are wonderful dogs.'

'Well, what I've discovered through extensive research,' said Marcus, almost at fever pitch, 'is that they are great at spotting things.'

Belinda and Harry looked at Emma.

She gave a nod. 'They're good for hunting, that's true enough.'

'And guess what they're remarkable at spotting?' said Marcus, rubbing his hands together.

'Rabbits,' said Emma.

'Gold,' said Belinda.

'Lamp posts,' said Harry.

'Lamp posts is quite ridiculous,' said Marcus. 'If you give up, I'll tell you.' He paused, threw his arms wide and said, 'Parking spaces!'

'What?' said Emma.

'You're a moron,' said Belinda.

'What they both said,' said Harry, rubbing at his own temples.

'Don't you get it?' said Marcus. 'You go shopping in a busy town centre, struggle to find somewhere to park, and then Fido starts to bark, telling you there's a space up ahead.'

'There's certainly a space in your head,' said Emma. 'I'm off.'

'You can't leave,' said Marcus. 'What about my dogs?'

She turned sharply towards him, the warm smile now a dim and distant memory.

Marcus gulped as Emma took a measured step towards him.

'Firstly, peanut brain,' she said, 'they are *my* dogs, and you will never make money selling *my* rescue dogs after all they've been through for such a ludicrous, hare-brained scheme. Secondly, you cannot leave a dog in a car while you go shopping. At best, you'll saunter back from Marks and Spencer's only to find the dog has eaten your upholstery, or at worst, died in the car from the heat. So there is no way on this earth I will allow you to condemn dogs to a certain death just to make yourself some money. Finally, I—'

'Thirdly,' said Marcus with a smile. 'You said firstly, then secondly and then finally – it's thirdly.'

Belinda and Harry had to look away. Even Colonel lay down, paws over his eyes.

Emma stepped closer. Her nose was almost touching Marcus's chin.

'FINALLY, I have come out of my way after a particularly long journey, having driven thirty dogs across Europe and delivered them safely, only to have my time wasted by *you*.'

Belinda stepped forward to say something and felt Harry's hand on her arm. She hesitated and then waited for the onslaught to continue.

'Here's what you're going to do, Penshurst,' said Emma. 'In exchange for wasting my time, and more importantly the dogs' time – every minute I'm here with you, I'm not with them – you'll donate bags of food to our charity.'

'That does sound fair,' said Marcus. 'Only the thing is, can you stay until morning to pick them up? If I have to have them sent on to Bulgaria, there's all sorts of red tape and paperwork.'

Even from a few feet away, Belinda and Harry could see the fury in Emma's eyes.

'I can't look,' whispered Harry in Belinda's ear.

'Which I'd be delighted to take care of,' said Marcus.

With that, Emma eased herself back and put her hand in her pocket, a movement that caused Marcus to pale significantly until she pulled out a dog biscuit.

'May I?' she asked, looking from Belinda to Harry with a smile at Colonel.

'Of course,' said Harry as Emma held the gravy bone biscuit out for the Great Dane, who appeared to hoover it up without even noticing it.

'It was nice to meet you,' said Emma to Harry and Belinda again.

She gave Marcus a withering stare and said, 'I'll text you a suitable amount of dog food when I've worked out the cost of my time.'

With that, she was in the van and driving away.

'That went as well as could be expected,' said Marcus. 'I think a beer's in order.'

'Hang on there, Marcus,' said Harry.

Marcus appeared a little taken aback, as if he had forgotten Harry was even there.

'Yes,' said Marcus. 'Oh, don't worry, I'll definitely be buying my punishment dog food from your good self.'

'There's the small matter of what you were discussing with Tipper,' said Harry. 'Directly before he was murdered.'

'My guess,' said Belinda, 'is that it was something to do with local dogs going missing before being returned to their owners, most of whom were none the wiser what their dog had been up to.'

Marcus smiled at her. 'The dogs were much simpler to deal with than the bitches, obviously.'

'Please don't tell me you were a part of this,' said Belinda, screwing her eyes shut.

He walked over to her and said, 'The only times I ever had anything to do with breeding dogs were all above board, definitely nothing to do with Tipper. His plan was to steal the dogs – temporarily, of course.' He looked over at Harry, down at Colonel and back at his sister.

'What part did you play in this?' said Belinda.

'None whatsoever,' said Marcus, staring her straight in the eye. 'I told the drunken fool that I had been involved in breeding dogs for years and I wouldn't have it, I wouldn't stand for him using dogs in this way without their owners' knowledge. Who would come up with such a ridiculous idea?'

'Well, you were going to use Bulgarian weasel retrievers to spot parking spaces,' said Harry.

Colonel growled again.

'Please make him stop doing that!' said Marcus.

'Both of you, please focus,' said Belinda. 'Why didn't you go to the police and tell them what Tipper was doing?'

'The first time he told me about it was the day he died and that was only because he was desperate to find a new business partner,' said Marcus. 'I swear. If he hadn't died, I would have reported him but there seemed little point once he was dead.'

'Did he tell you why he needed a new business partner?' said Harry.

Marcus shrugged. 'I don't have any idea but I would guess it was something to do with his drinking and becoming a liability to whoever was fool enough to be in business with him in the first place.'

'We think the dognapping was probably the reason he was killed,' said Harry, 'and he wanted you to join him. So if you know who else was involved, it's a good time to tell us.'

'I'm sorry, Tipper didn't give me any names,' said Marcus. 'I didn't like the sound of it then and I don't like the sound of it now. Dognapping is almost as bad as murder.'

'I overheard some of your conversation with Tipper, Marcus,' said Belinda. 'I've been avoiding asking you ever since because I wasn't sure I'd like the answer, but what was he blackmailing you over?'

She watched Marcus give a soft smile, all dimples and blue eyes.

'Once I told him I'd go to the police,' said Marcus, 'he told me it wasn't right that I'd threatened him. My reply was that I'd been breeding dogs for years, so his opinions didn't count for much. The daft fool had heard about my connection with Emma and thought he could blackmail me for using uncertificated and unlicensed foreign dogs for breeding. He had no idea about my parking space idea. The man was an idiot.'

Belinda ignored the sigh from Harry and said, 'Why did you smell of beer that day when you picked me up?'

'I told you I'd been for a pint. I'd been in the Dog and Duck talking to George,' said Marcus, genuine surprise on his face. 'I was asking him if he could keep me, well, the dogs, of course, supplied with scraps. From the sounds of things, I won't have to worry about approaching George again.'

'George?' said Belinda. 'So, he was telling me the truth after all.'

'Oh, yes,' said Marcus. 'Totally upstanding fellow. Why wouldn't anyone believe what he's got to say?'

'He did chase someone out of his butcher's shop with a knife,' said Harry.

'He did?' said Marcus. 'I did always think his eyes are too close together and some of his tattoos have grammatical errors in them.'

CHAPTER FORTY-ONE

'Are you OK?' said Harry as Belinda drove them back down to the village, Colonel on the back seat, his head sticking up between them.

'Fine. In fact, better than fine. I'm relieved that Marcus was simply being plain daft old Marcus and not some sort of dog thief.'

'And not a murderer.'

'Oh, yes,' she said. 'But knowing he's a dog thief would have been so much harder for me to live with.'

'You make it sound as though you wouldn't have turned him in whatever his crimes.'

'Of course I would have,' she said, 'but luckily I don't have to do something that would have broken my…'

She caught him staring in the direction of the post office. Across the green, past a family playing football and Angie Manning and Max Fish holding hands, were two figures, one a man in a red jacket and the other a younger man in a blue hoodie.

'That's the one who attacked me,' said Belinda.

'Drive around the green!' shouted Harry as she pressed her foot to the accelerator. 'Drop me nearer the hoodie. I bet it's Joe. We can come back and speak to Cotter.'

Belinda didn't hesitate this time; she made it around the green in record time. She barely had time to slow down when Harry opened his door and jumped from the Land Rover, hitting the pavement with more velocity than was advisable at his age. Nevertheless, it didn't stop Harry from giving chase to the hoodie-wearing man, who made off at quite a speed of his own.

Whether it was adrenalin, not wishing to lose face or Harry being spryer than he looked, it didn't take long before he had hold of the escapee by the arm.

'Let go, let go,' he whined, trying to pull away.

Belinda had stopped beside them with her mobile phone in her hand, ready to call the police.

'You!' she said, pointing at him. 'You hit me in the face and kicked me.'

'I'm sorry,' he said, bottom lip trembling. 'Please don't call the police. It was an accident.'

By this stage, Anthony Cotter had joined them, no doubt keen to find out the gossip first-hand.

'And don't set your dog on me!' said the young man.

Until that point, Belinda had been oblivious that Colonel had got out under his own steam. She glanced down to where the faithful dog stood, huge head almost to her waist.

'He won't hurt you,' said Harry.

The young man's shoulders relaxed.

'Not unless I tell him to,' said Belinda.

'Belinda,' said Anthony, placing himself between the docile dog and the terrified teenager, 'you do know who this is, don't you?'

'I certainly do,' she said. 'He's the thug who elbowed me in the face and then kicked me when I was on the floor. Joe, I presume.'

'You did what, Joey?' said Anthony.

'Honest, it was an accident, Uncle Anthony,' said Joe.

'Uncle Anthony?' said Belinda and Harry in unison.

'I'm not really his uncle,' said Anthony. 'I helped out with him a lot when he was a boy, what with his dad being a… liking a drink or two.'

Harry stared a little closer at the young man, scrutinising his features.

'My dad is… he was Tipper,' said Joe, lip trembling again.

Harry let go of him.

'He's been staying with me,' said Anthony. 'He does that from time to time when his mum needs a break and Tipper was, you know, busy with the pub.'

Belinda glanced up at Anthony to see him miming downing a drink as Joe hung his head so low, she feared his neck would never recover.

'Right, let me get this straight,' said Harry. 'How long have you been staying at the microbrewery?'

Joe shrugged. 'A few days, since before my dad died. I didn't go to the New Inn very often, I preferred to be at Uncle Anthony's. Whenever I was at Dad's, I tended to spend the time looking out of the window. The pub was boring with Dad always working.'

'It was you I saw in the flat above the pub the day Sandra got arrested?' said Belinda.

'Yes,' said Joe, with a hang-dog expression.

'Anthony, why didn't you tell anyone he was staying with you?' said Harry.

'He asked me not to,' said Anthony. 'He likes to make sure his dad is doing all right and then take off again.'

'Only he was far from all right,' said Belinda. 'He was dead, and yet you didn't say anything about being in Little Challham.'

'You wouldn't understand,' said Joe. 'I knew my dad was into some bad stuff and I know what everyone thinks of him, talking behind his back about him being a drunk, but he tried really hard. Have you any idea how tough it was for him to run a pub surrounded by booze? He couldn't leave, he had nothing else he was skilled for, and besides, it kept a roof over his head too.'

'The police were in the pub, in Little Challham,' said Harry, 'and you didn't come forward.'

Joe scuffed the toe of his trainer on the pavement and shrugged.

'Look,' said Anthony, 'this is very difficult for the lad to hear, but Tipper needed money and I used to help him out by paying him for Joe's help in the microbrewery.'

'What work did you do?' said Harry.

Joe risked a peek at Anthony.

'Go on,' said Anthony.

'I didn't really do anything,' he said, misery weighing down his every word. 'It kept my dad off my back and meant I could stay somewhere decent, not have to worry about anything.'

'It also meant his mum knew he was seeing his dad from time to time without, you know, complications,' said Anthony.

'So why were you in Harry's house?' said Belinda.

'I'm really sorry I did that,' he said, his focus returning to Belinda. 'I needed the stuff from his garage.'

A gasp from Belinda. 'You mean drugs?'

This earned her a tut of epic proportions. 'Don't be stupid. From that old geezer? No, I was after the dog treats.'

'Aha,' said Harry. 'I knew someone was pilfering them.'

'Well done, Poirot,' said Belinda, 'and by the way, no one says "pilfering". Not even me.'

'In a way, I was hoping you'd catch me,' said Joe, with a shy glance at Harry. 'You used to be a police officer and I thought you'd be able to help me.'

'Was it you I saw a couple of days ago on the edge of the village?' said Harry. 'You looked like you were up to no good with another lad in a hoodie.'

'That's Del,' said Joe. 'His parents have got three dogs, so I swap him Lego cards for dog treats.'

'Three dogs, you say?' said Harry, stroking his chin. 'And where do they get their dog food from?'

'This is not a business opportunity, Harry,' said Belinda.

Even Joe rolled his eyes.

'Hang on a moment,' said Belinda. 'Why exactly were you stealing dog treats?'

Joe looked at her as if she were the stupid one.

'For my dog, obviously,' he said.

'Your dog,' said Harry. 'Of course. Where did you get your dog from?'

This simple question made Joe crumble before their eyes.

'You OK, mate?' said Anthony, putting a large arm around Joe's shoulders.

The young man took a few deep breaths and said, 'After the last year, it's about time I got this out in the open.'

Anthony said in Joe's ear, 'If you're sure.'

This was met with frantic nodding and Joe said, 'I need to speak to the police. As petrified as I was back then about what they'd do to my dad, and as petrified as I am now about what will happen to my dog, I need to tell someone this. It was an accident, I swear. My dad didn't mean to hurt anyone, especially not kill that man.'

Joe blinked back the tears. 'It was my dad's fault, though. He was drunk that day and should never have been driving. I should have taken his keys or something, anything. My dad lost control in the lane and drove his car into Peter Clayton. He panicked, I panicked, so we drove off and left him. I went back for Scooter, and as much as I love that dog, every time I look at him, it reminds me of what we did.'

'It was you that took him to the dog shelter?' said Belinda.

'Yes,' said Anthony, arm now firmly around the young lad, 'it was him. And it was Joe who went back and got him, trying to make amends. We swore Cynthia to secrecy. She's an absolute star and we can trust her to keep quiet.'

'More than others,' mumbled Joe.

'Two people have been murdered, Joe,' said Harry. 'If you know something, anything, now's the time to tell us.'

With a worried glance at Anthony, who gave a nod in response, Joe said, 'I thought that I could trust Sandra, because she knew where Scooter came from but never told anyone. Lately it seemed she was playing my dad, trying to see what she could get out of him, and when that wasn't enough, she threatened to leave and go and work for Lennie.'

'Lennie in the Dog and Duck?' said Belinda. 'But wasn't that after your dad… we found your dad…'

'No,' said Joe, shaking his head. 'She threatened to leave before my dad died. I heard her tell him that she had been offered a job and it was a much better job with a better boss. After all he did for her.'

'It's important you tell us anything else at all you heard,' said Harry. 'Including anything you know about dognapping.'

'Dognapping?' said Joe, looking from Harry to Belinda. 'I don't know anything about dognapping. All I know is that Sandra was looking to leave the New Inn.'

'He's telling the truth,' said Anthony, giving Joe's shoulder a squeeze. 'You asked me before about Sandra talking to Dawn Jones and showing an interest in her Great Dane. I'm sorry I lied, but Sandra had come in that day asking for a job. Well, I hardly wanted her in my bar bothering the customers and being nosy, so I asked her to leave and told her I'd tell Tipper. I'm glad I didn't give her a job, not after I later found out about her and Tipper's involvement with the dognapping. I swear, Joe knew nothing about it and I wasn't involved in it. Stealing people's pets is little better than murder. I only didn't come forward because it might have meant Joe giving up Scooter if the truth came out. He's suffered enough.'

The open-mouthed stare Joe was giving Anthony left little doubt in Belinda's mind that he was telling the truth.

'Sandra told my dad that Lennie's bar supervisor had quit,' said Joe, 'and she was going to work for him.'

'That's probably why Sandra was at the Dog and Duck right before she was killed,' said Belinda.

'Well, that's one thing cleared up,' said Harry. 'She was going to speak to someone there about the bar supervisor job, so no great mystery, except it couldn't have been Lennie who killed her as he's still in hospital.'

'The only thing is,' said Belinda, narrowing her eyes at Anthony and Joe, 'only a few people knew she was going there this morning. And that includes you, Anthony Cotter.'

'Hang on a minute,' said Joe, wiping his nose with the back of his hand. 'I saw Uncle Anthony talking to Sandra outside the pub, and when he left her, he came straight back across the green to where I was waiting with two takeaway teas from the tea room.'

Slightly deflated, Belinda hid it with aplomb by pointing her finger at Anthony and saying, 'That's easily checkable in the tea room, so don't leave town.'

'Either of you,' said Harry.

'Either of you,' repeated Belinda, determined to have the last word.

CHAPTER FORTY-TWO

Harry glanced down at his phone alerting him to a message as they drove away from Joe Johnson and Anthony Cotter.

'It's Dawn,' he said to Belinda. 'We should take Colonel back before we go anywhere else.'

'OK,' said Belinda. 'Our next port of call after Dawn's should be the Dog and Duck to check to see if Lennie's home. Let's have a run through of what we know and see if anything we've missed comes to mind. We've already got one murdered landlord from the New Inn, drowned in a barrel of beer, pink threads in the crime scene that could have come from most of the occupants of Little Challham, plus Tipper's son hiding out in the flat and sometimes staying at the microbrewery with Anthony Cotter.'

'Not forgetting,' said Harry, 'that Joe, Tipper's son, has Scooter, the dog owned by Peter Clayton, killed by Tipper's drunk driving.'

'Someone tried to kill Lennie by hitting him on the head in his own pub, and the barmaid who connected the two of them is also dead,' said Belinda.

Harry gave this a moment's thought and said, 'The two things tying this all together are dogs and pubs. Whether we believe Anthony and Joe or not, you're right about checking on Lennie.'

'I couldn't agree more,' said Belinda, 'but as we seem to be trying to rule people out as murder suspects, what about who else is involved in the dognapping? It must be why Tipper and Sandra were killed. We know that Eric was aware of what was going on with the dogs.'

'Marcus knew too,' said Harry.

'Only right at the death,' said Belinda. 'Sorry, terrible choice of words.'

'If Sandra and Tipper were stealing dogs to order, using them for breeding and selling them on, there must have been someone else behind it,' said Harry. 'The New Inn would have been overrun with dogs otherwise.'

'Yes,' said Belinda. 'Someone, somewhere, was running the show from afar.'

'If we're going to believe Anthony's side of things,' said Harry, 'rule him and Joe out, that doesn't really get us any further.'

They spent the rest of the journey in relative silence until they turned into Dawn's street.

'All we have so far,' said Harry, 'is local people having their dogs stolen, thinking they're about to get stolen or, in Ivy White's case, a mystery litter of puppies on the way.'

Belinda's mobile phone bleeped. She pulled over outside Dawn's house, read the message and said to Harry, 'That's good timing: Lennie is just about to be released from hospital so we can head straight there once we've dropped Colonel off.'

'Do you have that sinking feeling that right at the moment,' said Harry, 'everyone's a potential suspect?'

He peered through the window to the front of Dawn's house, where Alicia was running along the garden path, her arms wide open, shouting, 'Colonel!'

'Even her?' said Belinda, nodding at the nine-year-old skipping gaily towards them.

Colonel's barking obscured Harry's answer and he thought it better they get out before it damaged their hearing.

Once inside, Belinda and Harry watched through the kitchen window as Alicia and Colonel chased each other happily across the lawn.

'Are you sure you won't stay for a cuppa?' said Dawn.

'Thanks, but no,' said Harry, unsure whether he should reveal more about their next destination to Dawn.

'Anything else out of the ordinary happened?' asked Belinda. 'You know, cars hanging around, that sort of thing?'

Harry shot her a look.

As Dawn continued to watch her daughter and their dog zipping around, she failed to see the shrug Belinda returned Harry.

'Not here, no,' said Dawn. 'I did hear that the Stones' black Lab ran off this morning on his walk. They're beside themselves and they've looked everywhere. They're even offering a reward.'

'Perhaps we should go and speak to the Stones,' said Belinda, exchanging a look with Harry. 'Find out if the dog ran off or someone was seen hanging around in a black SUV.'

Dawn turned away from the window.

'I'm petrified something will happen to Colonel,' said Dawn, running her fingers through her hair. 'I've tried not to say anything in front of Alicia but it's unlikely she hasn't picked up on my anxiety.'

'Don't worry,' said Belinda. 'We're asking around the village, trying to find out anything we can about the dognappers. We know that Tipper and Sandra were involved.'

'Really?' said Dawn. She glanced back to the garden, where Alicia and Colonel were still merrily playing with a deflated football that the overzealous dog must have punctured. 'Sandra *and* Tipper? I can't believe it. If that's who was doing this, why are dogs still going missing?'

'That's what we need to find out,' said Harry.

'You'll be fine here with Alicia and Colonel,' said Belinda. 'Leave it with us. Not one more dog is going AWOL from Little Challham, not with us working the case.'

Harry thought about sighing at Belinda's ridiculous choice of words but knew it would get him told off, so he settled for rolling his eyes instead. Only behind her back – he wasn't feeling that brave.

CHAPTER FORTY-THREE

Harry would have preferred to go to the Dog and Duck by himself. That was an opinion he knew he couldn't share with Belinda. The thought of her icy stare at the mere suggestion of going alone was chilling enough, without the sarcasm that would surely follow. Besides, allowing her to go off by herself would likely end in disaster. He still worried about her when she was out of his sight, despite knowing that getting too close to her might end badly for his own still-bruised heart.

'So, if Sandra was killed because of her involvement with dognapping, why do it in the pub kitchen?' said Belinda as they made their way to the Dog and Duck, all the while keeping an eye out for anyone out of place or anything new in Little Challham.

'Did you notice anything unusual in there when you found her body?' said Harry.

'Other than the industrial-sized roll of cling film and half of its contents wrapped around Sandra, not really. It was the sort of thing you'd expect to find there: milk, cheese, meats, a couple of dozen containers with sandwich fillings, that sort of thing. At least if the labels were anything to go by.'

'We don't know if someone seized the chance or knew she was going to be there,' said Harry as they reached the pub's entrance. 'Or maybe someone was coming back for Lennie if they thought he'd already been released from hospital.'

Although they saw no unknown faces on their short journey to the pub, that soon changed as they pushed open the door and saw a woman behind the bar neither of them recognised.

'Afternoon,' she said. 'What can I get you?'

'Hello,' said Harry, 'we've come to see how Lennie's doing.'

The woman put her head at an angle and eyeballed them in turn, like a pigeon with jowls, thought Harry. Something he kept to himself.

'He's doing as OK as can be expected,' she said. 'I'm Polly, his sister. He's not here at the moment.'

'We understood he was being sent home from the hospital,' said Belinda, her most winning smile on display.

'Sorry, who did you say you were?' said Polly, less pigeon, more hawk now.

'I'm Belinda and this is Harry,' she said. 'We're neighbours, customers, as well as friends. We were here the night he was rushed off to hospital.'

'Riiight,' said Polly as if the penny had dropped. 'He didn't mention either of you, but I'll be sure to pass on your well wishes.'

Then she was off to serve a customer.

Harry stepped away from the bar and got halfway across the pub floor before he realised that Belinda wasn't with him. She had moved along to where Polly was pouring a glass of lemonade from the pump.

Even from that distance, he heard Polly say, 'I've already told you that he's not here and I'm not telling you where he is. I've heard all about your attention-seeking amateur detective work, and five minutes of entertainment for you should not get in the way of my brother's recovery. He's not well, now go away.'

This time, Polly turned her back on Belinda and poured a gin from the optics, all the while staring at Belinda via the mirror behind the shelves.

Harry walked back over to Belinda and said, 'Come on, I've got an idea.'

Once outside, Harry said, 'Let's drop your car off and then go back to mine to talk it over.'

He watched her mouth stretch into a grin and felt his cheeks redden when she said, 'Let me guess: death by whiteboard?'

At times, she could really be too much. It was one of her many charms.

Seated once more at Harry's kitchen table, mugs of coffee in front of them, Harry said, 'Where do you reckon Lennie is?'

'I think he's in the pub, lying low,' said Belinda, taking a tentative sip of her drink. Her face was a picture of delighted surprise. 'This is good coffee.'

'I changed brands.'

Harry knew he had given in and it would make Belinda a tad smug, and stop any more comments about preferring filter coffee to instant. Not for the first time, he realised he was doing his best to accommodate her, ingratiate himself. No, he had to be honest with himself – he wanted to make her happy and that thought petrified him more than murder.

'Anyway,' he said, clearing his throat so as to concentrate on the crime and not get too distracted by Belinda, 'Tipper and Sandra are dead, probably because they were involved in dognapping, Lennie has just been released from hospital after someone tried to kill him, possibly because of dognapping—'

'I'm still not entirely convinced,' said Belinda. 'He loved his dog so much, I don't think he'd want anyone else to be separated from their pet.'

'If it'll help,' said Harry, 'I can get the wh—'

'If you say whiteboard, I won't be responsible for my actions.'

'I was going to say, er, whitener, the coffee whitener.'

She raised an eyebrow at him. 'And if Joe is telling the truth about Tipper, he accidently drunkenly killed Peter Clayton and that's why Joe has Scooter.'

'Cynthia Walker from the dog rescue centre might be behind wiping out the dognappers,' said Harry.

'She doesn't strike me as the sort,' said Belinda, putting down her coffee mug.

'Whoever it was, there's a chance they'll come back soon and finish what they started with Lennie.'

'What we'll do,' she said, 'is hide out in the Women's Institute until the pub closes and watch and see if anyone tries to break in.'

'We've got no reason to think someone will try something tonight,' said Harry, 'so I'll go on my own. There's no need for you to come along.'

'Oh, Harry, poor naive Harry. Do you think for one minute the good ladies of Little Challham would take kindly to a *man* wandering around their WI hall? Absolutely no chance of that happening. Besides, I've got the keys and you haven't.'

He gave it less than a heartbeat before he said, 'Fair enough, but I warn you, it could be boring and a long night.'

'Our very first team stakeout,' said Belinda with what Harry recognised as a twinkle in her eye.

Belinda and Harry's trip to the WI could hardly have been billed as clandestine. Harry stopped to say good evening to Mr and Mrs Sanderson, a lovely couple walking their cockapoo; Kulvinder and Steve Parry drew up in their car to tell them they had just come back from a meal in Upper Wallop; and Delia Hawking was in the car park picking up litter.

'Delia,' said Belinda. 'It's very late to be out cleaning up.'

She drew herself up to her five foot three and a half inches and said, 'It's the best time. It's quiet and no one's around. Speaking of which, what are you two doing here?'

'Nothing, nothing,' said Belinda. 'We're out for a stroll, that's all.'

'With a flask of coffee,' said the self-appointed community guardian, with a snort towards the stainless-steel container Harry had tucked under his arm.

With a furtive glance left and right, Harry pressed his finger to his lips and said, 'We've heard that tonight's the night the badgers and the foxes all get together in the woods for their annual meet-up. Once in a lifetime opportunity for a townie like me.'

'Yes, er, that's right,' said Belinda, tapping the side of her nose. 'I've been telling Harry here all about it, what with him not being from around here. I'm going to show him the best spot and leave him to it for the night.'

'You're doing wh—' said Delia. Then she put her hand over her mouth and, trying to suppress a laugh, added, 'You have fun now, Powell.'

They walked away from the car park and the eighty-year-old who was busy chasing a stray paper tissue across the tarmac, cleaning up an already almost perfect space.

When they were out of sight in the darkness on the edge of the woods, Belinda whispered, 'Seriously? That was the best you could come up with?'

'Under the circumstances, yes it was,' he whispered back. 'And now Delia thinks I'm a half-wit.'

'Keep your voice down,' she said. 'Everyone else has gone home except Delia. Once she leaves, at least we can go inside and keep out of sight.'

After a couple of minutes, she said, 'So, how long do you think this will take?'

Now a touch more accustomed to the gloom of the evening, Harry stared at her.

'What is it?' she said when she realised.

'I tried to warn you that this would be boring,' he said. 'We've been here seconds.'

'It's minutes, not seconds,' she said. 'Besides, I—'

'Shush.'

'Did you just "shush" me?' said Belinda.

'There's someone coming out of the back of the pub,' said Harry, creeping forwards from his hiding place.

Belinda moved towards Harry, desperate to see who was leaving the pub.

'It's Lennie,' said Belinda.

'And he's got a dog with him,' said Harry, dropping the flask of coffee.

'It's a Great Dane,' she said. 'He's got Colonel.'

Before Harry could move, Belinda sprinted towards Lennie and the Great Dane he was leading out of the back of the pub.

CHAPTER FORTY-FOUR

Belinda had not felt so furious in a long time. The realisation of what she was seeing propelled her forward. She swallowed the ground between her and Lennie in remarkable time.

'Stop!' she shouted as Lennie led the dog towards a white transit van.

Lennie turned in the direction of Belinda, who was hollering and running full pelt towards him.

His face changed from surprise to annoyance, eyebrows arched, mouth open. As if picking up on his mood, the dog let out a loud bark. Something about the sound stopped Harry short as he charged to Belinda's side.

'Where do you think you're going with that dog?' said Belinda.

'Not that it's any of your business,' said Lennie, 'but I'm taking the dog to the vets.'

'Oh, you are, are you?' she said. 'That dog's stolen. Isn't that right, Harry?'

Belinda glanced across to where Harry should have been standing next to her.

Instead, he was kneeling on the tarmac.

'She's not stolen,' said Lennie, his fury plain for all to see.

'She?' said Belinda, confused.

'She's a she, all right,' Harry said, looking up at her from his kneeling position.

'What?' said Belinda. She had half a mind to have a look herself, but then quickly realised that this didn't really call for a second opinion. 'How did that happen?'

'Nature, I guess,' said Harry.

'When you pair of circus clowns have finished,' said Lennie, 'I've got to get her to the vets. She's eaten something that's disagreed with her. We're worried.'

'You told me that you didn't want to get another dog,' said Belinda.

Lennie shook his head and moved towards the transit van. 'I don't have time for this. She's my sister's dog if you must know. I dog-sit her from time to time, and given Polly's looking after my pub, the least I can do is feed and look after her dog. Now, get out of my way.'

'What if someone killed Sandra because they saw her talking to you?' said Belinda. 'And then tried to kill you?'

Lennie paused and looked from Belinda to Harry. 'What part of "I've got to get the dog to the vets" are you having trouble with? She's sick so leave me alone.'

Lennie opened the back of the van, pulled down a ramp for the Great Dane to walk up and closed her in a cage. When he was satisfied that she was safely stowed inside, he went to the driver's door.

'And by the way,' he said, one hand on the door, the other holding the keys, 'if you really want to help, find out who I saw driving away from the New Inn in a black SUV the day Tipper was murdered.'

A touch crestfallen, Belinda and Harry walked back across the green to the Gatehouse.

'You really don't have to drive me home,' said Belinda.

'There's no need to sound so defiant,' said Harry. 'It's late, we've had a long day, and other than working out that Lennie had dog food in the pub to feed his sister's dog, we're both feeling as though we've chased our tails today. Besides, there's a murderer around.'

'I've not forgotten,' she said, aware there was a spring in her step. It wasn't entirely evident to her whether it was Harry's company or solving a murder that was making her walk as if the pavement was underlay and her inlays made of memory foam.

'Are you smiling?' he asked as they passed close to the illuminated frontage of the tea room.

'It's the late-night walk,' she said. 'I find it invigorating, don't you? And I'm amused by your "chasing our tails" comment.'

Still, Belinda turned her head away from Harry as they crossed the road to his home. Reluctant as she was to let him see how keen she was, this was the most satisfying escapade that she had been involved in for some time. Little Challham truly did have everything she wanted from life. She couldn't leave things there with Harry. She owed it to herself to at least try.

They reached his garage and, seizing her opportunity when she realised there would be no 'come in for a coffee', Belinda took her chance.

'When all of this is over, you know, when we've solved the crime and the culprit's on their way to prison,' she said, 'how about we go for a drink?'

Harry looked over into the trees and the darkness. 'We've already been for a drink, something like three times. Besides, it might take a while before we work out who the killer is.'

'So, is that a no?'

He gave her a smile she couldn't read.

Belinda closed her eyes, took a deep breath. She wondered if she'd misinterpreted the spark between them when all along it was Harry's passion for catching killers.

'Looks as though you've got a headache coming on,' said Harry. 'You should definitely leave your car here and let me give you a lift home.'

'Good idea,' murmured Belinda as she opened the car door and got in.

CHAPTER FORTY-FIVE

Harry probably could have driven with his eyes closed. But he wanted to seem as though he was paying as much attention as possible to the road, to give Belinda the chance to rid herself of a headache.

Harry knew that she didn't really have a headache. He sometimes came across as a touch bullish and like things were passing him by, but he was always attuned to other people's feelings and emotions.

It had been clear Belinda was asking him out on a date, but he simply couldn't do that at the moment. The last thing he had wanted to do was turn her down flat. That seemed too callous, but he'd panicked when she'd put him on the spot. Give him a dead body and he was in charge. An amazing woman asking him out for a drink didn't come with a police manual. He knew he had messed things up with her. He supposed he did owe her an explanation at the very least.

Harry had told Belinda that his last relationship had ended suddenly but he had left out the part about the ugly divorce he had gone through prior to that. Neither his ex-wife nor his ex-girlfriend had left him unscathed, something he didn't think he could cope with again.

The thought of the quandary he was in forced a sigh of such magnitude it took him by surprise. Belinda too, it seemed.

'It sounds as though you're attempting to blow up a bouncy castle with one puff,' she said.

'Talking of castles,' he said, 'we're here. Do you want me to drop you at the front or kitchen entrance?'

Belinda sat up in her seat and peered through the windscreen. 'There aren't many lights on,' she said, 'so the front will be locked, probably the kitchen too. Drop me here; I'll wander round the back.'

This startled Harry. 'You don't have a key?'

'Mostly, no.'

Belinda cracked open the door.

'No,' said Harry, 'I said I'd drive you home, and if you can't get in, well, then…'

'What?'

Harry honestly wasn't sure: he didn't want Belinda coming back to his house, that was for certain, yet he couldn't leave her here. Worse still, she might want him to climb a drainpipe.

'Don't worry about it,' said Belinda, 'there's a key under a plant pot at the back of the house.'

'You've got to be kidding me?'

Belinda turned around to face him, moonlight lighting up her beautiful face.

'No one ever thinks of looking there,' she said. 'It's such a cliché.'

'Oh, you'd be surprised,' he said as he put the car in gear. 'At the very least, I'm driving you round there and making sure you get in OK.'

'Harry Powell, always the gentleman,' she said.

Once again, he pretended to be absorbed in the complexities of driving several hundred feet, all the while hoping that there really was a key so he could make a getaway.

At the back of the castle, Harry parked and Belinda went in search of the badly hidden key.

Harry stood next to his car, watching her move from pot to pot. The peace and quiet of the late evening was easy to take for granted when it surrounded you on a nightly basis. He breathed in the freshness of the air, unsure whether he could feel spots of rain or if it was simply the dampness creeping in.

When he saw Belinda move the fifth pot to no avail, he took a step in her direction.

Then Belinda froze and stared into the distance, towards the barn.

He looked to see what had caught her attention but all he could see was blackness.

Harry continued to gaze into the night and then saw a light go on.

'We need to get over to the barn,' said Belinda. 'Something's not right. I just heard a dog bark and this time, I'm certain it's Colonel.'

The ground between the castle and the barn wasn't ideal terrain for the Audi, which bounced and lurched around, but Harry made as quick time as he dared. Belinda sat on the edge of her seat, hand on the dashboard to support herself as she leaned forward to peer at the barn.

'If Marcus has lied to me,' she said through gritted teeth, 'I won't be responsible for my actions.'

'Take it easy now,' said Harry. He felt an urge to put his hand on her arm, but thought better of it. 'You've already... well, I mean, we've already made one mistake tonight about Colonel's incorrect identity. Let's get all of the facts this time.'

By this stage, they were beside the barn, Belinda releasing her seat belt with one hand, opening the door with the other and then running towards the barn doors.

Harry came to a stop close behind her, slipping on the ground now the rain had begun to turn the dirt to mud.

The sound of several dogs barking excitedly made them turn to one another, their rain-soaked faces showing complete bewilderment as Belinda grappled with the metal bar across the door.

With Harry's help, she got the door open, swung it back and stared at two Labradors, two Cavalier King Charles spaniels and two Great Danes, one of which bounded forward and sat on Harry's feet.

Harry reached down for his collar, read the name tag and said to Belinda, 'It's Colonel.'

CHAPTER FORTY-SIX

Belinda felt she would explode with rage. The red mist had engulfed her to the point that she wanted to scream.

'Sis, what on earth are you doing out here at this time of night?' said a voice some feet behind her.

She turned a half-circle to see a flashlight bouncing towards her as Marcus's voice said, 'And you too, Harry. I don't know why you're…'

Marcus stopped talking as he swung the light towards the barn's interior. A parade of dogs was making its way towards the three of them, four counting Colonel.

'There is no explanation, Marcus,' she shouted, 'that can even come close to excusing why we have a barn full of dogs we don't own!'

Belinda was now nose to nose with her brother, her entire body shaking with fury.

'The barn… It was… The dogs… I don't know,' said Marcus, taking a small step towards Harry.

'I think you've got some explaining to do,' said Harry, 'but how about we do it inside the barn and out of the rain? We're getting soaked.'

The sound of the rain hammering on the roof made conversation at a normal level pointless, but Belinda was all about the hollering by this stage.

'What do you think you're doing?' she said, poking Marcus in the chest with her finger. 'Are you out of your mind? Stealing other people's dogs! I believed you, Marcus. What on earth has got into you?'

'Firstly, Bel,' said Marcus, 'I had no idea about the dogs being here, so I'm as surprised as you are. Secondly, I was about to fly out to Bulgaria and I would hardly leave a pack of hounds here in the barn.'

As he spoke, Marcus pulled his phone from his back pocket.

'I've got the flight ticket here, see.' He held the phone up to her and Harry. 'I need to fly out there and make some amends. Besides, I showed this barn to Emma only the other day and it was empty then. I've been out and only this minute got back. You know that we hardly ever come out here, it's a waste of space really.'

Marcus stood with his hands on his hips, craning his neck to see up into the corners of the barn.

'You know what we should do?' said Marcus. 'A barn dance, or something like that. You know, make proper use of this space. I'll give it some thought over—'

'Marcus,' snapped Belinda, 'for goodness' sake, what about these dogs?'

'We need to lock them in, and call the police,' said Harry. 'As long as they're safe, we can trace the owners without too much…' He trailed off.

'What is it?' said Belinda.

'I know that some dogs look the same, but I'm sure I recognise some of these ones,' said Harry.

He pointed to the black Labradors. 'They look very much like some of my clients' dogs. I think that's Carol and Richard Stone's Scooby, who Dawn said went missing this morning – I can tell by his ears. And that one there is Matt and Sarah's Ellie.'

'Are you saying these are all supposed to be breeding pairs?' said Marcus.

'If Harry's right,' said Belinda, 'then they're likely to all be Doggie Delight clients' dogs.'

The three of them were huddled together to make themselves heard over the noise of the rain crashing down from outside, so engrossed in their conversation that the barn door being swung back caught all three of them unawares.

Not Colonel. He barked, leaped to his feet and wagged his tail furiously, managing to catch Harry's thigh as he ran to greet Dawn and Alicia.

'Colonel, Colonel,' cried Alicia as she threw her arms around their dog and let him lick her face.

Dawn put a trembling hand out on his enormous head, tears spilling down her cheeks.

Belinda, Harry and Marcus were frozen to the spot watching the happy reunion unfold, before Belinda broke the spell. She walked up to Dawn and gave her a hug.

'I never thought I'd see him again, Bel,' said Dawn. 'I really thought they'd got him. He was in the garden, and then he was gone. I only left him for one minute.'

'How did you know he was here?' said Belinda.

A sad little face looked up at them, nestled next to Colonel's gigantic head.

'Sorry I didn't tell you earlier, Mum, but I thought you'd be angry,' said Alicia, teary eyes trying to meet Dawn's.

'We'll talk about the unauthorised credit card transaction later,' said Dawn, taking a tissue from her raincoat pocket and wiping her eyes. 'The important thing is, he's safe.'

For the first time since hurtling through the door, Dawn took stock of the situation they were in.

'What's going on? And where have all these dogs come from?' she said with a frown aimed at Harry.

'Why are you looking at me? It's their barn,' he said, nodding at the Penshurst siblings.

'We're not entirely certain how Colonel or these other dogs ended up here,' said Belinda. 'We were in the middle of working that out when you arrived. Tell me how you knew Colonel was here, and what unauthorised credit card transaction?'

Dawn dabbed at her moist cheeks again and said, 'Turns out that my nine-year-old daughter, detective-in-training, knows my passwords for my online shopping and bought a tracker for Colonel's collar.'

'Ah,' said Belinda and Harry, followed two seconds later by Marcus.

'All the time he was on the move, the signal kept dropping out,' said Dawn. 'Then about twenty minutes ago, it showed him here in your barn.'

'Ah,' said Marcus.

'Please stop that,' said Belinda to her brother, 'the moment's over.'

Dawn looked down at her daughter lying on the floor beside their furry family member, who was on his back, legs in the air, relishing every second of having his tummy tickled.

Suddenly, Colonel rolled over, stared into a far corner of the barn and began to bark.

Alicia stood up and moved next to her mum.

Every pair of eyes, human and canine, peered into the darkness.

Marcus crept forward with his flashlight, swinging the brightness from side to side.

'Hello,' he called. 'Anyone there? Do come out, if so.'

'Stop flapping around,' said Belinda as she grabbed a pitchfork and surged towards the far corner, Colonel standing alongside her, now barking and growling.

'I'm coming out,' called a voice. 'Don't hurt me.'

Everyone stood stock-still, Harry with a metal wrench, the nearest and heaviest object he could find, Dawn with the point of her umbrella thrust forwards, her other hand pushing Alicia behind her.

'Eric?' said Harry. 'What are you doing here?'

'I told you it was Eric,' Belinda told Harry.

'No, no, you've got it all wrong,' said Eric, stepping out of the shadows.

'Stay where you are,' said Belinda, jabbing the prongs of her weapon.

'He made me do it,' said Eric, holding his hands up in surrender.

'Marcus?' said Belinda.

'Why do you always think the worst of me, Bel?' said Marcus, letting the torch beam fall to the floor.

A sudden scurrying sound from the dingy depths of Eric's hideout made Marcus refocus the light and Harry step in front of Belinda.

'I don't think trying to make a run for it is a good idea, do you, Eric?' said Harry.

'Tipper got me involved,' said Eric, sinking to the floor and resting his elbows on his knees. 'Now I'm petrified I'll be murdered next.'

'Tipper's dead so he's hardly a threat,' said Harry. 'Come on, what's been going on?'

'Tipper and Sandra hatched a scheme to breed dogs by borrowing them from the owners for a day or so,' said Eric, looking up into the faces of his audience. 'Mostly, people got their dogs back, but if they produced good litters, they stayed. They were using them to get bitches pregnant. I didn't exactly agree with it. And it wasn't puppy farming before you accuse us of that. These were legitimate bitches.'

'Likely story,' said Belinda. 'Who used to pick the dogs up?'

'It was me and Tipper, or me and Sandra,' said Eric miserably. 'She didn't have a car.'

'And let me guess,' said Harry, 'as well as your work van, you own an SUV and Tipper was happy to leave the driving to you.'

'I drove because Tipper was, well, usually drunk,' said Eric. 'A couple of times, he took a bitch instead of a dog. Easy mistake to make.'

'Not really,' said Belinda, Harry, Dawn and Marcus.

'At least we all agree on something,' said Belinda, glancing at her team.

'Go on,' said Harry.

'Tipper still wanted to go ahead with the plan, Sandra more so, and by that stage, thinking it wasn't going to cause much upset, I'd been pulled into it,' said Eric, attempting a wry smile until he met Belinda's gaze. Her raised eyebrows and the pitchfork forced his face into a more solemn expression.

'How?' said Belinda.

'I'd given them the names of the owners whose dogs they could borrow,' said Eric.

Belinda jumped forward and pushed the pitchfork against his throat. 'You cannot borrow people's dogs and use them in that way,' she said, enunciating every word. 'I would guess that you got paid for this information?'

'I only did it a few times, I promise,' Eric said, rapid blinking and incessant swallowing giving away any attempt at hiding his nerves. 'They took it in turns marking on the road outside the prospective houses with paint as most of the properties had names instead of numbers, they didn't want to get the wrong house. And then the other one would go and borrow the dog.'

'Although it didn't seem to stop them taking the wrong dog,' said Dawn, still shielding Alicia from Eric on the floor and Belinda wielding the pitchfork.

'I had nothing to do with marking the houses,' said Eric. 'I got pulled into this whole sorry thing. It was bigger than Tipper and much bigger than Sandra and you've got to believe me when I say I don't know who's behind it.'

'We're supposed to trust you?' said Belinda.

'Belinda,' said Harry as he stepped in to take the pitchfork from her. 'The important thing is why Eric is here now.'

'Yes,' said Belinda, snatching the pitchfork back from Harry. 'Why are you cowering in our barn?'

'I was keeping out of the way,' said Eric, unable to look anyone in the eye. 'Holding some of the dogs here until it was time.'

'Time for what?' said Harry.

'He's stalling,' said Belinda. 'Right, I've had enough of this.' She leaped forward, thrusting the pitchfork at his chest, pinning Eric into the corner.

'I say, Bel,' said Marcus. 'That's a bit strong. And please don't forget there's a child present.'

Alicia was trying her best to catch the show, and Dawn's best attempts to stop her daughter witnessing a man getting run through with a farmyard weapon were failing spectacularly.

Belinda glanced behind her, saw Alicia peering around her mother and lowered the pitchfork.

Eric took that as his chance to lunge forward and try to pry it from her hand. As she stumbled sideways, completely taken off guard, Harry kicked Eric in the chest, sending him sprawling backwards.

'When we came to see you at the depot,' said Harry, sole of his boot on Eric's neck, 'you mentioned something about opening a doggie day care crèche for the staff. Are you keeping dogs at the depot?'

Panic ran riot across Eric's face as he looked at them. He slowly closed his eyes and started to cry. 'He's going to kill me, he's going to kill me,' wailed Eric.

'Oh, shut up, you pathetic freak,' said Belinda.

'If Eric's hiding here in your barn with some of the dogs,' said Harry, 'perhaps someone's on their way to the depot to pick up the other ones.'

Eric gave a frightened sob and covered his eyes with his hands.

'OK, Bel,' said Marcus, now grinding his own foot into Eric's chest and indicating that Harry could remove his foot. 'You and Harry get over to the depot while I stay here and call the police.'

Belinda rushed across to her brother, kissed him on the cheek and said, 'Thanks, Marcus. Looks like Harry and I have work to do.'

CHAPTER FORTY-SEVEN

Belinda's stomach lurched at the thought of what could be happening in the depot.

'Harry,' she said. 'I think you're right about the dog crèche at the depot. It would be the perfect spot to keep them and pick them up in the dead of night. You said yourself that the gates were hardly ever locked, and Eric cut back on night security. Saving money wasn't the only reason.'

'Whoever's taking these dogs must have drowned Tipper and then killed Sandra,' said Harry.

'If Sandra was scared and told Lennie something, that might have made him a target,' said Belinda.

'I think we can guess that Tipper was killed for trying to get too many people involved,' said Harry. 'He told Eric what they were up to, as well as Marcus. Someone's desperate to take care of loose ends.'

'We don't know that for sure,' said Belinda, 'but we need to make sure whoever it is doesn't hurt anyone else, or steal another dog.'

'Belinda, wait for me,' called Harry as she raced across the muddy ground, rain soaking her. She jumped into the seat and reached for the car keys.

Harry pulled open the door.

'I need the keys,' she said.

'I haven't got them,' he said. 'I left them in the ignition. If you can leave the keys to a castle under a flowerpot, I guessed my car keys would be safe.'

Despite the drumming of the rain, Belinda still heard a defensive tone to Harry's voice.

'Belinda,' he said, leaning into the car, letting the rain cascade onto his car seats, 'I left them in the ignition. If they've gone, someone's taken them while we were in the barn.'

The wind momentarily subsided, allowing the noise of an engine gunning at some considerable speed in the distance to reach their ears.

'My car's at yours so we'll have to use Marcus's Land Rover,' said Belinda. 'Someone's been on my land, in my barns, and they think it's acceptable to steal dogs. We have to do something; they can't get away with this.'

'Show me where his Land Rover is,' said Harry, raising his voice again as the wind picked up.

'Follow me.'

Belinda jumped from the car, ran past the barn door to an open-sided lean-to, switched on a light and fumbled on the hooks inside the door.

Her hand hit upon the Land Rover keys and she yanked open the car door, got in and drove out onto the now boggy grass.

'Wait for me,' said Harry as she slowed the Land Rover, got out and ran around the back, pulling open the rear door.

'Get in then,' she said, rain making her hair and clothes stick to her. She pulled a pair of wellies from the back of the Land Rover, practicalities far outweighing fashionable footwear.

She leaned against the car, kicked off her heels, leaving them where they fell, and pushed her feet into Marcus's Wellington boots. They were a touch too large, but needs must.

Now she was ready.

'Belinda,' called Marcus from where he was keeping watch over Eric.

'Not now!' she shouted at him. 'We need to go, and we need to go now.'

As she threw the door open to jump into the driver's seat, the force of the wind almost yanked the handle from her grip. Harry had opened the passenger door at the same time.

'I've already said that you're not going by yourself,' he said as she climbed in. 'Whoever's behind this is a lunatic and we know he's already murdered. He won't hesitate to do it again.'

A face appeared at the window next to Belinda, startling her as she went to drive off.

'Good grief, Dawn!' she shrieked. 'You and Alicia wait here for the police. Harry and I are off to the depot.'

Dawn tried to bang on the window, but Belinda was too focused to heed her words as they sped away into the night.

The red mist had most definitely come down and Belinda was stopping for no one.

'If anyone harms a hair on any of those dogs, their life won't be worth living,' said Belinda through gritted teeth.

'Over there,' said Harry, pointing towards the glow of a taillight as a vehicle in the distance bumped towards the remote access road to the Doggie Delight depot. He was frantically pressing 999, but the signal only allowed him to get as far as telling the operator that he needed the police before being cut off again.

'Who on earth is it?' Belinda shouted over the noise of the engine, the rattling and shaking of the Land Rover and the whistling wind.

A sharp cry from Harry momentarily distracted her. She looked across to see him holding the top of his head.

'Sorry, Harry,' she said. 'You should probably duck down a little.'

Belinda was not entirely sure that his answer was a clean one, so she chose to ignore it and gain a little ground on the vehicle speeding away in front of them.

'They must have heard us talking in the barn and know we're on to them,' she said, peering past the wipers frantically trying to clear the incessant rain from the windscreen.

'This horrendous weather isn't helping,' said Harry.

'Well, whoever it is, they're definitely heading to the depot,' Belinda said. 'Some of the dogs must be there.'

Belinda pushed the Land Rover on, forging towards the access road, pleased when at last the mud gave way to tarmac.

'From what Eric told us, it sounded as though this was a big shipment of dogs,' she said.

'If, of course, Eric was telling the truth,' said Harry, one hand clinging to the seat belt, the other braced against the dashboard.

'Someone killed Tipper and then Sandra,' said Belinda, risking another look across at him. 'If Eric's the only other one still alive who was involved in the dognapping and unofficial breeding programme, that means we're about to find out who the murderer is.'

'We're chasing a lunatic,' said Harry. 'That's such good news.'

'Let's hope we get there in time to stop him,' said Belinda as she steered the vehicle sharply to the left towards the Doggie Delight front gate, only slightly amused by the way Harry wrapped both arms over his head in anticipation of a collision that didn't come.

In the distance, the vehicle in front drove at the gates, which were only pushed closed, not held together by a chain. The driver forged on, barely slowing despite the bang of metal on metal.

'It looks like a van,' said Harry as the night lights of the depot lit up the driveway and the loading yard.

'A van?' said Belinda. 'Would it be too much of a coincidence that earlier we saw—'

'He's stopping,' said Harry. 'And why is there a delivery van here blocking the bays? That's not right.'

Belinda put her foot down and drove the Land Rover as close as she could get to the transit van.

'It's Lennie!' shouted Belinda. 'I can't believe it! What's he doing here?'

The sight of Lennie jumping from the transit van and running towards the locked side door, pausing only momentarily to smash at the lock with something he pulled from his pocket, made Belinda's blood run cold.

Belinda wasn't sure whether she was more horrified that a dog lover was involved in something so cruel or that she had been fooled so easily. He had been on her land, about to take dogs from her barn, and was now breaking into the depot.

As Harry opened his door to get out, she grabbed his arm and said, 'H, be careful. I don't know what he was holding, it might be a gun.'

Harry paused. Looked across at her, their faces inches apart, lips a breath away.

'Belinda?'

'Yes?'

'Something in the car smells like a wrestler's towel.'

Right on cue, the car was filled with the sounds of Colonel's bark.

'How did he get in here?' said Belinda, looking over to the back seat.

'Never mind,' said Harry as he passed her his mobile. 'I'll go after Lennie and you call the police as soon as you can get a signal.'

He jumped out of the car and ran across the yard, followed swiftly by Colonel.

'If he thinks I'm leaving him here, he's got another thing coming,' said Belinda, leaping from the driver's seat to follow Harry inside.

Belinda barely had time to register the signage on the delivery van blocking the loading bay before rushing after Harry, although something about it seemed very familiar.

CHAPTER FORTY-EIGHT

Once Belinda was through the door, her eyes took several seconds to accustom to the gloom of the warehouse, lit only by the faint eerie glow of emergency lighting. Her ears were a touch quicker at picking out the noise of running feet, although she could have sworn it was more than two people and one dog she could hear.

Belinda's brain was buzzing with many thoughts, including about the driver of the delivery van parked outside.

Trying to focus, she kept as close as she could to the pallets of dog food stacked ten feet high, surprisingly nimble for someone unused to late-night skulduggery and wearing Wellington boots several times too large. She ran towards the sounds of shouting and Colonel's barking.

From her earlier visit to the depot with Harry, Belinda knew that the office and the crèche area were at the back of the enormous warehouse, and besides, it wasn't difficult to work out the direction everyone was heading in from the sounds reverberating through the warehouse.

Belinda got closer and closer, listening out for footsteps.

'Stay the hell where you are,' hollered Harry.

The sound of running feet told her that the last thing Lennie was prepared to do was to heed any kind of warning. That, and the way the pair of them were crashing into everything as they ran along the aisles.

Again, she felt sure someone other than Lennie was in here with them, and that wouldn't end well.

Belinda peered around the heaped-up dog food, concern mounting all the time at what she might see.

The sight that greeted her was worse than she could have anticipated: Harry was nowhere to be seen but, in the distance, about thirty feet away, she could see two people wrestling each other.

As they swung from side to side, arms and legs flailing in the melee, the dimness of the overhead emergency lights flashed across Lennie's face, while the other was still partially obscured.

Unless her eyes were deceiving her, though, she knew the other person grappling with Lennie.

But it couldn't be, could it?

Lennie Aisling, unhinged pub landlord, was fighting with Max Fish, the delivery driver who supplied goods to Belinda's own tea room. Not to mention half of Little Challham.

'You think you can get away with stealing people's dogs and using them to breed from?' screamed Lennie as he delivered a series of jab punches to Max's stomach. 'I should have killed you like I killed Tipper and Sandra. I at least gave her fair warning, but she wouldn't listen to me.'

Max staggered backwards, holding his ribs. His pale, freckly complexion appeared a little freakish in the semidarkness.

'You always were pathetic,' said Max, breath coming in rasps. 'Most of the puppies went to good homes, and most of the dogs got returned to their owners. We could have been rich.'

From the farthest side of the warehouse, Belinda heard the sound of a metal concertina door slide open, Harry pushing it with all of his might. The harsh glare from the strip lighting inside the crèche showed up his silhouette in all its out-of-shape glory, as well as the gaggle of overexcited dogs that burst forth and ran in all directions.

The cacophony of barking and whining and nails clipping on the concrete floor momentarily distracted the crazed fighters.

'Leave the dogs alone,' shouted Lennie. 'I'll kill anyone who hurts the dogs.'

Taking full advantage, Max landed a right hook on Lennie's jaw and lunged towards Harry.

The couple of seconds were enough time for Harry to grab a two-kilo bag of dog biscuits from a nearby stack and run towards the two men. While Lennie had staggered backwards from the impact of the punch, Max was nearly on top of Harry.

Unfortunately for Max, Harry swung the bag of assorted shapes and smashed it into his face.

Max hit the floor, the bag split and twenty excited and somewhat hungry dogs made straight for him, some eating the snacks from where they'd landed on his body.

Belinda saw her chance to dash from her cover, running towards them and shouting at Harry to look out. She was a beat too slow, her voice lost in the all-round merriment of twenty dogs eating biscuits.

Lennie grabbed Harry in a headlock, punched him in the side of his face, and Belinda watched helplessly as her friend fell to the ground.

Lennie stood over him, kicking him. Belinda had only gone a few steps when Colonel came bounding from the other direction, all ears and teeth.

He headed straight for the two men on the floor, not seeming to differentiate who was who. For a terrible moment, Belinda thought he was about to attack Harry as he lay prone, desperately fending off Lennie's blows.

Instead, the wonderful Great Dane, usually so placid, latched his jaws onto Lennie's trouser leg. A few shakes of the leg weren't nearly enough to displace the disgruntled hound. Colonel hung on until a swift kick in the ribs had him whimpering and cowering in the shadow of a pallet.

That Belinda simply could not stand.

She ran forward at the same time as Lennie jumped backwards, emergency lighting illuminating his face in a half-crazed, half-sinister way.

Unable to stop herself, she shouted, 'No!' at the top of her lungs, watching, afraid to get any closer, as Lennie turned to the pallets piled high beside him and put all of his weight into rocking them backwards and forwards.

The maniacal glee on his face as he realised that the object of his hate was directly beneath the pallets was horrifying. Soon the entire stack would fall on top of Harry.

Belinda ran towards Lennie, shouting, 'The police are on their way.' It was very probably true from Harry's abandoned 999 calls, but even Lennie wasn't deranged enough to be fooled that their arrival was imminent.

And it didn't stop the rocking of the kibble tower either. The tower that was dangerously close to an already injured Harry.

With one more almighty grunt, Lennie gave another shove and the ten-foot-high heap of dry dog food started to topple.

Belinda watched Harry crawl across the floor, one hand holding his ribcage. He was still directly within its trajectory. Three feet further and he would be safe. But three feet with the slow progress he was making might as well be a mile.

Both she and Harry were aware that the distance he was gaining was nowhere near enough to make him safe, yet it was better than no distance at all.

As Lennie gave the side of the dog food mountain another push, not caring for her own safety, Belinda surged forward, bag of Doggie Delight treats held above her head, a scream on her lips.

'I'll kill you both!' shouted Lennie, shoulder behind the corner of the tower looming over Harry, his concentration shifting to Belinda.

Belinda reached Lennie, her only protection a bag of turkey twizzlers, which she threw at him. They hit his head and fell to the floor.

It had the desired effect in that it briefly distracted Lennie. He propelled himself away from the bags of food, no longer the neat, straight, orderly stack they had once been.

Instinctively, Belinda went to call out to Harry for help, but all she managed was 'Har—' before Lennie's hands were around her throat.

'I didn't smack myself on the head with the lead piping to have you two idiots stop me now,' said Lennie, his hands squeezing tighter. 'I'll kill you both before I spend my days in prison.'

From the corner of her eye, she saw a grey mass spring into view and launch itself at Lennie's left arm.

Colonel sank his teeth straight into Lennie's flesh, forcing Lennie to release his grip on Belinda.

Her hands flew up to her neck and she watched in horror as Lennie fell backwards against the precarious mound of dog food.

Sensing his work was not finished, Colonel let go of Lennie, who collapsed to the floor weeping and holding his bloody arm. The Great Dane raced around the wobbling heap of dog food, sank his teeth into Harry's backside and pulled with all his might.

With no time to spare, Colonel pulled Harry free of the toppling mountain of dog food as it hit the floor. An explosion of thousands of dog food pellets hit the floor and scattered in every direction. Colonel took the chance to get his reward for being a good boy, put his head to the floor and started to eat.

That was the moment that Lennie decided to make a run for it. His feet failed to get any purchase on the concrete floor now littered with tiny round pellets and he tripped, landing on his head and knocking himself out.

'That is what you get for messing with us,' said Belinda over the prone bodies of Max and Lennie, Harry standing beside her.

The rain had stopped hammering on the corrugated roof. Belinda could make out the sound of a number of cars pulling up and several people shouting as they raced to the three of them standing guard over the unconscious duo. Well, only two of them were keeping watch – the third was eating dog food off the floor when the first police officers reached them.

'How come the murderer only gets his arm bitten,' said Harry, 'while I get bitten on the—'

'Officers, over here,' shouted Belinda. 'Oh, look, it's PC Green. Cooee.'

CHAPTER FORTY-NINE

'So,' said Belinda as she stood next to Harry, the blue lights of the police cars and ambulances lighting up the warehouse.

'So,' said Harry, rubbing his backside.

'You should probably get one of the paramedics to take a look at that.'

'I'll be fine,' he said. 'It smarts a bit, but I don't think Colonel did too much damage. It's him I was worried about. Fortunately, he's a robust old boy and it doesn't look as if he's hurt in the slightest. I owe that dog a lot.'

Harry missed Belinda dabbing at her eyes with a tissue; he was too busy looking out for Dawn and Alicia.

'There's a dog handler here,' said Harry. 'She's offered to take a look at Colonel, much to her own land shark's disgust. You can probably hear Police Dog Milo barking his head off, showing his displeasure. Anyway, Sally the handler is trying to make sure Colonel is perfectly comfortable until we can get him to a vet and checked. In the meantime—'

'Harry,' said Belinda.

'Oh, that looks like Dawn and Alicia trying to get through the police cordon. They're having a spot of bother. I'd better—'

'Harry.'

'They should probably mention my name. I may be retired, but I still—'

'Harry!' she said. 'For goodness' sake, please listen to me. Dawn will be here any moment.'

Belinda stopped. She was a little concerned that now she had his attention, her resolve would fail her.

'What is it?' said Harry.

Belinda stared at him, unblinking and determined.

'That drink I mentioned, oh, I don't know, I think it was a lifetime ago,' said Belinda. 'Any chance you fancy doing that at some point?'

Everything went quiet: the wailing of the police sirens, the barking dogs, the shouting police officers – it was as if they were all silenced from her world.

Nothing stirred for a few perfect moments.

Belinda watched Harry look away from her and shake his head.

'I'm so sorry but I really can't do that. The relationship break-up I mentioned was brutal.' Harry had the start of tears in his eyes. 'In a frenzy of romantic gestures, I booked us a holiday,' he said, mouth so downturned it must have been difficult to speak. 'The good old U S of A. Oh, yeah, I had it all planned, including Las Vegas and a down-on-my-knee proposal in front of a crowd.'

It was Belinda's turn to look away. She couldn't stand the pain ravaging his kind face. She could tell how that story ended.

'So, as much as I'd like to go for a drink,' said Harry, 'only as friends. Please.'

With as bright a smile as she could manage, Belinda said, 'I meant as friends, clearly I meant as friends. I thought that once the dust has settled, we could mull it over, pool our resources and pick over what we've learned in case my amateur detective skills are ever called on again.'

'Then I'd really love that,' said Harry, a wonky smile on his face.

Harry started to move towards the police officers and the blue-and-white tape of the cordon. Then he looked back at her.

'Next time you ask me, B, I don't think I'll be stupid enough to say no.'

Belinda watched him grow in stature as he stopped to talk to the boys and girls in blue, at one with his own kind. There was muffled inappropriate laughter and some backslapping.

It was the first time he had called her 'B' and not Belinda. That could only mean one thing, surely.

For a moment, Belinda allowed herself to bask in the idea of Harry turning round and beckoning her over, except he seemed to have forgotten her already now he was surrounded by police officers.

With a sigh, she took a step in the direction of Marcus's Land Rover, abandoned with its doors open and no doubt rain-sodden.

'Belinda, Belinda,' shouted Harry with a wave in her direction.

Harry was pointing at something PC Green was holding up.

Despite the distance and the darkness lit only by car headlights, Belinda could see it was a police evidence bag with something inside it.

She walked over to the group and stepped inside the huddle.

'We got the CCTV from outside the hospital,' said PC Green. 'Lennie Aisling left the hospital several hours before he was officially discharged and then sneaked back in.'

'I'd put money on the times he was gone coinciding with Sandra's murder,' said Belinda.

'You'd be absolutely spot on,' said PC Green. He was momentarily distracted by a flurry of activity as the paramedic crews carried Lennie out on one stretcher, Max on another. Each was shepherded by a police officer who climbed in the back of their respective ambulance with them.

'It would appear,' said PC Green, indicating the ambulance Max was in, 'that Max Fish was about to take all of these stolen dogs out of here to be sold on. Some for breeding, no doubt, some to unwitting new owners.'

'I knew there was something odd about Max and his bun delivery,' said Harry.

'You knew nothing of the sort,' said Belinda. 'We had him down as a perfectly harmless man. I can't believe we didn't notice what he was up to and add him to the list of suspects.'

'We need a bigger whiteboard,' said Harry.

'Anyway, Lennie got wind of what was going on,' said Belinda. 'We heard him tell Max that he'd killed Tipper and Sandra for what they'd done to the dogs.'

'Until Lennie turned up at the barn tonight and overheard what Eric told us,' said Harry, 'it doesn't seem he knew that someone else was involved either.'

'Max probably owes you both his life,' said PC Green. 'Once they both come to, they'll have some answering to do.'

'Could this all be because Lennie was so upset by the death of his dog?' said Harry.

'I don't know,' said PC Green. 'I've been in the Dog and Duck a number of times over the years, and he always seemed so, well, normal.'

'Just as long as you didn't have the soup with the croutons,' said Belinda, loving that only Harry got the joke.

CHAPTER FIFTY

Belinda sat in her favourite spot, the attic on the third floor, sun lighting up the dreariest spots usually so hard to reach. Nowhere was going to be dark and gloomy today; she wouldn't let it happen.

Marcus was home, Harry was back delivering dog food under a new manager, the village had returned to normal and the dogs were all safe and sound.

'Sound as a hound.' She smiled to herself, watching her eleven-week-old Labrador puppy Horatio, who was nestled down on his bed, his tiny mouth hanging open and his pink little tongue lolling to the side.

His tail thudded on the bed as he slumbered, causing her smile to turn into an ear-to-ear grin.

Sure, Horatio had bitten her about six times that day and chewed one of the best rugs in the living room, and Marcus was still furious that the pup had emptied his tanks in his slippers, but asleep, the dog was perfection itself.

Belinda had the presence of mind to move her wicker box of memories out of Horatio's way. That was safely tucked up on the bookshelf. As much as she could already feel her heart being torn in two by her love for her dog, she knew she would not be able to fully forgive him for nibbling through her most treasured possessions.

Horatio yawned and blinked open his cute little brown eyes. He stared up at her for the briefest of moments, until he remembered he was a puppy with far too much energy who'd just had a refreshing nap. He was up and heading straight for her.

Belinda knew it had been fate that brought Harry back into her life. All those years ago in Dover docks, he had helped her on her path. While he had tried to talk her into taking the easy way out with a police caution, she saw in him a man of principle who didn't walk away when things got tough. Harry had told PC Green that it was Belinda who'd stood up for what she believed in and refused the police caution she had been offered. The strength she had found to do that had come from seeing that quality in him. They didn't come more principled and decent than Harry.

Now personal things looked somewhat bleak for Harry, the least she could do for him was be the kind of supportive friend who would look out for him. He was obviously struggling with his transition from detective inspector to dog food delivery driver, to say nothing of mending a broken heart.

That made two of them. Hers hadn't healed from her break-up with Ivan. She had thought Ivan and Harry were similar in character, but it was clear now that they weren't as alike as she had first believed. Harry was everything Ivan wasn't, and more importantly, Harry was here in Kent, not South Africa.

While Harry stood up for what he believed in, she knew he had a line and he wouldn't cross it. She had seen a change in Ivan she hadn't liked and a glimpse of the kind of behaviour he would stoop to to get what he wanted. Harry would never do that. Certainly not to her.

Belinda was determined to help Harry.

That would be the easy bit; the difficult part was her doing it in a way so that he never suspected what she was up to.

Still, her plan was almost hatched, and Harry wouldn't be able to resist. One way or another, he was going for that drink with her.

Without even realising it, on the night they'd stopped Lennie and rid Little Challham of dognapping evil, her brother had planted the seeds of an idea Harry was bound to accept. After all, who wouldn't kill to come to a Little Challham wine-tasting event right here in the castle grounds?

Even if it meant disguising it as a business transaction, Belinda and Harry would raise a glass together and begin their next adventure.

In the meantime, Belinda had a lively Labrador puppy to walk.

A LETTER FROM LISA

Dear reader,

Thank you so much for choosing to read *Murder in the Village*. I had great fun writing it and really hope you enjoyed reading it. If you'd like to keep up to date with all my latest releases, just sign up at the following link. Your email address will never be shared and you can unsubscribe at any time.

www.bookouture.com/lisa-cutts

Living and working in the beautiful county of Kent inspired me to create a thriving village where neighbours help each other out, pop to the pub, shop locally and sometimes kill each other. After all, when you've a background in murder, why not put it to good use? Like Harry Powell, I've spent some time investigating murders for a living, and wondered how he'd cope with retirement. Of course, it was all the more pleasant for him with Belinda Penshurst's amateur sleuth skills guiding him along.

I've loved creating a world for Belinda and Harry, plus murders to solve. If you would be kind enough to leave a short review for the first in the Little Challham mysteries, your time would be greatly appreciated. Feedback from readers is so important and if you've enjoyed the book, letting other readers know would introduce them to the series too.

Belinda, Harry and the dogs will be back soon.

Thank you so much,
Lisa

 @LisaCuttsAuthor

 @lisa_cutts

lisa.cutts.505

ACKNOWLEDGEMENTS

Firstly, a huge thank you to readers everywhere. Without you, there is little point and the whole process would involve me laughing at my own jokes – in the style of Harry Powell.

How fortunate I am to have my book edited by Ruth Tross. I've loved every second of working with Ruth and know how extremely lucky I am to have such an amazing editor. The book is all the better for her expertise and fantastic suggestions. I know that there is a whole team at Bookouture who work tirelessly and many of them I have met only in a virtual capacity. As well as Ruth's superb editorial skills, I'm grateful to every member of the team for all the behind-the-scenes work that takes place to get the book released and find its way to you. Thanks go to Alex Holmes and Martina Arzu in editorial, Kim Nash, Noelle Holten and Sarah Hardy in publicity, Lisa Brewster for the cover, Alex Crow and Hannah Deuce in marketing, and DeAndra Lupu and Rachel Rowlands for copyediting and proofreading. I've admired Bookouture for many years and can't quite believe I'm now in the safe hands of such an extraordinary publisher.

You'll have noticed that dogs have a starring role in this book. Major was our family dog when my brother and I were growing up, and as fantastic as I thought he was, he was always my mum's dog. It's impossible to think of my mum without thinking of Major, which is peculiar when you consider how short a dog's lifespan is. That's the impact they have on our lives and our hearts.

It was years until I was in the position to have another dog, and in 2011 my husband and I bought a fox-red Labrador puppy and named him after a dog from a Laurel and Hardy film. On Tuesday, 8 March 2011, Laughing Gravy came home to live with us. For many years he was the centre of our universe, and then on Sunday, 8 December 2019, we had our hearts broken when we had to say our final goodbyes.

Dogs love unconditionally without the problems humans bring to the party. I think of my mum – and Major – with happiness and fond memories, and I still sob when I think of Laughing Gravy and his short life.

I cried when my friends Richard and Carol Stone's gorgeous boy Scooby died; I cried when Monty Don's dog Nigel died. I cheer endlessly when I see the work that the wonderful folks at Street Hearts, Bulgaria, Emma and Anthony Smith, carry out for the stray dogs in the area of Dryanovo, rescuing more than one dog at a time. A huge thank you to Emma for allowing herself to be a character in the book. I could picture you reacting in the same way if you thought someone was taking liberties with your dogs!

My husband and I now have our own rescue dog from the UK. Barney is a nervous but sweet boy, and a year and a bit later, he's growing in confidence and loving gravy bones.

I'm on social media but shy away from politics, anything contentious and just about anything that will get me in trouble at work, but please tag me in photos of your dogs. Those I want to see.

Take care and thanks again for reading.